THE STORY OF ELISA

The Story Of Elisa

FOREVER & ALWAYS

Chavanese Wint

Icons Media Publishing

Published by Icons Media Publishing in 2024

First Edition

Contents

Acknowledgements

To Shermaine Campbell

DEDICATION

Well, would you look at that! Giving up on writing seemed like such a brilliant idea three years ago, but then I had the audacity to dream about this book and it ruined everything. And now, against all odds, here we are, proving that dreams sometimes have a wicked sense of humor. Now I've gone and published my eighth book. Who needs sleep anyway right? I guess dreaming big has its perks, like sacrificing precious hours of rest to bring more literary masterpieces into the world.

With Love
Chavanese Wint

PROLOGUE

Journey of Reminiscence

As Elisa sat by the window, her thoughts drifted back to the vibrant days of her youth. The warmth of the summer sun kissed her cheeks, evoking a sense of nostalgia that filled her with bittersweet memories. Her gaze was fixed on the world outside, but her mind wandered through the corridors of time, trying to retrace the steps of her past. In the midst of her reverie, a soft whimper pulled her back to the present. A young woman stood beside her, tears glistening in her eyes. Elisa's heart ached with empathy as she observed the agony etched on the woman's face. A rush of compassion surged within her, propelling her to reach out and offer solace. As the younger woman poured out her sorrow, Elisa's mind swirled with empathy and understanding. It was as if the universe had woven their lives together in that precise moment, intertwining their emotions and experiences. The room was filled with an air of poignant vulnerability, and yet, the sunlight streamed in, casting a glow that symbolized hope and renewal. Elisa felt the weight of the emotions surrounding her, but also a sense of resilience and strength rising within her.

Elisa's mind wandered into the labyrinth of her past, where fragments of memories danced like spectres in the recesses of her mind. She felt the warmth of the sun's rays on her face, recalling long-forgotten days of laughter and innocence. But as the sunlight faded, so did the tranquillity of her recollections, replaced by the shadows of her well-kept bedroom, every crease and fold meticulously arranged. The young woman's voice pierced through the haze, pulling Elisa back to the present. Her eyes met those of the intruder, brimming with a fire that threatened to consume everything in its path. What had transpired to ignite such fury in the young woman's heart? As the drama unfolded before her, Elisa found herself drawn into the maelstrom of emotions, her own curiosity piqued. She longed to understand the genesis of the woman's rage, to unravel the enigma that had brought her to this tumultuous moment. The tension in the room crackled like electricity, each breath pregnant with the weight of untold secrets. As Elisa sat in her hospital chair, surrounded by the familiar yet unfamiliar faces of her family in the photographs adorning her walls, she couldn't help but wonder about the stories behind those frozen moments in time. Who were these people smiling back at her with warmth and love? She wished she could remember, but for now, she found solace in the feeling of familiarity they brought to this place.

The aroma of a savoury casserole wafted into her room, igniting her senses and bringing with it a flood of memories. The tantalizing scent danced through the air, triggering something deep within her subconscious. It was as if that particular blend of spices held the key to unlocking a world she had forgotten. Jelly pots and ice cream for dessert – a simple, yet comforting combination that never failed to bring a smile to her face. As she savoured the sweet memory, flashes of laughter and joy flickered in her mind, elusive and just out of reach. On the nightstand beside her bed, a faded photograph caught her eye. It was a picture of her as a child, her small hands reaching eagerly for a spoonful of jelly and ice cream. The image tugged at something buried deep within her, a yearning for a time when life was simpler and filled with innocent delight. Elisa found herself at the centre of a peculiar spectacle. The lady before her kept shouting, her words slicing through the air like a whirlwind. In her hands, she clutched a crumpled white paper, the source of her distress. Elisa stood there, bewildered, trying to comprehend the situation unfolding before her.

The lady, with her long brown hair tied back in a ponytail and piercing blue eyes, seemed to be on the brink of unravelling. Her face flushed with emotion, she hurled words at Elisa, yet the meaning eluded her. Who was she? And why did she look so upset? As Elisa cast a sympathetic glance towards the lady, something unexpected happened. The woman's tirade came to an abrupt halt, her eyes meeting Elisa's in an intense gaze. The chaos subsided, replaced by an eerie calm that hung in the air like a thick fog. The hospital room was eerily quiet, the only sound the rhythmic beeping of the heart monitor. Elisa sat in the chair, her face contorted in pain, her hand outstretched toward the mysterious lady standing before her. The lady's eyes held a mix of concern and fear as she watched Elisa struggle.

As Elisa's breathing became shallow, a sharp pain pierced her chest, causing her to double over. The smile that had graced her face moments before twisted into a grimace of agony. It was as if an invisible force was tearing her apart from the inside out. The mysterious lady knelt next to Elisa, taking her hand in a gentle, reassuring grip. Elisa's eyes locked onto hers, silently pleading for help. With a sense of urgency, the lady sprang into action, dashing out of the room to summon the doctors. In a matter of seconds, a team of medical professionals descended upon the room, their trained eyes assessing the situation with a rapid precision. Tubes and wires were swiftly adjusted, medication administered, and prayers whispered under breaths. Time seemed to blur as the battle against Elisa's suffering raged on, her fate hanging in the balance. The room became a rapid response of activity, as the doctors and nurses worked tirelessly to restore Elisa to health. As the tension mounted, a glimmer of hope emerged. Elisa's laboured breathing began to ease, the lines of pain on her face gradually softening. The heart monitor's steady beeping was joined by the sound of her deep, steady breaths. Doctor Myers, with an air of quiet intensity, adjusted his stethoscope and placed it against Elisa's chest, listening intently to the life-giving symphony within her. The sound of that heartbeat held the key to Elisa's fate, a delicate melody that resonated with the weight of hope and uncertainty. As the doctor analysed the rhythm and cadence, his brow furrowed with concern. The heartbeat was slow, its once robust strength waning. With a sense of urgency, he swiftly administered medication to stabilize her oxygen levels, ward off potential infections, and tend to her fluctuating blood pressure and temperature. Every move was calculated, every action purposeful, all in a race against time to safeguard the precious life beating within Elisa's chest.

The room hummed with the mechanical symphony of medical equipment, the soft murmur of the medical team, and the palpable tension that hung thick in the air. Doctor Myers, unwavering in his determination, placed the heart monitor on Elisa's chest, the device serving as a conduit to the vital rhythm that danced within her. The overhead lights flickered ominously as the medical team scrambled to stabilize her.

"Her heartbeat is slow and not as strong as it should be. We need to get her into surgery now," the lead doctor's voice cut through the hushed urgency, the weight of those words hanging heavy in the air. The room was a rush of fear, each person holding their breath as they processed the gravity of the situation.

As Elisa was wheeled away the tension was evident. The team of surgeons and nurses worked with precision and a sense of urgency, their focused expressions illuminated by the sterile glow of the surgical lights. As the woman's hand clenched around Elisa's, a strange sensation washed over her. It was as if an invisible thread connected them, pulling Elisa into the storm of emotions swirling within the woman. Her beauty juxtaposed with the ferocity of her anger left Elisa mesmerized, almost wishing for the woman to never release her grip. But as suddenly as it had begun, the woman let go, and Elisa felt a wave of relief flood through her. The paradox of emotions left her perplexed and strangely drawn to the woman. Was it fear that made her heart race, or was it a strange admiration for the woman's unbridled passion? Elisa felt a small smile tugging at the corners of her lips.

The woman looked on, tears streaming down her face, she knew that her life would never be the same again. She closed her eyes, surrendering to the inevitable, as the doctors swiftly whisked Elisa away from the arid white room. In that moment, time seemed to stretch and fold, leaving her to dwell in her thoughts, wondering if she could ever find peace.

One

Savoring the Subconscious

A s the sun rose over the bustling city, the sound of children's laughter echoed through the neighbourhood. The morning air was alive with energy, and the playground was a whirlwind of excitement. As the children played, the morning sun cast a golden glow over the worn playground equipment. The air was heavy with the promise of another scorching day, and yet the children played with unrivalled energy, their laughter filling the air. Amidst the backdrop of towering buildings and cramped streets, a sense of joyful chaos reigned. As the children laughed and played, the mothers hurriedly prepared their little ones for the day ahead, their voices carrying through the open windows of the modest apartments.

While other families hurried through their morning routines, the inhabitants of one home moved at a more leisurely pace. Inside another home, the aroma of freshly brewed coffee filled the air, mingling with the sounds of sizzling bacon and chirping birds from outside. Meanwhile another family sat around the table, the morning light streaming through the windows, there was an air of peacefulness that seemed to envelop the room. The off-white doors, worn and discoloured with age, stood as a silent testament to the passage of time. They had weathered summers and winters, witnessed laughter and tears, and yet, they stood strong, guarding the secrets of the house within.

Carolina, a woman with a determined glint in her eyes, was on a mission to ensure that her son, Daniel, made it to school on time. With bleached blonde hair tied back in a ponytail, she exuded an aura of no-nonsense determination as she tried to rouse her son from his slumber.

"Daniel, you need to hustle if you don't want to be late for school!" Carolina's voice resonated through the house, carrying a sense of urgency that mirrored her swift movements. She dashed up the stairs, her footsteps echoing along the hallway as she made her way to her son's room.

"I'm coming, Ma!" Daniel's voice rang out, a hint of grogginess betraying his small frame as he struggled to rise from the warmth of his bed.

As Carolina entered his room, her eyes flashed with determination.

"Don't you talk to me that way, young man! I am not one of your silly friends. Now get up and get ready quickly!" Her stern tone filled the room, echoing off the walls as she flung open the curtains to let the morning light flood in.

As Daniel reluctantly began to rouse himself, a sense of purpose gripped Carolina. She was intent on ensuring that her son didn't miss the bus, a feeling of urgency propelling her forward as she helped him get ready. The gust of fresh air swept through his abode, it was clear that the window needed to be left open. Over on the other side of the apartment building, young Elisa lay, burrowed in her bed and completely buried under the covers. She could just about make out the sound of her alarm ringing, so she stuck one arm out from underneath the sheets and slapped it off with her palm. Rolling over onto her back, she opened her eyes slowly and gazed up at the ceiling for a few seconds. She'd had a delightful dream; this one was far better than her earlier nightmare in which she was running away from something. This time, she'd been eating seafood- something she adored yet never indulged in due to lack of funds.

As a gentle smile spread across her face, she licked her lips as if savouring the memory of the delicious meal.

"Mmm yum, seafood".

Elisa's heart raced as she glanced at the alarm clock; it was 7:30am and she had to be at work on time. Throwing back the covers, Elisa scrambled out of bed and rushed into the bathroom. The warm shower soothed her tense muscles as she works shampoo into her hair and lathered her washcloth with soap, scrubbing every inch of her skin. After rinsing out her mouth with toothpaste, Elisa grabbed a towel from the rack and dried off. She then placed the blow dryer on its dock and blew out her freshly washed hair, throwing it down when done.

Moving to her dresser, she opened it and takes out a bra which she quickly put on before dashing to the wardrobe. As she tried to put one foot into her pants, Elisa tripped up.

"God dammit," she muttered.

Elisa still half-asleep, screamed as she stumbled to her feet. Her hair stuck to her face in damp tendrils that smelled like tea tree oil shampoo, rivulets of water ran down her neck and collected between her breasts. After finally putting on her clothes, she grabbed her keys and purse and immediately rushed out the door, locking it behind her. As she hustled past the other, run-down apartments, which were worn down brick buildings crammed together like box cars, she noticed how they leaned over the filthy streets and sometimes collapsed into them. One of the apartment across from Elisa's door was covered in gang tags and spray paint, which Carolina her neighbour usually tries to clean up as best as she could. She continued to rush but Carolina and her son David caught sight of her.

"Well look who decided to wake up for work this morning," Carolina said as she shut the door of her apartment. Her son, enthralled in his game, paid no attention to the conversation.

"Not now Carolina! I'm late," Elisa shot back as she ran down the seven flights of stairs.

"Maybe if you got up earlier you wouldn't have this problem, you're just like my son! Anyway, remember to call me later so we can get drinks, these nosy neighbours are driving me crazy. I think old Mrs. Smith might be dead again—her house still smells like that go-dawful mix of broccoli and gone off cheese. We should check on her." Shouted Carolina down the fifty flights of stairs.

"Okay I'll look into it later," Elisa answered back before continuing down the steps with her things in tow.

She finally reached her bright red Honda which had definitely seen better days. She hastily threw her stuff in the passenger seat and inserted the key into the ignition. There were deep scratches on the paint and several parts of the interior were held together with duct tape and magic markers. After a few seconds of coughing and sputtering, the engine finally rumbled to life.

"Yes! That's my baby!" Elisa shouted excitedly as she pulled away from the curb.

Two

Lovelace Elementary: Nurturing Young Minds

E lisa approached Lovelace Elementary School with a mixture of apprehension and excitement. She looked ahead at the school that she had dedicated years of her life to. The autumn leaves danced in the wind, creating a picturesque scene. As she parked her car, she couldn't help but notice the flurry of activity around her. Students and their parents hurried past, sharing hugs and hurried goodbyes, their energy contagious. Gathering her belongings, she glanced ahead at the school building she called her workplace. It stood modestly, painted in a pristine white, its simplicity belying the magic that awaited within.

Entering the building, Elisa walked past the silver locker rooms, catching glimpses of children stowing away their belongings in a rush. Some were engrossed in animated conversations, their laughter filling the air. The vibrant energy of the students pulsed through the hallways, echoing with the promise of another day filled with wonder and discovery. As Elisa made her way towards her classroom, she found herself face to face with the formidable figure of the principal, a stern expression etched on her face.

"Good morning, Rodriguez," the principal greeted, her tone tinged with both annoyance and familiarity. "I see that you were nearly late, yet again."

Elisa smiled sheepishly, aware of her recurring tardiness. She had always been a free spirit, struggling to adhere to rigid schedules. But there was something about Lovelace Elementary School that captivated her. It wasn't just the cheerful children or the welcoming atmosphere – it was also the people too.

"Technically, I am not late, the bell hasn't rung yet, and you know how Cleveland traffic is, it's the absolute worst," replied Elisa with a hint of defiance in her voice.

"Yeah, tell me about it," responded the principal with a knowing look.

She watches Elisa as she rushes towards her classroom, an amused smile playing on her lips.

"That girl will be late for her own funeral", she thought to herself. With a quick nod, the principal gathers the students in the hallway.

"Okay students, let's go, straight to class please, thank you." As they begin to disperse, the principal keeps an eye on Elisa, curious to see if she will indeed make it on time.

Elisa walked into her open classroom, her footsteps echoing as she made her way to the front of the room. The morning sunlight streamed in through the large windows, casting a warm glow on the desks and textbooks scattered throughout the room. With a sense of purpose, she quickly set about getting everything ready for the day ahead. She deftly placed her belongings in a neat row on her desk, their familiar presence bringing her a sense of comfort. Then, grabbing a pile of textbooks from her bag, she methodically placed each book on the desk in front of every student's seat. As she reached back to her table, her fingers brushed against a set of markers, ready to be used to bring life to the whiteboard. As she turned around to write on the large white board in front of her, the bell rings and her students rushed to their seats. Taking a deep breath, Elisa turned to face her students. With a smile playing on her lips, she wrote the date in bold. As the bell finally rings, signalling the start of class, she looks at her expectant students.

"So, who's ready to embark on a journey of discovery?" The students, captivated by Elisa's enigmatic presence, eagerly raise their hands. The classroom fills with an excited buzz, and the adventure begins.

"Today, we dive into the magical world of maths." Intriguing questions formed on the board under her skilled hand.

"4x4 =?" she wrote, the numbers standing tall and proud, ready to be solved. Elisa knew that this simple equation held the power to unlock a world of possibilities for her students. It was the gateway to understanding, critical thinking, and problem-solving. Feeling a sudden wave of exhaustion, Elisa retrieved a bottle of water from her bag. She unscrewed the cap and took a long, refreshing sip, feeling the cool liquid soothe her throat. As the water rejuvenated her, she couldn't help but wonder about the incredible journey that awaited her students.

....

It was lunch time, and students scattered throughout the playground to enjoy their much-needed snack. Elisa made her way to the snacks section to fetch some treats for her students. With a gentle smile, she carefully selected a variety of snacks and placed them in a basket. As she arranged the snacks, her best friend Charlene walked into the classroom, her presence immediately brightening the room. Elisa couldn't help but admire Charlene's stunning appearance. Charlene was wearing a vibrant pink dress that seemed to radiate with life. The dress clung to her figure like a melody, accentuating her graceful movements. She completed her ensemble with matching earrings that effortlessly complemented the dress.

"Wow, Charlene, you look absolutely beautiful in that dress," Elisa exclaimed, unable to contain her admiration. "Can I borrow it sometime? I would love to feel as elegant as you."

Charlene chuckled, the sound melodic and warm.

"Of course, Elisa! You know you're always welcome to borrow anything from my wardrobe. We'll definitely make that happen. "On one exception, you have to come out with me tonight," her friend begged, a sense of urgency in her tone.

Elisa sighed, glancing at the clock on the wall. It was already early afternoon, and her workload seemed endless.

"You know I hate going out, girl," Elisa replied, her voice tinged with exhaustion. "Plus, I have so much work to get through." Responded Elisa.

Her friend pouted walking over to the table where Elisa was standing. She began arranging snacks for the children, who were patiently waiting on the ground to be fed. With each small treat she placed in a child's hand, she gave them a warm smile. Charlene couldn't help but be moved by her friend's kindness. She was so naturally beautiful and kind. Her long brown hair held into a perfectly neat bun. "If only Elisa knew how beautiful she was", thought Charlene.

"Come on, that's what you say every weekend," Charlene moaned, her voice filled with determination. "I'm not taking no for an answer this time."

Elisa paused, her mind racing with excuses and reasons why she should decline the invitation. But as she watched her friend's selfless actions, a small voice inside her began to whisper. Maybe, just maybe, she could use a break from her monotonous routine.

"Well, I haven't been out in like a decade," Elisa finally muttered, contemplating the idea. "I'll think about it." Her friend shook her head, a playful glint in her eyes.

"Nope, you will no longer tell me that you are thinking about it. I want you over at my house by six tonight."

Elisa's initial resistance slowly dissolved as she gazed at her friend's genuine smile. She made up her mind, ready to embrace the unexpected. There was something alluring about stepping out of her comfort zone, even if just for an evening. But she knew her friend would not give up this time. Their conversation was interrupted as the bell rang, signalling the end of break time. Elisa reluctantly put the idea of going out aside, knowing that the rest of the day awaited her.

Three

Ready Set Go

Charlene was lost in her own little world, dancing and singing along to her favourite tunes. She couldn't help but feel the excitement bubbling inside her as she prepared for a much-anticipated night out. As the music filled the room, she carefully browsed through her wardrobe, desperately searching for the perfect outfit that would make heads turn. Just as she was about to give up and settle for her usual attire, the doorbell rang, abruptly interrupting her solo dance party. Charlene's heart skipped a beat. Who could it be? With hurried steps, she dashed down the stairs, her curiosity growing with each passing second. With a bright smile, she flung open the door and was greeted by the sight of her dear friend Elisa.

The thrill that filled Charlene's eyes was undeniable as she exclaimed.

"You're here! I thought you weren't going to show up, like you always do."

Elisa rolled her eyes playfully, her lips curling into a mischievous smile.

"Well, I wasn't planning on coming, but here I am, ready to join in on your wild adventures," she teased.

Charlene's excitement soared, and she couldn't help but let out a contagious laugh.

"Come on then, where's your outfit? You didn't bring anything with you?" she quizzed, curious about Elisa's spontaneous decision to accompany her. Elisa simply shrugged, a glimmer of rebellion in her eyes.

"No, why would I? I'll be wearing this," she responded, gesturing to her simple yet striking attire.

"You have got to be kidding, girl. There is no way you will be walking around in that next to me," exclaimed Charlene, eying Elisa's choice of attire with a mix of amusement and horror.

Elisa looked down at her comfortable jeans and oversized hoodie and shrugged, "I thought we were just going to grab a casual dinner, Char. Nothing fancy."

Charlene scoffed and grabbed Elisa's hand, dragging her up the stairs towards her boudoir.

"Come on, let's go and choose something from my wardrobe. We're not settling for casual tonight, my friend."

As they reached the top of the stairs, Charlene swung open her closet doors, revealing a dazzling array of dresses, blouses, and skirts. Her wardrobe was a testament to her impeccable taste and love for fashion. They rummaged through the racks, picking out outfits for each other. Charlene had a knack for knowing what would suit Elisa perfectly.

"Look at this skirt, oh my! This would look absolutely lovely on you," Charlene exclaimed, holding up a flowy floral skirt to Elisa's waist. "And look, I have a nice top that can go with this. Yes, this is the outfit for you," she declared with a smile.

Elisa hesitated, looking at herself in the mirror. She had always been more comfortable in her own skin, shying away from attention and flashy clothing. But tonight was different. Tonight, Charlene wanted her to shine.

"Erm, I don't think so," Elisa said, her voice filled with uncertainty. Charlene's eyes sparkled with determination as she locked eyes with Elisa in the mirror.

"Trust me, Elisa. You deserve to feel beautiful and confident. Tonight, we're stepping out of our comfort zones, together."

Elisa took a deep breath, realizing that her friend's intentions were pure. Elisa's heart swelled with gratitude as she slipped into the skirt, feeling the soft fabric brush against her skin. It hugged her curves in all the right places, making her feel confident and beautiful. As Charlene helped her with the final touches, adding a touch of elegance with delicate jewellery and a pair of heels, Elisa's reflection seemed to transform before her eyes. In the mirror, she saw a woman who exuded grace and confidence. The skirt had brought out a side of her that she never knew existed. With each step, she felt a newfound sense of empowerment and freedom. The two friends finished getting ready and headed out for the time of their lives. The city streets were alive with energy, as if they were attuned to the magic that was about to unfold.

Four

Embracing the Unexpected

Approaching the bar, Elisa and Charlene turned heads with their stunning presence. Elisa, dressed in a skirt and blouse that accentuated her assets, and Charlene, in an elegant dress, exuded an air of confidence and allure. The club was pulsating with music as they made their way through the crowd, captivating all who laid eyes on them. Finding a cosy spot to sit, they settled down, ready to begin their night of excitement. Charlene, always the proactive one, decided to fetch them both a round of drinks. She gracefully walked over to the bar, catching the attention of the bartender and the patrons alike. Ordering a couple of shots, she collected them with a charming smile and made her way back to Elisa.

As the glasses clinked, the two friends raised their shots in a toast to the night that lay ahead. The liquid shimmered enticingly, promising a taste of exhilaration. With a silent agreement, they downed the shots in one swift motion, feeling the warmth spread through their bodies. The club buzzed with energy as they embraced the intoxicating atmosphere. The music, a hypnotic blend of beats, guided their movements as they danced, their bodies flowing in perfect harmony. Every eye in the room was drawn to Elisa and Charlene, their passion and chemistry electrifying the air. Amidst the revelry, a mysterious figure caught

Elisa's attention. A dark presence seemed to emanate from the shadowy corner of the club. Elisa couldn't help but be intrigued, her curiosity piqued by the allure of the unknown. The dimly lit room was filled with pulsating music and the clinking of glasses, but this mysterious duo caught Elisa's attention like nothing else that night.

Elisa turned to Charlene, a mischievous grin playing on her lips.

"Look, there are two men staring at you over there," she said, pointing subtly with her eyes.

Charlene's eyes widened with excitement as she turned around, not even trying to be discreet.

"Where?" she asked, her voice filled with anticipation.

Elisa chuckled at Charlene's eagerness.

"Damn, girl, you didn't have to look back that fast," shouted Elisa, both of them giggling drunkenly amidst the lively ambiance of the club.

As Elisa and Charlene continued to revel in their evening, unaware of the mysterious duo's presence, the two men exchanged a glance that didn't go unnoticed. Their eyes held a lingering intensity, filled with secrets waiting to be unveiled. An unspoken connection seemed to bind them, drawing them closer to Elisa and Charlene. Intrigued, Elisa couldn't help but feel a shiver run down her spine. There was something inexplicable about those men, something that stirred a sense of danger and excitement within her. As the night wore on, Elisa found herself stealing glances in their direction, unable to resist their magnetic pull. The mysterious duo played their part, occasionally glancing back at Elisa and Charlene, their eyes gleaming with a hidden agenda. It was as if they were following an unwritten script, waiting for the perfect moment to make their move.

As Elisa and Charlene sat in the club sipping on their drinks, the atmosphere was filled with an air of excitement. Lost in conversation, the two friends were startled when the two strangers approached their table. The first stranger, a tall man with mesmerizing green eyes and a charming smile, caught Elisa's attention. His voice carried a hint of admiration as he spoke.

"Excuse me," he said, his gaze fixed on Elisa. "I couldn't help but notice how stunning you look in that skirt. It suits you perfectly."

Elisa's cheeks turned a delicate shade of pink, her heart unexpectedly fluttering at the surprising compliment. A quick glance was exchanged between Elisa and Charlene, who was beaming with delight. They were both intrigued by the sudden attention they were receiving.

With a curious smile Elisa replied, "Thank you, that's very kind of you." The second stranger, a suave gentleman with a mischievous twinkle in his eyes, turned his attention to Charlene.

"Is it alright if we join you ladies for a drink?" he asked, his voice filled with a subtle hint of charm.

Elisa and Charlene exchanged glances once more, their responses reflecting their contrasting personalities. Elisa, cautious and reserved, hesitated for a moment before nodding in agreement.

However, Charlene, always adventurous and open to new experiences, enthusiastically exclaimed.

"Absolutely! We'd love some company." As the strangers took their seats, the conversation flowed effortlessly.

The green-eyed man engaged Elisa in a captivating discussion about art, while the mischievous gentleman entertained Charlene with witty anecdotes and stories. The evening seemed magical, as if fate had orchestrated this chance encounter.

"Don't tell anyone I said this, but I'm a little bit of a weirdo too, I hate going out," said Donald.

Elisa looked at him in astonishment.

"How did he know? "How could he sense her unease?" "Was she really that transparent?" Elisa thought to herself. She tried to form the words to ask him, but before she could speak, Donald chuckled, "Oh, I'm a little bit of a psychic by the way."

Elisa burst into laughter, surprised and intrigued by Donald's ability to break the ice with humour. They continued talking, their conversation flowing effortlessly, as if they had known each other for years. They shared stories, dreams, and fears, creating an instant connection. As the night went on, Elisa found herself laughing, dancing, and letting go of her worries in a way she had never experienced before. Donald's quirky personality and genuine understanding made her feel comfortable in her own skin. Hours passed and soon, they were the last ones left in the bar.

As the bartender announced the closing time, Elisa's curiosity was aroused. She glanced over at Donald, His eyes met hers, and a mischievous smile danced on his lips.

"Why don't you come back to mine?" he whispered, his voice dripping with anticipation.

Elisa hesitated, her mind racing with thoughts of work awaiting her on Monday. She couldn't afford to go off on an adventure tonight, or could she?

"Oh no, I have work on Monday, I can't," she replied, her voice filled with regret. "I'm sorry."

Donald's smile widened, and he leaned in closer. "Just one drink, I promise," he reassured her.

Charlene, Elisa's best friend, chimed in from the neighbouring seat.

"Go on girl, you haven't been out in years, go and have yourself a wonderful night. I'll call you in the morning, and we can get some breakfast or something."

Elisa pondered for a few seconds, torn between responsibility and the allure of the unknown. Finally, she gave in to the whispers of excitement tugging at her heart.

"Okay, but just one drink, and that's all," she agreed cautiously.

"Just one, I promise," Donald said, his eyes sparkling with mischief. "And if you want another one, then you can have six more." With laughter in their hearts and anticipation in the air, they both walked away from the dimly lit bar and into the starlit night.

They walked through the park, watching the moon and gazing at the stars. Suddenly, amidst the serenity of the park, a commotion caught their attention. A group of rowdy teenagers were causing a ruckus, their jeers echoing through the peaceful surroundings. Elisa's eyes narrowed in concern as she noticed them encircling a homeless man, their gestures menacing and cruel. They seemed to find pleasure in tormenting the vulnerable soul, callously flinging his meagre belongings onto the ground.

"Don't you kids have anything better to do? Leave me alone," the homeless man pleaded, his voice tinged with desperation.

Without a moment's hesitation, Elisa sprang into action. She swiftly made her way towards the unfolding scene, her voice cutting through the air like a clarion call.

"Hey, leave him alone!" she exclaimed, her words laced with a fierce determination.

Ignoring the scoffs of the teenagers, she bent down to assist the homeless man, tenderly gathering his scattered possessions and placing them back into his trolley with utmost care.

"I'm so sorry about them," she murmured softly, her eyes reflecting a wellspring of compassion.

As the teenagers slunk away, their bravado fading in the wake of Elisa's unwavering intervention, the homeless man gazed at her with profound gratitude shining in his tired eyes. A palpable silence enveloped the park, broken only by the gentle rustling of leaves and the distant hum of city life.

"It's alright, I'm okay," the homeless man said to Elisa, "they are young kids, they don't understand life just yet. Thank you, young lady, you are such a nice girl."

Elisa smiled warmly at the man and wished him a good night.

"Thank you, you too," she replied.

Watching Elisa's interaction with the homeless man, Donald felt a surge of admiration for her. She wasn't just beautiful; she was a wonderful person too.

"Look at you, superwoman," Donald teased, "can you save me too?"

Elisa chuckled.

"Well, If you want me too, I sure can."

As they walked on, the night wrapped them in its embrace, and they found themselves lost in deep conversation. They talked about their dreams, their fears, and their shared love for adventure. The park was their playground, and the moon their spotlight as they danced through the night. As the night grew later, they sat on a bench overlooking the city skyline. The city that never sleeps was alive with activity, but in that moment, it felt like the world belonged to just the two of them.

Five

The Ripple Effect

Elisa and Donald entered into his apartment, still laughing and having fun. Elisa couldn't help but admire the size and beauty of the place as her gaze roamed around the room. She was captivated by the sight of a staircase in the middle of the apartment that led to another level. The white tiles on the floor kept her feet cool. On the upper level, three bedrooms lay in wait, all decorated entirely in white with matching curtains and furniture. She then went into the kitchen, where there was a bar lined with alcohol bottles and surrounded by white bar stools. A large kitchen table and a six-burner stove completed the setup, making Elisa ponder what it would be like to cook here.

"This is the most spectacular apartment I have ever seen," Elisa marvelled as she explored the space. "It must have cost a fortune!"

"It's alright, I guess," Donald modestly replied.

"You are so humble! This place is incredible. If it were mine, I'd be jumping up on every counter," Elisa joked.

"Feel free then," Donald said.

"What do you mean?" Elisa was confused.

"Make yourself at home - whatever I own, is yours too," Donald clarified.

Elisa chuckled and took a seat at the table. Then, Donald removed his jacket and hung it up, before taking off his shoes and heading towards the bar area.

"Let's have a drink - what would you like?" he asked.

"I think I'll just stick to Champagne; no need to get too out of it when I need to go to work in the morning," Elisa answered.

Donald laughed.

"Actually I just came back from the Dominican Republic where they make an old concoction that dates back five hundred years; it's forbidden in the USA but I managed to sneak it in with some friends. It's called mamajuana – not marijuana!"

Elisa grinned,.

"Well if you're going to give me a history lesson on this drink, I guess I'll have to try some now."

"You're definitely going to love it," Donald assured her.

He stepped forward, taking the bottle of mamajuana and pouring Elisa her first glass of the liquor. Then he poured himself a drink and sat down next to her to drink it. She took a small sip, prompting him to urge her to take a bigger one.

"Oh come on, you can do better than that." Said Donald.

Taking a larger gulp, she remarked on how strong it was.

"WHOA! That's the strongest drink I have ever tasted in my life."

Elisa exclaimed, her voice filled with a combination of surprise and excitement. She tried to shake off the shivers that the potent concoction gave her, yet it was an exhilarating experience. The drink lived up to its reputation and her wild expectations.

Making his way over to the phonograph, he turned on the speakers and music began to fill the room as he finished off his glass. Performing an impromptu dance, he made his way back to the bar area and poured another drink. Swirling around the space, he came closer to Elisa and asked her to join him in dancing, but she demurred.

"No, no, I'm not good at dancing, please, I'll just watch you," she protested.

"Oh, stop it, are you telling me that the most beautiful girl in the world can't dance? Come on," teased Donald, reaching out to her with a contagious grin. His hand was warm and inviting, coaxing the reluctant Elisa from her seat.

A feeling of uncertainty washed over her as she rose, tentative yet intrigued. Elisa felt her cheeks flushed, but Donald's reassuring presence made her forget her inhibitions.

Donald held her close, their movements in perfect harmony.

"You are the most beautiful girl in the world. I think I might be in love already," he confessed, the room's chatter fading into white noise.

Elisa looked up at him, her heart thudding in her chest. His eyes held an intensity that made her breath hitch; the sincerity was impossible to ignore. Donald leaned in, bridging the gap between their lips. The tension crumbled, and Elisa found herself lost in the soft, warm taste of him. Their music providing a fitting backdrop to the unfolding romance. Elisa kissed him back, the murmurings of her uncertainty swept away with the melody. Although she was inebriated, Elisa was cognizant enough to know the man before her wasn't devoted to her. But he sure was attractive. He gently held the back of her head and her knees buckled from his embrace. Donald opened his eyes slowly to witness her reaction, pleased that she was enjoying it as much as he was. After a few seconds, they released each other's lips. Elisa's stomach churned with delight; it felt nice to be embraced again especially by such a handsome man.

"Let me pour you another drink," Donald said.

"Erm, I think I've had enough; I still have to work tomorrow." Responded Elisa.

"Don't worry, I'll make sure you get home safe; I don't want a beautiful girl like yourself out there all alone!" He thought about undressing her as he spoke these words.

"That would be great, thank you," Elisa replied when he handed her an extra glass.

"I'm going to freshen up a little," Donald announced, noting his excessive perspiration and unappealing smell. "I feel like that homeless man you just rescued!"

Elisa wasn't too happy about his comment, but she shrugged it off.

"Alright," Elisa replied as she took a sip of her drink.

Donald then left the room and walked over to the bathroom. Elisa stood up from her chair and walked around the expansive apartment.

"What she wouldn't give to live in a place like this!" she thought to herself. In the middle of the lounge was a huge glass table with a white rug below it.

The curtains were white, expensive-looking, and very luxurious. The white tiles on the floor sparkled like they had been freshly scrubbed—so clean that Elisa could even see her reflection in them. There weren't any personal photos around, just pricey drawings of naked men and women. As Elisa gazed at one of these images, she couldn't look away. It showed a woman lying face up—tears streaming down her left cheek; bruises on both her wrists and ankles; her skin glowing, almost as if someone had washed her; and one leg propped up, with what appeared to be blood coming from it. Elisa leaned in closer, mesmerized by the picture.

"Was she menstruating? That would be an odd way to take a photo of someone," Elisa thought. But the strangest part was that the woman was smiling—though not genuinely or against her will, Elisa couldn't tell which. Had someone hurt this woman? She wondered.

As she sank into her thoughts, Donald emerged from the bathroom in his white dressing gown. He looked ravishing. There was something special about him; he looked cleaner than before. Elisa couldn't help but smile as she admired him.

"I see you noticing that iconic photo," said Donald, a glimmer of joy in his voice as he walks over to stand beside her.

"It's beautiful, who took it?" asked Elisa.

"That would be me," he replied with pride. "Now, shall we have some fun?"

Donald poured them each another drink and placed hers on the glass table.

"You seem different somehow," said Elisa thoughtfully.

"Yeah, I don't want to be walking around this amazing place smelling like a bum," joked Donald.

Elisa laughed nervously; even though she wasn't too fond of the joke. Hugging her tightly, he then opened up a small packet and put some powder in her glass. Stirring it gently so it could dissolve quickly, he flashed her a grin. He cupped her face in both hands and kissed her sweetly.

"God, your lips are amazing. I could kiss you all day," Donald murmured with admiration.

He turned up the music and started grooving to its rhythm, performing rock star-like dance moves. Elisa gulped down the rest of her drink before placing the glass back on the table. She walked across to where Donald was standing and joined him in dancing together in harmony, enjoying themselves immensely.

A few minutes had passed and Elisa was starting to feel woozy. The drink was beginning to take hold, and she needed to rest for a bit.

"I need to sit down for a moment, that Dominican beverage certainly did the trick," Elisa stated as her head started to spin.

"Take a seat and let me grab you some water," Donald said as he walked over to the sink.

He ran the faucet and grabbed an empty cup from the cupboard before filling it with water. He then opened the freezer and took out some cubes of ice which he put in the glass before reaching into his pocket to get something else. He sprinkled some drugs into the glass, stirring it until it dissolved. Walking over to Elisa on the couch, he could tell she was dozing off but still conscious of her surroundings.

"Oh you poor thing, you don't go out much, do you? here have this," Donald said as he handed her the glass of water.

"No, I haven't been out in four years, nor have I been with anyone during that time," Elisa replied as she accepted the drink. The liquid tasted strange in her mouth, but perhaps that was because of all the alcohol still lingering on her breath. She quickly finished it off before attempting to lie down again.

"Let me help you back to the bedroom so you can rest this off." Donald offered, picking her up with his right arm around her shoulders; Elisa's body felt limp, as if she could no longer stand. It seemed he was right; she had had too much to drink.

As they arrived at Donald's bedroom, Elisa noticed its immense size; he placed her on the bed and stroked her hair. His fingers moved across her face, pressing against her lips with passionate intimacy. Elisa didn't know how to react. She hadn't been touched in years and it felt so good, yet wrong at the same time. Her body felt heavier in his embrace, getting warmer by the second.

"I need some air. I think I'm going to be sick," Elisa said, attempting to raise herself from the bed.

"Just relax, baby," Donald replied.

Lying on the bed, Elisa was alone with her thoughts, hoping that tomorrow would be a better day. Suddenly she felt Donald's hands encircle her neck. Rage and desire coursed through Donald's veins as he moves toward Elisa, his hands tightening around her neck. His grip didn't loosen until it travelled down to her chest and began tugging at her shirt, ripping it off of her in a single swift motion. Her skirt followed shortly after until Elisa's body was fully exposed in nothing but a bra and G-string. Donald stood back and ogle her body in admiration of its beauty. He soon moved over to where Elisa was laid out and found that she had no strength or reaction when he picked up her arms and tested them for responsiveness. Elisa lay exposed in nothing but a bra and G-string. Her soft, feminine curves were enough to drive him wild. Craving to taste her, he wanted his manhood deep inside of her now as he knelt between Elisa's opened legs.

With his robe removed, he was ready to pleasure her. He parted her vaginal lips, wanting to feel the pleasure of his touch as he caresses inside of her. His lips kissed hers with a tenderness that was almost indistinguishable from kissing regular lips. Taking in her aroma of lavender, he sucked on her clitoris. Elisa made no movement as Donald continued to pleasure her. He then forced his tongue inside of her, savouring the taste of her wetness. Seconds later, Donald dragged his fingertips around Elisa's anus, exploring its contours before inserting two of them. He tasted the digits on his index and middle fingers as he was swept away by her pleasure. Every part of her felt and tasted incredible, like a goddess in human form. Seconds passed as he moved up to the base of her spine, his hand sliding down to her vagina. With every breath she took, her breathing grew slower and deeper. Donald grabbed onto her arms and stretched them above her head, positioning himself between her legs. After spending a few moments with her vagina and anus, he planted a kiss on Elisa's lips while gripping her chin softly. Lying atop of her, he started devouring her breasts before thrusting himself inside of Elisa's body.

"Please stop..." she murmured in a half-awake state.

"It's okay baby, Daddy is going to take good care of you," Donald promised while continuing to rape her as she moved up and down with the thrusting of his penis within her walls.

Even though he expected it to be pleasurable for him, Donald did not anticipate just how good Elisa's pussy would feel. Before reaching climax, he quickly pulled out and laughed.

"Oh bitch, you almost caught me there didn't you!" As he spoke, his hands rhythmically worked his shaft back and forth.

He towered above Elisa's motionless body like a wild animal, his eyes wide and shining with a maniacal glee as he thrust his hips while clutching his erect penis. He released a guttural groan followed by a spray of warm ejaculation that landed on her chest and face. His chest heaved as he panted heavily, relishing in the afterglow of his perverse delight.

"We've got to do that again, sweetheart. You liked it don't you? Tell me how much you fucking enjoyed it!" He spat before taking hold of Elisa's delicate jawbone and forcing her to look at him.

No words escaped her lips, only vacant eyes stared back at him. Releasing his grip, he made his way over to an old wooden table in the corner of the room and carefully poured a thin line of white powder onto its surface. Placing one nostril directly above this make-shift drug line, he inhaled hard before slamming his fist into the wall and shouting.

"Let the fucking party begin!! Yeah!" as he threw his gaze towards the ceiling.

....

Elisa jolted awake, her head pounding and throat dry as a desert. She tried to move, only to be met with an unyielding tug from the ropes that bound her wrists and ankles, suspending her above the hard wooden headboard. Her wide eyes scanned the room. It was the only room in the house that was black. Fully black. There was nothing but darkness before her. Taking in every detail of her terrifying situation, restraints cut deep into her flesh, her feet spread uncomfortably wide, the entirety of her unclothed body exposed. In the centre of the room sat a table; its top littered with dark objects -- whips, dildos, guns, boxing gloves -- an array of pleasure and pain waiting to be experienced by Elisa's tender skin. A deep fear settled over her as she realized there was no escape through these twisted pleasures.

"Help! Someone help me, please!" Elisa gasped and tried to open her eyes and cry out.

Despite the strength of her plea, it seemed scarcely audible--the walls simply swallowed up her words. Moments later, Donald stepped into the room.

"Well, well, look who's finally awake! Welcome to my dungeon you sexy little thing!" he declared with a grin as he walked closer to Elisa.

As she attempted to lift her head upright, droplets of moisture oozed from her mouth. She looked at the man before her, he no longer appeared as handsome as before; instead, he had transformed into a monster. Red lines lined his eyes, and he was obviously intoxicated yet somehow seemed to stay on his feet.

"God, you are gorgeous," he breathed before he grabbed her face tightly and kissed her lips forcefully, then slid his tongue down into her throat.

Weak and powerless to resist, Elisa begged for him to free her.

"Let me go, please let me go..."

His reply was an echoing shout that filled the air.

"Let you go? We're only getting started baby! You rested for four hours already—now it's time for me to have my fun."

Donald shuffled over to the table and snorted a line of cocaine then washed it down with some hard liquor. He poured another glass and brought it back over to Elisa.

"Here you go—you love this mamajuana right? I've got more for you baby," he says as he yanked open her mouth and made her swallow the alcohol.

After chugging the drink and spilling some of it on her chest, Donald leaned in and lapped up the liquid from her skin with his tongue. His lips felt like fire against her body as he moved around her sensually.

His breathing grew heavier as he let out a loud moan before pulling away.

"FUCK YOU ARE SO HOT! You know what, I think I might keep you here for a little while longer. Shall we start?"

He grabbed the remote off the side table and increased the music to its loudest volume. Rock music began blaring from the speakers, filling the room with a frenetic energy. Looking like a real boxer, Donald walked over to a nearby table and reached for two boxing gloves which he tied tightly to his wrists with one swift movement. Then he started swaying his body around like a professional fighter would during their

first round. His smile faded as a more serious expression took over –
eyes narrowed; face contorted into deep thought. With a smirk on his
face, he hollered:

"I would be a pretty good boxer don't you think?" Getting no
response he then raised his voice even louder: "BITCH, I SAID I
WOULD BE A PRETTY GOOD BOXER DON'T YOU THINK?"

Immediately after his words left his mouth he threw an unexpected
punch at Elisa's left ribs, causing her to yell out in pain. He followed
up with several more punches until blood began pooling from an open
wound on her face. Elisa was screaming in agony with every blow.

"There's no use in screaming, sweetheart; I CREATED THESE
WALLS WITH MY BARE HANDS and made them perfect," he
bellowed, followed by another punch to Elisa's stomach. Her body
trembled as she threw up all over the floor.

"Scream louder! It turns me on!" he jeered before landing another
blow to her head.

This knocked Elisa out cold, leaving her tied to the machine. Minutes later, he threw a bucket of cold water on her, jolting her back
to reality. Her body shook uncontrollably. Donald couldn't look away
from Elisa, who was now beaten and bloodied in front of him. He
wanted her to suffer more - yet at the same time he couldn't help but
feel a strong attraction for her. He reached for the whip on the torture
table and hissed with pleasure as he struck her with it. Seeing her pain
made him feel powerful, almost invincible.

Cocaine and cannabis filled the air around them as Donald stripped
down and began to make strange incisions into his arm. The drugs
raced through his veins, pushing him further into a euphoric state as
he sunk deeper into his chair. Elisa's bruised body fascinated him, and

he marvelled at how beautiful she looked even after all that she had endured.

"I'm fucking amazing, just look at you!" he said as smoke billowed from his mouth.

He felt torn between wanting her to stay and wanting her to go – both desires raging within him.

"AHHHH, DAMN. I'VE UNLEASHED THE DEVIL IN ME BABY. Wake up". Donald shouted as he noticed that Elisa was becoming unconscious.

He rushed to her side with the whip in his hands. The whip was long and black with a one-inch-wide strip of leather at the end, which was wrapped in small metal rings. He then dipped the whip in cold water as he sprinkled cocaine on it. With each swing, it made a whistling sound like a bird or an airplane passing by. He lifted his arm back behind him and lashed out hard against her breasts with the whip held tightly between his thumb and forefinger. Elisa's skin was being removed from her body with every slash.

"Do you really think that Jesus was sleeping when He died for us?" he asked.

He was now shouting in a complete manic state, almost as if he was having a psychotic breakdown. Donald asked her questions over and over, while swinging again and again, effectively lacerating her smooth skin. He slashed at her chest seven more times before letting go of the bruised flesh on her chest so she could feel the intensified pain. With the last slash, he then held the whip in his hands, he saw that a bigger piece of flesh was removed from her skin, he stared at it with glee. He then removed the small piece of flesh from the whip and place it into his mouth. Chewing on it delicately, he smiled to himself. Seconds later he untied her arms and legs, first the left feet then the right - before releasing her hands. As she fell into a deep state of unconsciousness, she imagined meeting her dead parents who passed away in a car accident when she was six years old. She wanted to hug her mother again and taste her delicious cinnamon cake on a Thursday afternoon for lunch. Her mother's face smiled at Elisa as darkness took over.

He picked her up and carried her back to his room, her body limp in his arms. Flashes of her life flickered through her mind as she drifted in and out of consciousness. He laid her on the bed, face down, before rubbing her butt and planting kisses on it. His fingers moved inside her anus before he forcefully inserted his penis. Feeling her tightness around him, he suspected that this might be the first time she had something inside her ass. Removing his penis, he reached for a bottle of champagne and used his fingers to open her anus wider as he started pushing the bottleneck inside. As he continued to forcefully push the bottle inside of her, the bottle breaks inside of her anus. Elisa screamed in pain. Discarding the bottle, he turned her over onto her back. Her beauty still captivated him as he opened her mouth and stuck his penis inside it, telling her to suck it.

"You stupid bitch," he shouted, "I've been pleasuring you all night and you don't want to please me. I hate you, you fucking whore." As he forced his member further down Elisa's throat, she was powerless to resist.

Elisa attempted to force open her eyes and when she did, she noticed a small birth mark located near his genitalia.

"If you please me enough, I'll let you live. But if you fail to do so, then death will be your fate," he said in a threatening tone, trying desperately to keep her conscious.

Elisa tried her best but failed; she no longer had the energy required to satisfy him. This enraged him, and he thrashed her head with a powerful punch that knocked her out completely.

....

It was not long before Elisa found herself fully dressed on Donald's bed. He picks up her body and tries to shake her awake, but to no avail. Collecting her few belongings, he stood her up and wrapped his arms around her waist as they made their way to the door of his apartment. After speaking with someone for a few minutes, he handed Elisa over to them before shutting the door behind him and lighting up a cigarette. Sitting around the glass table, he turned on the television while pulling out his cell phone to message someone.

Six

A Journey Into The Luminosity of Existence

Elisa lay contorted in the back seat of the car in radiating pain. Her eyes felt raw and swollen; her skin, like it had been soaked in acid. The slightest motion sent shockwaves of agony through her body, and the smell of drugs and alcohol hung in the air around her. She tried to push herself up but her muscles were so weak she could barely move. As Elisa forced her eyes open, flickering streetlamps lit up the interior of the vehicle, only serving to emphasize how alone she felt. The car came to a jarring halt, and Elisa was thrown slightly forward before her body retched and she threw up inside. An unfamiliar man turned around from the driver's seat with a look of deep concern in his eyes. Calming her down he switched on the radio, filling the atmosphere with calm music that soothed her soul. Her mother's face filled her vision for one last time before deep sleep took over.

Moments later they arrived at her destination and the tall figure of 6-foot 4 got out of the car and grabbed a bag from the passenger seat before closing the door behind him. Reaching into the backseat, he noticed Elisa's vomit covering the car floor but with a shrug of his broad shoulders he decided to deal with it later. Fishing out her house keys from her bag, he tucked them into his pocket and lifted her up in his powerful arms with ease. With only one hand supporting her weight, he kicked open the door and quickly carried her off towards the apartment building without much effort. Pulling out her keys from his pocket, he effortlessly unlocked the door and pushed it opened. Walking over to the elevator, he pressed the button for Elisa's floor. Waiting for a few seconds, the elevator eventually arrived. As the elevator opens, he could smell a foul scent, his face screwed up in disgust, he stepped into the elevator. Just as the doors were about to shut, Carolina's voice called out behind him. She was carrying shopping bags and had just come off her shift; exhausted, she wanted to get home quickly. Panicked at being seen, he instinctively hit the buttons multiple times. Fortunately, Carolina didn't make it in time and the elevator doors closed, taking him where he wanted to go.

"Well fuck you then. Go to hell, you bastard!" Carolina yelled.

He stepped out of the elevator and inserted the key into Elisa's door. It was worn-out from the outside but he could still tell that she had decorated her apartment to suit her tastes. After laying Elisa's body down on her bed, he noticed how ravishingly beautiful she was. Her long dark hair spread across her face like a curtain; he couldn't believe his eyes. But, like always, he had a job to do and he wasn't going to let emotions get in the way. He then undressed her, taking off her shirt first and then her trousers. He removed her bra and panties, leaving her completely nude. The man observed Elisa's bruised body with shock; it had never been this bad before. Something seemed different about this one—she didn't deserve this kind of treatment. Searching around the room for a bathroom, he put his gloves back on before running the shower to make sure the temperature was right. He walked back to the bedroom and lifted Elisa's weak body up into the shower, letting the water wash over her battered skin. Blood streamed out of her pores as he washed her down with soap and chemicals, his fingers skimming gently over her body as if they were feathers. He ran shampoo through her hair before opening up her legs and delicately inserting his fingers inside her in an attempt to erase any evidence of what had happened the previous night.

Minutes later, he holds a towel close to her body and lifts her up. He lays her down on the bed and gently begins drying her off, careful to avoid pressing too hard on any of her scars. As he wipes her skin clean, he couldn't help but admire her figure. He then takes her hairbrush from the nightstand and starts brushing her hair. He looks at her in awe, wondering how anyone could create something so beautiful. Even as she lies there helpless and naked, his heart tells him that he must protect this woman. He finishes brushing out her hair and arranges the pillows beneath her head to make sure she's comfortable. He takes one last look at all of the wounds dotting her body before he tenderly kisses each one. From her feet which were bound together to the other side of what was likely a long list of bruises - his lips caress every single one. When he reaches for her face, he hesitates, not wanting to take things too far. Instead, he turns around and leaves a kiss on her exposed backside.

The unidentified man kissed every cut on her body, and then knelt down and opened her anus. He lingered here longer, knowing this was where she had endured greater suffering. Turning Elisa over, he became overwhelmed with emotions that he couldn't explain. He'd never felt anything like this before for a stranger. Gazing at her broken form, he tenderly kissed her neck then removed his clothing and lay beside her. With slow, deliberate movements, he straddled Elisa. She was still unable to move or speak; the drugs in her system were strong and her head pounded as if she had been hit by a car. In his mind, he wanted to soothe all of Elisa's pain so that she could forget about it forever. His blue eyes stared at her as he pushed inside of her slowly in rhythmical motions. He then cupped her right breast in his hands and gently sucked on each nipple before repeating the same actions on the left side.

An hour passed and he was still working to calm her body. When finished, he pressed a gentle kiss on her lips; something that he would've never done before. He rose from the bed, revealing his own nakedness. Moving Elisa in his arms, he brought her into the bathroom and turned the shower on. He washed her from head to toe with his cleaning supplies, taking care that not a single strand of DNA remained on her. Afterwards, he carried Elisa back to the bedroom and brushed her hair tenderly as he stared at her face. Donning his clothes again, he went over to the closet and found another set of sheets. Lifting Elisa's body once more, he put her down on the sofa and switched out all of the bed linen before wiping down the room with his products, making certain that no evidence was left behind. Back in the bedroom, he covered Elisa up with a duvet and rearranged her pillow for good measure. His next task was to find and bag up her clothing that she had been wearing earlier. In addition, he thoroughly scrubbed the bathroom top-to-bottom before gathering his cleaning supplies and any other traces of himself left in the apartment. With his gloves still on, he took one long look at Elisa before heading out for his long drive home.

Seven

Unseen & Unheard

A gust of cool, autumnal morning air swept past as Charlene's sensible shoes crunched on the gravel. Lovelace Elementary School stood majestically before her, almost as if it was an age-old shrine of learning seeped in history, yet teeming with the vivacious energy of youth. Its ivory walls, etched in time, bore the mark of countless giggles, shared secrets, and dreams of generations neatly etched within its silent throbbing heart.

"Good morning, Miss Bennett!" A spirited voice hollered, pulling her out of her thoughts.

That was Cynthia, a precocious third grader with a mischievous twinkle in her eyes. The child was sprinting, her Velcro shoes barely touching the ground. Charlene smiled warmly, buttoning up her cardigan.

"Good morning, Cynthia. Don't forget to do your homework this week - no excuses! Not even that your dog ate it."

As she chuckled, her eyes, hidden behind a pair of chic glasses, sparkled with joy. She loved this, the everyday hustle and bustle, the hopes and dreams that echoed in this corridor - this was her realm, her sanctuary.

Walking into her classroom, her heart echoing with familiar warmth, the stern visage of the Principal came into view. Her grey hair was neatly pinned up, her floral dress fluttered softly as she moved - a timeless blend of authority and grace.

"Charlene," Principal Morrison's voice broke the silence, a slight hint of urgency in her tone. "Let me borrow you for a minute please."

Intrigued, Charlene followed her into the office, her mind constructing myriad possibilities. Was it about the new curriculum? Or perhaps the upcoming charity drive? Or was it something more serious? As she stepped into the office, the door closed behind her, the whispers of nostalgia replaced by an puzzling silence. The venerable, oak desk stood as an island amidst the sea of uncertainty, the world outside forgotten for a moment. The bright morning sunlight filtered through the blinds in the principal's office, casting an eerie glow around her.

She looked at Charlene, her usually jovial face masked with concern. "How are you doing today?" she asked, leaning back in her plush chair, her fingers tapping a rhythm of unease on her mahogany desk.

Charlene, usually so bubbly and effervescent, paused before she answered.

"I'm doing well, thanks. I had a great time with Elisa on the weekend, then I slept for most of the day when I arrived back, I am not as young as I used to be I tell you, I need at least a week to recover from my hangovers." Her voice trailed off, her eyes clouding over as she remembered their weekend of laughter and camaraderie.

The principal frowned, her thick eyebrows furrowing in a sigh of relief.

"That sounds great, Charlene. Thankfully you don't work Mondays, otherwise, you would have been utterly exhausted!" She attempted a half-hearted smile, but her concern was palpable.

"Have you seen Elisa lately?" she asked, shifting in her chair. "She didn't show up yesterday and I haven't seen her this morning either. Normally she could be heard rushing through the doors like a headless chicken trying not to be late but I've been calling her phone since yesterday and there's been no answer."

Charlene's heart pounded in her chest. Seeing her principal's distress, she tried to remain composed.

"Yeah, that doesn't sound like her..." she said as casually as she could muster. "I'll go have a look for her this afternoon." Said Charlene, a woman known for her sharp mind, and empathetic heart. She was the most respected teacher at the school, owing as much to her exemplary knowledge as to her congenial nature.

"Do you think you could do it now? I can get Mrs. Carter to pick up your morning class. That way we don't need to call out a wellness check – you know how long and tedious those take," the principal interjected, her voice saturated with worry. The teacher's absence was unsettling, especially knowing that Elisa was a person of impeccable punctuality.

With no room for arguments, Charlene grabbed her things, leaving her half-filled coffee cup behind, which was unlike her. She was a lady of routine, but today was different. Today, the concern for her co-worker and best friend overpowered everything else.

"And if she is sick, make sure she calls in – I don't want to have to file an incident report on this one," the principal's voice echoed behind her as she hurriedly made her way through the hallways and out into the schoolyard.

"Will do!" Charlene shouted back, her voice a blend of determination and apprehension.

The summer leaves crunched under her feet as she made her way out of the school gates, the chill in the air encapsulating the anxiety that hung over her. As the schoolyard faded behind her, the uncertainty of what awaited her loomed overhead. Little did she know, the day ahead had a sequence of events in store that would leave a lasting impression not only on her but on the entire world. The fate of the missing teacher and the impending chain of events were now spiralling into an abyss of endless possibilities, and all Charlene could do was brace herself for what was to come.

Eight

Overwhelming Catastrophes

As Charlene pulls up to Elisa's apartment building, she couldn't help but notice how tight the parking space was. Her car barely fitting into the small spot, but she managed to manoeuvre it with ease. Taking a deep breath, she turned off her vehicle and gathered her belongings - her phone, her handbag, and most importantly, her car keys. With a sigh, Charlene opened the driver's side door and stepped out of the car, turning around to lock it, she places the key in the car and turns it to the left once. Checking to see if she closed it right, she pulls the car handle. As she walks towards Elisa's building, she couldn't help but be disappointed by the state of the place.

The smell hit her the moment she entered, a nauseating combination of urine and faeces that seemed to permeate every inch of the stair-well. Elisa's apartment, on the other hand, was a different story. It was a place to die for - stylishly decorated, with a hit of cinnamon always floating through the air. Charlene couldn't help but envy her friend's taste and ability to transform the space into a haven amidst the dilapidated building. It was a stark contrast that left her perplexed. She couldn't comprehend how someone could live in such a rundown building, and yet create a sanctuary within their own four walls. It was as if Elisa had managed to shield herself from the external horrors, turning a blind eye to the unpleasantness that surrounded her.

Pressing the button, the lift immediately opens. She was happy that the lift was already on the ground floor; the quicker she could get Elisa out of bed, the better, she thought to herself, a sense of urgency engulfing her. The lift smoothly ascends, carrying her up to Elisa's apartment floor. As she walks towards the door, she couldn't help but feel a sense of unease. Knocking loudly, she waits, expecting a swift response. A minute passes, and then another, but there is no answer. She chews her gum rapidly, a nervous habit that she couldn't seem to shake off. Without any indication that Elisa is awake, she tries again, knocking with more force this time. Silence engulfs the corridor as she waits, her heart pounding against her chest. One more attempt, she thinks to herself, as her hand rises to knock on the door for the third time.

The anticipation builds as she pauses, hoping to hear the sound of footsteps or the creaking of the door opening. But there was nothing. Utter silence surrounds her, like a thick fog that refuses to dissipate. Confusion creeps into her mind. Elisa is usually prompt with her morning routine, always ready to take on the day. This sudden absence from the door is unusual, perplexing even.

Questions flooded her thoughts.

"Is Elisa still asleep?" "Did she leave without informing anyone?" The possibilities swirl in her mind, creating a whirlwind of uncertainty.

Unable to contain her curiosity any longer, she reaches into her pocket and pulls out her phone. With trembling fingers, she dials Elisa's number, hoping for a response. The anticipation builds with each ring. One... two... three... and then, voicemail.

"Where could she be? Why isn't she answering?" A sense of unease washes over her, the unanswered questions gnawing at her core.

As she could not get any response, she removes her bags from her shoulders. She was wearing a black handbag with a large butterfly in the middle. Opening the zip of the bag, she searches through it. putting the bag on the ground she tries once again.

"God dammit, I don't have the spare key she gave me. How the hell am I going to get in now". she moans.

As she stands up, she then bangs on the door a few more times. She contemplates her next move, feeling an overwhelming responsibility to ensure Elisa's well-being. Should she wait outside the door a little longer? Should she seek help from the building management? The options play out in her mind like a strategic game, each move carrying its own risks and uncertainties. As she stands outside the apartment door, she bangs again a few more times, As her bangs became louder, Carolina opens her apartment door, with a very frustrating and angry look on her face.

"What the fuck is going on out here, are you the God damn police, why are you banging down the door like that, I have a headache and I am trying to sleep, this is the only day that I have off work." Shouted Carolina has she looked at Charlene.

"Oh hey Carolina, I'm so sorry, I've been trying to contact Elisa, but I haven't been able to get hold of her, and she hasn't turned up to work in two days. Have you seen her?" asked Charlene.

"No I haven't seen her since she went out over the weekend, this was after I told her to meet me for a few drinks, and to check on our neighbour because she might be dead, but she went out instead, don't you have a spare key or something?" responded Carolina.

"Yes, I do, but I left it at home, I thought she would've answered the door my now." Answered Charlene.

"Well, don't let anyone know that I did this for you, hold on one second." Says Carolina, as she walks to her apartment and returned with a sharp object in her hands.

Moving closer to Elisa's apartment door, she places the sharp object into the keyhole, within seconds the door was open, and Charlene had an astonished look on her face.

"Wow, how the hell did you learn how to do that?" asked Charlene.

"Listen honey, this is the ghetto. You have to learn how to stay safe and protect yourself, you also have to know how to make some money, you know what I mean? Joked Carolina. "Now, don't go around telling anyone either because I will deny all criminal charges". She responded.

"I won't, as long as you promise to break into my Ex's house and steal all the shit I gave him, I won't tell a soul." Chuckled Charlene.

They both joked as Charlene entered the apartment. As Charlene enters Elisa's apartment, there was nothing out of the ordinary, her apartment was clean as always and as she looked on, she could see Elisa laying peacefully in her bed. As she approached Elisa, she thought that she was fully sleeping, and was still out of it from the weekend.

"Knowing that Elisa did not drink too much, she must've had a wonderful time with that man she went home with," thought Charlene.

"I can't believe you actually over slept Elisa, I'm not taking you anywhere again," she says as she walks closer to her bed.

As she approaches Elisa she could see a very pale look on her face, it looked almost like she was going black and blue. She then bent down and looked at Elisa face, pulling back her duvet slowly, she realised that Elisa's whole body was changing colour and she was not breathing. It was also shocking to realise that Elisa's body was battered and bruised all over. Dropping her handbag and belongings on the ground, she held Elisa in her arms, screaming for help, she was almost in a manic state as tears runs down her cheeks.

"HELPPP.... HELP ME PLEASE, SOMEONE CALL THE AMBU-LANCE, SHE'S NOT BREATHING. HELP ME!" Charlene desperate plea rang through the corridor, carrying a sense of urgency that reso-nated with her neighbours.

Within moments, the sound of running footsteps filled the hallway. Concerned neighbours, their faces etched with worry, flocked to Elisa's apartment door. Panic rippled through the air as Carolina rushed back to her neighbours side, her heart pounding in her chest. Time seemed to stand still as Charlene cradled Elisa in her arms, her tears mixing with the rush of voices around her. The weight of the situation bore down on her, and an overwhelming sense of helplessness consumed her. As the minutes ticked by, Charlene's pleas for help grew louder, her voice straining against the weight of the moment. Elisa's lifeless form lay before her, a stark contrast to the lively friend she had known. Her pale skin, tinged with a haunting blue, revealed the severity of the situation, while the bruises on her body told a story of pain and suffer-ing. The neighbours watched in silence, their eyes filled with disbelief and concern. The urgency in the air was palpable, as if the very heart-beat of the community depended on Elisa's survival.

"PLEASE GET SOMEONE HERE NOW, SHE'S NOT BREATH-ING, PLEASE". Yelled Carolina as she held her hands up and runs it through her hair. Carolina could not believe what she was seeing.

And while still being on the phone with the police, she slowly walks over to Elisa's body and covers if with the sheet that was on the bed. As the minutes stretched on, an eerie hush fell over the crowd. The collective breath of hope hung in the air, mingling with the silent prayers whispered by those who stood witness to the unfolding tragedy. Each passing moment felt like an eternity, anticipation building, and hearts beating in collective unison. Finally, the wailing sound of sirens pierced through the silence, growing louder and closer with each passing second. A wave of relief washed over Carolina as she realized help has arrived. The paramedics burst through the door, their expertise and determination shining through their eyes.

With skilled hands and a swift sense of urgency, the paramedics took over, working tirelessly to revive Elisa's fragile body. Carolina watched, her eyes welling up with tears, her heart filled with a blend of gratitude and anxiety. Every beat of Elisa's heart felt like a precious gift, a second chance at life. Just when all hope seemed lost, a gasp escaped Elisa's lips, breaking the spell of despair that had enveloped the room. Everyone held their breath, their eyes locked on the miracle unfolding before them. Elisa's chest rose and fell, each breath a testament to the resilience of the human spirit. As Elisa was whisked away in the ambulance, surrounded by a team of caring professionals, Carolina stood there, her face etched with a mix of relief and uncertainty. The neighbourhood fell into an uneasy silence as the ambulance disappeared into the day, leaving behind unanswered questions and a lingering sense of wonder.

Nine

A Place of Hope

U nder the harsh illumination of the fluorescent lights, in an unending white corridor of the hospital, a drama unfolded. Rushing her body on a stretcher through the hospital, doctors surrounded Elisa as she laid motionless. The white corridor echoed with urgent footsteps and hushed voices. Panic filled the air. The hospital reverberated with their swift, heavy footsteps, like the ominous beat of a war drum, punctuating the tension that hung in the air.

"Elisa, can you hear me?" the anxious voices of the doctors echoed through the sterile hallway.

Elisa's lifeless form lay there, unresponsive, her ghostly pale face was a stark contrast against the crisp hospital sheets. There was palpable urgency in the air, and the incessant beep of the heart monitor was the only proof that she was still clinging onto life.

"She's not responding, her vitals and pulse are plummeting. We need to operate immediately. There might be a bleed in her brain," a senior doctor's voice cut through the tense room, his eyes reflecting the seriousness of the situation.

"A bleed in her brain, what does that mean? Will she be okay?" Charlene, Elisa's best friend, stammered, her fear evident in her trembling voice and tear-streaked face.

The medical team was swift, their professional veneer never faltering even as the urgency in the room cranked up a notch. They started to wheel Elisa into the OR, leaving Charlene in the cold, unsettling silence of the waiting area, her mind teeming with worst-case scenarios. With the hands of the clock hanging on the wall seeming to tick with peculiar urgency, every passing second was a siren call, a reminder of the fragileness of human life teetering on the edge. Dr. Langton, a man marked by the trials and triumphs of a life spent in the emergency room, held the gaze of a distraught woman standing before him.

His voice, usually steady and reassuring, wavered just briefly as he confronted the severity of the situation.

"I can't say for sure. She's in critical condition, but our team will do everything we can. We have to act quickly," he breathed out, each word a solemn promise from a healer to a desperate friend. Charlene could only respond with a strangled gasp as a wave of fear washed over her.

"Ma'am, please step back. You have to wait here. I'm sorry," the doctor urged Charlene as she hovered just a step behind him, her desperate need to be with Elisa creating a visible tension in the air.

Obediently, Charlene took one step back, then another, each movement seeming to echo around the sterile confines of the hospital corridor. As she watched the flurry of white coats surround her dear friend and whisk her away, her heart pounded mercilessly against her rib-cage.

A silent plea slipped past her trembling lips as she whispered her friend's name, "Elisa", into the tense atmosphere.

In her mind's eye, she could see Elisa laughing, a radiant image of vitality and life, their shared memories flooding Charlene's mind in stark contrast to the reality of the moment. From their college days filled with dreams of the future to their shared joy of corporate victories, their friendship had been a series of highs and lows, triumphs, and tears. Charlene felt a lump in her throat as the stark hospital lights faded into a disorienting blur. A warm tear trickled down her cheek, a silent testament to the worry consuming her. And there she waited, her heart wrapped in a blanket of uncertainty and fear, her mind replaying the echo of the doctor's words. The frantic rhythm of the hospital kept time with her racing thoughts, each tick tock a reminder of Elisa's precarious balance between life and death.

....

There was something unsettling about the stillness of the hospital halls at night. It was as though time had chosen to hold its breath, awaiting an outcome that could tilt the scales of fate. Against this eerily quiet backdrop, Charlene paced restlessly, anxiety contorting her normally calm features. The world outside progressed at a normal pace, oblivious to her ordeal. But for Charlene, time had slowed down to a torturous crawl, each tick of the clock echoing loudly in her head. The scent of the hospital burned in her nostrils but it was the oppressive silence that disturbed her the most. In those moments, silence wasn't golden, it was a glaring neon sign of the uncertainty that gnawed relentlessly at her.

Every passing second was like a stone added to the weight she felt pressing down on her, as she continued her silent vigil in the waiting room. Her mind was a labyrinth of worry, with a thousand questions ricocheting inside her head, leaving her winded, and her patience threadbare. Then, finally, the silence was broken. With a slow, creaking sound that resonated through the quiet hallway, the operation room doors swung open. Dr. Langton a usually buoyant man, emerged. Today, however, there was a firm restraint in his step, and his face was etched with exhaustion. As Charlene rushed towards him, her heart pounded against her chest like a wild drum. Her eyes, wide and expectant, searched his for signs of hope. He took off his glasses and wiped the sweat off his brow before he acknowledged her silent plea. He opened his mouth to speak, and Charlene's heart seemed to stop, waiting for the words that would determine her fate.

"Is she okay?" she asked, her voice trembling with anticipation.

The silence in the hospital corridor was broken only by the haunting echo of her desperate question. The suspense hung heavy in the air, like an unseen mantle of dread. Every tick of the looming wall clock seemed to crash into the eerie silence like a dull drum, accentuating the gravity of the situation. Dr. Langton, a man with decades of experience etched on his face, met her anxious eyes with a gaze softened by compassion.

"We managed to control the bleed and stabilize her condition. But she's still unconscious. We'll have to wait and see," he explained, his tone not promising, but filled with a hint of cautious optimism.

Relief washed over Charlene, temporary though it was. It was like a parched traveller finding a murky puddle in an endless desert. The solace that the worst had been averted was marred by the uncertainty of what lay ahead. Charlene took a deep breath, shoving away the dark clouds of despair, clutching onto the glimmering silver lining of hope. Her heart ached as she thought of her friend, Elisa. A woman who was always so full of life, now lay lifeless on a cold hospital bed.

....

Days turned into weeks and weeks turned into months, as Charlene remained steadfast by Elisa's side. She became a fixture in the room, the silent sentinel who refused to leave her friend's bedside. The doctors, fuelled by the indomitable spirit of their profession, worked tirelessly, monitoring Elisa's condition. Their faces, initially guarded and grim, began to reflect a glimmer of hope. Charlene, on the other hand, found herself oscillating between bouts of despair and hope. It was a distressing dance on a tightrope, where on one side lay the abyss of despair and on the other, the chasm of false hope. In the quiet moments when Elisa's room was empty and saved for the two of them, Charlene found herself beseeching any higher power that would listen. She bartered, begged and pleaded for a miracle.

Months continued, and Elisa remained in her comatose state. Yet, in the deafening silence, Charlene clung to one reassuring fact; her friend was still alive. And as long as that fact remained, her hope refused to die.

Ten

Echoing Visits

The cold chill of the hospital corridors seemed to seep into Charlene's very bones, a daily reminder of the perilous balance between life and death. Each tick of the clock echoed through the hospital white walls, a haunting symphony of seconds lost and minutes wasted. Every day, after the monotonous routine of work, Charlene found herself venturing into these unforgiving corridors, her heart burdened with worry for her friend Elisa.

Elisa, the vibrant soul whose laughter once echoed in their shared moments of joy, now laid silent and still, trapped within the confines of her own body, after the incident that had snuffed out her vitality, leaving her in a deep, impenetrable coma. Elisa had no family to call her own, and therefore it fell on Charlene, and occasionally Carolina, to endure the harsh reality of her stillness. Charlene's days became a repetitive sequence of tree-like hope and sinking despair. Hours turned into days, days into weeks, and weeks into agonizing months. Yet, within the muted grey of the hospital room, Charlene continued her vigil. She brought Elisa fragrant bouquets of peonies and roses, whispering sweet nothing's to her sleeping friend. Pillows were fluffed, blankets adjusted, every single detail attended to with a meticulous eye. She found herself frequently questioning Elisa's doctors, her voice desperate for some hint of improvement, some indication that Elisa was not lost to them.

As the days wore on, the monotonous hum of the life-support machine became a haunting lullaby for Charlene. She could almost hear the faint echoes of Elisa's laughter interwoven with the rhythm. Her mind began to spin tales of a future where Elisa would wake up, of days filled with shared laughter and companionship. Yet the harsh reality of the hospital room always pulled her back. In the stillness of one particular night, as Charlene sat by Elisa's side, she found herself whispering another prayer of desperate hope. The soft glow of the bedside lamp cast long shadows across Elisa's face, highlighting the unfair tranquillity of her slumber.

"Please," Charlene murmured, her voice barely a whisper. "Come back to us, Elisa."

As the words hung in the air, Charlene was left to wonder - what would the next day bring? Would her friend finally wake up or would she be forever lost to the depths of her eternal sleep? The unknown promise of tomorrow loomed ahead, leaving a poignant trail of curiosity in its wake.

Eleven

Time's Impact

Elisa's eyes fluttered open, a welcoming dance to the golden beams of morning sunlight that poured into the room, casting abstract patterns on the clean white walls. This was not her home. Drenched in a state of disarray, Elisa was like a solitary island in a sea of strange equipment. Cold, metallic arms connected her to a network of humming machines, their lights blinking in an alien rhythm. The tubes snaking across her body were conduits of life, yet a stark reminder of her yet-to-be-discovered predicament.

Confusion gnawed at her tired mind, her memories blurred like an abstract painting splattered with a riot of unrecognizable colours. With a heavy bandaged head, she made a valiant attempt to connect the loose threads of her cognition. A soft moan slipped past her cracked lips, the only language her pain-ridden body could speak. But amid the chaos, a comforting sight entered her periphery. There, in the nondescript station hospital chair, Charlene, her closest friend and confidante, slumbered peacefully. Her rose-tinted cheeks glowed softly in the sunlight, and her chest rose and fell rhythmically. Charlene seemed to carry a halo of tranquillity around her, a stark contrast to the tempest brewing within Elisa.

Seeing Charlene stirred a sense of comfort, a soothing balm over the sting of worry. Still, like a phantom in the dark, unease followed closely on the heels of this temporary peace. It lurked in the shadows, unseen but felt – an ever-pressing question mark on the end of every thought. Each second heavy with a mounting suspense. As the seconds passed, Elisa noticed the subtle changes in the room - the steady hum of machinery, the soft rustle of Charlene's breath and the occasional distant sound of footsteps. With each discovery, her worries seemed to grow, manifesting into a gnawing feeling of dread that curled itself around her heart, refusing to let go.

Elisa's eyes once again flickered open like an old-time movie projector, and she found herself swallowed in a concert of sunlight that showered through a misty window. The aesthetic of the room, while beautiful, felt alien and discomforting. A wave of bewilderment and uncertainty crashed over her as her gaze traced the flurry of tubes that seemed to have taken root within her. They sprawled across her frail form like a network of twisted vines, connecting her to humming machines that echoed the rhythm of her pulsating heart. Fighting the restrictions of her gauze-wrapped head, she attempted to make sense of the bizarre predicament she was knotted in. A soft whimper escaped her lips, a meek protest against the mystery that enveloped her existence.

But even as a wave of nostalgia washed over her, a chilling sense of unease clawed at her gut. A puzzle was forming in her mind, yet the pieces remained a jumbled, chaotic mess. What had happened? How had she ended up here? Her memory was like a cloudy mirror, images distorted and obscured. Elisa turned her head back to the ceiling, the sunlight highlighting the unspoken words on her lips. Her eyes fluttered closed again, as if praying for a revelation. The end was as sudden as a storm on a clear day. As quickly as the life seemed to burst back into her, it receded. Her breathing slowed, her eyes remained closed. The machines hummed their usual hymn, but there was a strange calm.

Charlene awoke with a start, her eyes wide as she took in the sight of her motionless friend.

"Elisa," Charlene whispered, her voice filled with disbelief.

She had spent countless nights beside her best friend's hospital bed, hoping for this very moment, yet never truly believing it would come. Tears welled up in Charlene's eyes as she reached out to hold Elisa's hand. Overwhelmed with emotion, she struggled to find words, her heart racing with a mixture of joy, relief, and lingering uncertainty. As the two friends locked eyes, a flood of questions swirled in Elisa's mind. What had led her to this moment? How had she come to be in such a vulnerable state? The room seemed to close in around her, suffocating her with its sterile presence.

The dimly lit hospital room buzzed with tension as Charlene watched over her best friend Elisa, who lay still on the bed. The rhythmic beeping of the heart monitor served as a constant reminder of the fragility of life. Charlene had been by Elisa's side day and night since she found her unconscious. But today was different. The room suddenly fell silent as Elisa's eyelids flickered, as if trying to break free from the heaviness that held them shut. Excitement surged through Charlene's veins as she reached out, her trembling hand gently brushing against Elisa's face. A spark of hope ignited within her, filling the room with an air of anticipation. Without wasting a second, Charlene dashed towards the door, her heart pounding in her chest. She sped through the hospital corridors, determined to find a nurse or doctor who could confirm what she had just witnessed. Panic and urgency clouded her mind, echoing through her footsteps. Finally, Charlene stumbled upon a group of doctors discussing a case at the end of the hallway. Her voice trembled as she called out for their attention, her words tumbling out in a jumble of desperation. The doctors, taken aback by her frantic demeanour, exchanged puzzled glances before following her back to Elisa's room. As the doctors entered the room, their astonishment mirrored Charlene's. Elisa, who had been motionless for what felt like an eternity, had somehow defied all odds and awakened from her deep slumber. It was as if a miracle had taken place right before their eyes. Amidst the commotion, doctors hurriedly checked Elisa's vitals, their eyebrows furrowed in disbelief. Each heartbeat seemed to whisper a tale of determination, as if Elisa's very soul fought to reclaim its place in the world. While one doctor rushed to inform the police department, Charlene held onto a glimmer of hope, her heart soaring with the possibilities that lay ahead.

Twelve

The Transformative Call

In the heart of a gritty city, the early dawn rolled a sheet of ethereal mist over the police station. Inside, Sergeant Soliman had just marked his presence, clutching a steaming cup of coffee in one hand, the other laden with a burgeoning pile of paperwork. The relentless chatter of typewriters, ringing telephones, and hushed conversations echoed through the station, sparking a swirl of nostalgia and fatigue within him.

His eyes gravitated towards the walls, a grisly gallery of unsolved cases. Every pinned photograph, each casualty of violence, represented a life yearning for closure and for justice. These were the faces that haunted him in the wee hours, the echoes of their unheard screams keeping him awake, determined to seek the elusive resolutions. Just as he had countless times before, he settled into his worn-out chair, the creaking of the leather a familiar melody. However, amongst the routine, there was a sudden shift. An unusual sense of astonishment washed over Sergeant Soliman. The sun peeked through the curtains, casting long streaks across the worn, mahogany desk nestled amid scribbled case notes and a mug of steaming coffee, he felt an unexpected wave of optimism swell within him. Sergeant Soliman was a man moulded by years of chasing shadows, fighting crime, and dealing with the worst humanity had to offer. Yet, today, the atmosphere seemed different, leaving even this hardened criminal detective feeling hopeful.

As the weight of his upcoming retirement loomed closer, he found himself yearning for an odd sense of resolution. Time was running out, the sands of the hourglass slipping away quickly. Now, he needed to bring closure, not only to the endless sea of faces etched in his memory —the victims and their grieving families—but also for himself. The loose ends of unsolved cases tugged at him, like a stinging reminder of battles left unfinished. Poised to attack the Everest of paperwork on his desk, he was interrupted by the sudden shrill of his phone. A sigh escaped him as he set down his black coffee, mid-sip. His wrinkled hand slowly reached towards the phone, like a sloth navigating through dense vegetation.

The moment the sun peeped over the horizon, that fourth ring of the phone echoed through the silence in his office. Fumbling through the pile of unsolved case files spread open on the table, he squinted at the caller ID. It glared back: "Saint Mary's Hospital." His heart began to reverberate like a drum inside his chest, playing the rhythm of his worst fears.

"Sergeant Soliman," he announced, his voice was as rusty as an old hinge, tension seeping into each syllable.

"Sergeant, it's Dr. Washington here," came the voice from the other end, firm and urgent, "I thought you should know. Elisa, the assault victim who fell in a coma a few months ago- she just woke up."

His world came to an abrupt standstill. The edges of his vision blurred. The case that had been his worst nightmare, his most persistent demon, now held a spark of hope. Elisa, the once vibrant teacher, now the key to unlocking a mystery that had sent shivers down the spine of the city, had emerged from the dark abyss of unconsciousness.

Her case was unlike any other Soliman had worked. A gifted teacher, Elisa was found in her apartment, brutalized and left in a coma. Her body, splattered with bruises, told a chilling story of a struggle, but fell short of revealing the identity of her assaulter. For months, Soliman had been grappling with dead ends, chasing shadows in the dark realm of the unknown. But now, Elisa was awake. His breath hitched as he registered the weight of this new development. His mind began to probe, to question, to hope. Could she remember? Could she identify her assaulter?

"Thank you, Doctor," Soliman managed to utter, his mind already racing ahead, assembling pieces of an incomplete puzzle.

He ended the call, his mind teeming with possibilities. An eerie silence hung in the room as the gravity of the situation slowly sank in. He looked around at the files, the pictures, the pieces of a broken life waiting to be pieced together. All at once, it seemed as though the walls of his apartment, previously filled with the stench of despair, had been jolted awake. As the aroma of freshly brewed coffee filled the station, Solomon hastily reached for his coat, ignoring the scalding sensation of the hot liquid in his hand. His eyes, usually calm like an undisturbed lake, were alive with a fire never before seen by his colleagues.

"Smith, let's go," Soliman's voice echoed through the office, disrupting the incessant mechanical clattering of the typewriters. His tone was ripe with a startling urgency that froze the normal humdrum of the precinct.

Smith looked up, a bewildered expression washing over his face. His tie was half-knotted, his shoes weren't fastened properly, but none of that mattered. He was drawn out of his bafflement by Soliman's peculiar behaviour - a man usually defined by his composure was now a picture of restless anticipation.

Smith, now fully alert, managed to stammer.

"What's going on, Sergeant? Where are we going?"

Soliman paused, letting the gravity of the moment build before he replied.

"Do you remember that assault victim, the one who was put in a coma a few months ago? She just woke up."

Smith's mouth fell open as a wave of astonishment swept over him. His mind raced to remember the details of the case. That poor woman, caught in a ruthless assault and left comatose. The case had gone cold, shrouded in the ambiguous grey of uncertainty. But now, the grey was starting to dissipate. Soliman's eyes glinted with a renewed sense of purpose, lighting up the gloominess of the police station. Smith's heart pounded in his chest as he rapidly laced up his shoes, understanding now why Solomon was in such a hurry. This was a game changer, an unexpected ray of hope in a case that had seemed hopeless.

As he followed Soliman through the maze of desks and out the station's grand front doors, the weight of the situation settled on him. What would the woman remember? Could she identify her attacker? A thousand questions swirled in his mind, leaving him both anxious and eager. The dawn was breaking, its golden rays filtering through the city's concrete jungle, symbolizing a new beginning.

Thirteen

The Quest for Answers

The detectives walked briskly through the speckless hallways of the hospital, their footsteps echoing off the cold, white walls. The urgency in their stride matched the gravity of the situation they were about to face. Arriving at the front desk, they approached the nurse with a sense of determination.

"Excuse me, we're looking for Elisa Rodriquez hospital room," Detective Smith said with a hint of impatience.

The nurse, busy with paperwork, looked up and quickly scanned through her computer screen.

"Room 215," she replied, her voice barely audible over the beeping machines. "Down the hallway, on the left."

The detectives nodded in gratitude and hurriedly made their way down the corridor. The white walls seemed to close in on them, creating a suffocating atmosphere that mirrored their anticipation. Each step brought them closer to Elisa's room, and the mystery that awaited within. As they reached the door marked 215, one detective hesitated before turning the handle.

"It's a miracle that she is awake, so let's take the questions easy on her," Sergeant Soliman whispered to his companion, his voice filled with a mix of wonder and disbelief.

With a deep breath, the detective pushed open the door, revealing a scene that defied explanation. Elisa, lying in the hospital bed, looked pale and weak, yet her eyes sparkled with an extraordinary light. The room was filled with an indescribable energy, almost tangible, as if something extraordinary had taken place. Elisa stared blankly at the ceiling, her body completely immobilized by the myriad of wires and tubes that snaked their way around her frail frame. It was nothing short of a miracle that she had emerged from her coma, but as Sergeant Soliman stood at her bedside, he knew that her battle was far from over. Detective Smith stood quietly beside him, a stoic and determined expression on his face, ready to assist in any way necessary. Turning their attention to the young woman lying before them, the two detectives exchanged a glance of sympathy. Elisa's friend, Charlene, sat faithfully by her side, clutching her hands tightly as if that simple act could somehow mend the broken pieces of her shattered existence. Breaking the silence, Sergeant Soliman introduced himself gently, his voice laced with compassion.

"Hi, my name is Sergeant Soliman, and this is my partner, Detective Smith. Can we speak with Elisa? We have a few questions that may help in our investigation." Charlene's eyes flickered with a mix of concern and relief.

She rose from her seat, a glimmer of hope dancing in her eyes as she addressed the police officers standing before her.

"Of course, please go ahead. Elisa has been through so much, but if it could help bring justice, we'll do whatever we can." Responded Charlene.

Sergeant Soliman nodded in understanding and leaned closer to Elisa, his voice barely above a whisper.

"Elisa, can you hear me?" Elisa's eyes fluttered weakly, a glimmer of recognition shining through her hazy gaze. With great effort, she managed to nod slightly, signalling her willingness to participate in their questioning.

"The incident that led to your coma," began Detective Smith, his voice steady and calm, "it remains a mystery. We've been trying to piece together the events leading up to that night, and we believe you may hold some crucial information. Can you remember anything?"

Elisa's brow furrowed, her mind struggling to grasp onto fleeting memories. There was darkness, a sense of fear, but the details remained elusive. A surge of frustration coursed through her veins as she desperately tried to recall even a single fragment of the puzzle that had stolen her memory. Tension hung heavy in the air, time ticking away as Elisa fought against the prison of her own mind. Every passing second felt like an eternity, both for Elisa and the detectives eagerly awaiting her response. Finally, a flicker of recognition lit up Elisa's eyes. She opened her mouth to speak, her voice barely a whisper. But before any words could escape her lips, the monitors connected to her body began to beep frantically, their urgent rhythm piercing the silence of the room. Panic filled the air as doctors and nurses rushed into the room, their urgent voices blending with the cacophony of alarms. As chaos unfolded around them, Sergeant Soliman and Detective Smith were forced to retreat, their unanswered questions hanging in the air like unsolved riddles.

....

Sergeant Soliman shifted restlessly in the uncomfortable hospital chair. His partner Officers Smith, stood nearby, his expressions just as anxious. As minutes turned into what felt like hours, Sergeant Soliman's mind filled with worry. He couldn't shake the image of Elisa when she was taken into the hospital, her face battered and bruised. The thought of her pain and suffering gnawed at his heart, fuelling his impatience. Finally, the moment everyone had been waiting for arrived. The doors swung open, and a middle-aged man with greying hair emerged. Sergeant Soliman approached him, his heart pounding with anticipation.

"How is she doing, Doctor?" he asked, his voice barely concealing his anxiety.

The doctor looked at him kindly, a small smile tugging at the corners of his mouth.

"She's stabilized, Sergeant," he replied. "But she needs her rest. It will take time for her to fully recover from the injuries she sustained."

Relief washed over Sergeant Soliman, but there was still a lingering concern. Officer Smith stepped forward, his voice full of genuine worry.

"What do her charts say, Doctor? Is there any cause for concern?"

The doctor sighed, his brow furrowing.

"She was beaten very badly, as you know," he began. "It will be a difficult journey to recovery. But there's something else you should know..."

Sergeant Soliman and his partners exchanged puzzled glances.

"What is it, Doctor?" Sergeant Soliman pressed; his tone firm yet tinged with trepidation.

The doctor hesitated for a moment before continuing.

"Elisa is four months pregnant," he revealed."

Sergeant Soliman's eyes widened in surprise. He had no idea Elisa was expecting a child. His mind raced with questions. Who was the father? Why didn't they share this news with any of them? And more importantly, could this pregnancy somehow be connected to the attack? The doctor seemed to sense the unspoken queries in the room.

"We'll need to conduct another round of tests," he said, his voice filled with concern. "But for now, Elisa needs to focus on her recovery."

"Okay, thank you doctor" responded Detective Smith.

As the doctor walks away, Sergeant Soliman mind whirled with a mix of emotions. He couldn't help but feel a deep sense of protectiveness towards Elisa and her unborn child. He knew he had to uncover the truth, not just for the sake of justice, but for the safety of Elisa and her baby.

Fourteen

In Pursuit of the Truth

The atmosphere at the police station was tense as Sergeant Soliman and a few other officers gathered around the whiteboard, their focus solely on the photo of Elisa. The mystery surrounding her brutal attack had consumed them all, and now, more than ever, they were determined to piece together the puzzle of what had happened to her. As they examined the evidence, the officers exchanged theories and ideas, jotting down notes and connecting the dots. It was clear that Elisa had gone out four months ago, enjoying a night of revelry in the local bar with her friend. But what happened next remained a haunting enigma.

"So, let's go over this again. Elisa left the bar with a mysterious man," Sergeant Soliman stated, his voice filled with a mix of curiosity and concern. "No one knows what transpired after that."

The officers exchanged glances, their minds racing with possibilities. Could this mysterious man hold the key to Elisa's attack? With a heaviness in his heart, Sergeant Soliman shared the horrifying findings:

"Elisa had been brutally assaulted. The evidence paints a heart-wrenching picture of the pain she had endured. Pieces of glass were found in her anus, serving as a horrifying testament to the forced entry inflicted upon her."

The thought alone left a shiver running down the spines of everyone present.

"Elisa's injuries were extensive and unimaginable. And the next time anyone saw or heard from Elisa again, was when her friend Charlene found her beaten and battered body in her room. Her fingers had been broken, her body bearing the physical scars of her traumatic ordeal. She also had a bleed on her brain served as a cruel reminder that her road to recovery would be long and uncertain. Not to mention, she is suffering memory loss, which doesn't help us or the investigation." Said Sergeant Soliman.

Detective Moony sat at his desk, his eyes fixed on the graphic photos of Elisa. The images were disturbing, but they triggered a memory buried deep within his subconscious. A memory from his time in New York, when he was working on a case so similar it sent chills down his spine. It was a warm summer night when the call came in—a young girl had been found beaten and assaulted. The details mirrored Elisa's case, except for one stark difference, this victim didn't make it; She didn't survive the horrifying ordeal. Moony's mind raced back to that fateful night. He had pursued every lead, scrutinized every piece of evidence, but the killer remained elusive. The case had haunted him, a constant reminder of the darkness that lurked in the shadows. Lost in his thoughts, Moony couldn't shake the feeling that there was a connection, a thread linking these two devastating crimes. He became obsessed, determined to uncover the truth and bring justice to Elisa.

"This case reminds me of a case that I was working on a few years ago." Says Detective Moony. A girl about the same age as Elisa was raped and beaten to death, her murder was so horrific, we couldn't identify her body for months, it was only due to dental records why we identified her, and that was from the only few teeth her attacker left in her mouth."

"Okay, but what connection do you think this have with Elisa's case?" Asked Detective Smith.

"Well, she was also clean, there was no evidence on her body, and I mean none, clean as a whistle. Her hair nails and body were spotless. But internally, she suffered brain damage, and was brutally raped." Exclaimed Detective Moony.

Everyone looked at each other in astonishment.

"Okay, well, I think we need to revisit that case, see if anything out of the blue pops up. We need to also re-interview Charlene, Elisa's friend, and understand what exactly went on that night." His tone echoed a sense of urgency and restlessness, the ticking clock providing an unwelcome rhythm to their deliberations.

Detective Smith, the empathetic one with an unparalleled emotional acumen, interjected.

"We've spoken with her in depth, I don't think we should take her through this again, she's the only person supporting Elisa at the moment." He had always been reluctant to question innocence, always sensitive to the emotional distress of the victims and witnesses.

Sergeant Soliman looked up, his eyes revealing an astonishment that swept across the room.

'Well, unfortunately, we will have to work together on this, and if that mean revisiting the case one hundred more times, that's what we will have to do. Talk to her, maybe there is something that she missed, a name, a face, something, we need to start over again and see if we missed anything. Also, let's go back to the bar where she was the last night she went out, interview everyone again. Remember, every nook and cranny, every whisper and chaos, they all have stories to tell.'

As everyone rushed off to restart their investigation, Sergeant Soliman looked around him, determination etched on his face. He didn't care what it took; he was going to find out who brutally attacked Elisa, even if it was the last thing he did.

Fifteen

Reigniting Old Friendships

Detective Moony stepped onto the bustling streets of New York with a mix of nostalgia and trepidation. It had been years since he had set foot in his old precinct, and as he walked through its familiar blue painted walls, memories flooded his mind. The air was thick with the lingering scent of unfinished cases and the weight of unfulfilled justice. Moony couldn't help but feel a pang of frustration as he remembered the understaffed police force that simply couldn't keep up with the ever-growing crime rate. Budget cuts had slashed the resources they so desperately needed, leaving them to fend for themselves in a city teeming with lawlessness.

As he surveyed the weary faces of his former colleagues, Moony couldn't help but be reminded of the unfair hierarchy that plagued the department. It wasn't about skill or dedication, but rather about who had the right connections. The system was broken, and the most talented detectives were often overshadowed by those who knew how to play the game. But it was the unsolved murder cases that haunted Moony the most. The victims' faces flashed before his eyes; their families left to grieve without closure. Lack of witnesses and rampant fear among the citizens had turned the pursuit of justice into a never-ending battle. He had seen the dark side of the city, the whispers and secrets that cast a veil over the truth. Drugs too, held a vice-like grip on the streets of New York. Undercover police officers were not immune to the seduction of easy money, leading to misplaced priorities. Rather than focusing on the relentless pursuit of justice, some saw an opportunity to line their own pockets. Moony had seen things in the field that no one should ever witness, corruption that tainted the good intentions of those sworn to protect and serve.

As Moony's footsteps echoed through the halls of his past, he couldn't help but feel a surge of determination. He had left this behind for a reason, seeking solace in a quieter life far from the chaos of the city. But now, standing amidst the echoes of forgotten cases and broken promises, he knew that he couldn't turn his back any longer. With a renewed purpose, Detective Moony vowed to confront the ghosts of his past. He would fight for justice, even if it meant battling against a broken system. As he walked through the precinct, the streets of New York seemed both familiar and unfamiliar, teeming with stories yet to be told. Detective Moony stared at the door in front of him, his heart pounding with anticipation. He had been away for years, but now he was finally here again, standing outside his former partner's office. He raised his hand and knocked, each tap echoing through the hallway.

Inside the room, Detective Carter glanced up from his paperwork, his eyes widening in surprise. It took a moment for the shock to wear off before he recognized the face that stood on the other side of the door.

"Moony, is that you?" Detective Carter exclaimed; his voice filled with disbelief. He jumped out of his chair, sending papers flying in all directions, and hastily approached the door. With a warmth that only old friends could share, he embraced Detective Moony in a tight, manly hug.

Detective Moony couldn't help but smile as he stepped inside the office, all the memories flooding back. The years had been long and eventful, but the bond between partners remained unbreakable. Both men took a seat, ready to catch up on lost time.

"Just thought I'd pay you a visit, how have you been? It's been years since I've seen you". Detective Moony said, his voice filled with genuine affection.

Detective Moony shifted uncomfortably in his chair as the memories flooded back. It had been years since he had seen his old partner, Detective Carter, and catching up was long overdue.

"I've been well, you know how it is. It's New York, nothing ever changes. How's it over there in Cleveland? They been treating you well?" Detective Carter replied, his voice betraying a hint of longing.

"Could be better, but I guess anywhere is better than this shithole," Moony laughed, trying to lighten the mood. "Hey, how's the wife and children? Everyone been good?" he asked, genuinely interested.

With a sigh, Detective Carter's hand began motioning through the air, as if trying to brush away the pain that clung to his past. A sad smile played on his lips as he spoke.

"Divorced. She tried to take me for everything I had, which was fucking nothing. Thank God I put nothing in my name, she tried to outsmart me, but it didn't work, left that whore for the streets where she belonged. But the kids are good though, thank God for that. Mia my oldest hates me, her mother just keeps feeding her lies. Anyway, I don't care, they can all join the Carter hate train. How about you? Are you still being a man whore"? Laughed Detective Carter.

Moony's eyes widened in surprise. He remembered Carter's warm smile, the way he used to talk about his family with so much love. It was hard to fathom that all of that had changed.

"I'm sorry to hear that, Carter," Moony paused, unsure of what else to say.

After a few seconds of talking and laughing, Detective Carter asked the much-needed question.

"So, what's going on man? What brings you here? We know you wanted to get the fuck up out of here years ago. It must be something that brought you back," asked Detective Carter, his eyes filled with curiosity.

"You're right," replied Moony, his voice filled with a mixture of hesitation and urgency. "Look, I need some help. You remember that case we worked on when I was a rookie? The one that was never solved."

Detective Carter, a seasoned investigator with a cynical demeanour, looked at him quizzically.

"My friend, you're going to have to be more technical than that. You know there's a shitload of unsolved crimes in this hellhole. Which one are you talking about?"

Detective Moony leaned against the worn-out desk, his eyes fixated on the case files staring at him on Carter's desk. The memory of one of the most haunting crimes resurfaced, sending shivers down his spine.

"That case," he murmured, his voice barely above a whisper, "where a young girl, about twenty-eight, was kidnapped, raped, and killed. Her teeth were knocked out, and her body was dumped in the river. It took her dental records for us to identify her. Erm, if I remember right, I think her father was suicidal after his daughter died, he had several visits to the hospital."

Detective Carter, engrossed in his work, looked up, his eyes filled with a mix of curiosity and dread.

"Oh, fuck yes," he exclaimed, his voice laden with a hint of trepidation. "I remember that case. It was brutal. What's going on? Why are you asking?"

Detective Moony's gaze intensified as he spoke.

"I need to look at that case again. We have a similar situation down in Cleveland, and there are a lot of uncanny resemblance."

Intrigue flickered in Carter's eyes, and a tinge of unease settled over the room. They both knew that revisiting this case could unravel dark secrets and open wounds that had never healed. As the two detectives delved deeper into the case, they discovered an eerie pattern emerging. The young girl's murder seemed to be part of a series, spreading its menacing web across different cities. Each victim suffered the same gruesome fate – teeth shattered, innocence stolen, and life violently extinguished.

"Alright, I'll get the detectives to send over the paperwork for you. I hope you can catch the mother fucker who did this. If there's anything else that I can do to help, you let me know." Says Detective Carter.

Detective Moony stood up from the dusty, worn-out chair, his hand firmly locked with his ex-partner's. The room reeked of stale coffee and desperation, a constant reminder of the countless unsolved cases that had come before them. As he thanked his ex-partner for accommodating him, Detective Moony's mind was already racing, eager to delve further into the puzzling case that had consumed their thoughts for years. Leaving the dimly lit room behind, Detective Moony stepped into the crisp night air. The moon shone brightly, casting an ethereal glow on the city streets. He could feel the familiar itch of curiosity creeping up his spine, challenging his resolve to leave no stone unturned.

Sixteen

Beneath the Surface

Sergeant Soliman and Detective Smith pulled up to the bar, their eyes scanning the bustling scene before them. The wind whistled through the empty street, adding an eerie touch to the already mysterious atmosphere. It was a cold night, and the dimly lit bar seemed to hold the secrets they were searching for. Stepping out of their sleek black vehicle, the detectives exchanged a determined glance. They knew the importance of this investigation and the urgency of helping Elisa. Shutting the car doors gently behind them, they approached the bar with a heightened sense of anticipation.

As they walk through the entrance, the sound of lively chatter filled the air. The bartenders and staff were in full swing, preparing for what seemed like a busy night ahead. Unloading trucks lined the back alley, delivering crates upon crates of drinks to be stocked and served. The doors of the bar swung open, revealing an enormous space that seemed to stretch on forever. It was a modern marvel, a place that had quickly become the talk of the town. Stepping inside, the first thing that caught the detective's eyes was the grand staircase leading to the upper level. It was a sight to behold, adorned with a cascading floral arrangement that added a touch of elegance to the already charming atmosphere. The wooden floors, polished to a shiny black, reflected the glimmering chandeliers that hung from the ceiling, casting a soft, enchanting light over the scene below.

The seating area downstairs was meticulously designed, with tables and chairs arranged in perfect symmetry. Cutlery and plates were neatly placed on the tables, ready to serve mouthwatering dishes to the eager guests. The aroma of culinary delights filled the air, tempting the taste buds and leaving hopelessly hungry patrons salivating in excitement. Large windows lined the walls, standing bright and immaculate as the sun's rays poured in, illuminating the entire place. The outside world seemed to fade away, replaced by an oasis of sophistication and style amidst the bustling city. Zack, a dedicated Caucasian male, dressed in his uniform, his dedication shone brighter than the neon signs that flickered outside the bar where he worked tirelessly. Unloading the drinks into the large fridges hidden behind counters, a task he approached with the meticulous precision of a craftsman. Despite the monotony, Zack never failed to infuse grace into each movement. His black work clothing hugged his slim frame, indicating the physical effort of his labour. Yards of freshly laundered fabric danced around his figure, fluttering as he moved, while his hand weaved stories in the air as they transported the bottles from boxes to their cooling abode.

At five foot nine inches, Zack wasn't the tallest in the room. Still, his presence filled the space, casting a shadow that danced across the wooden floors. His hair, the colour of midnight sky, was neatly tied back, revealing a pair of bright green eyes that captivated anyone who dared to look into them. They were the kind of eyes that were tirelessly working, seeking order amidst the chaos, effortlessly dictating his hands to their respective tasks. Behind those azure lenses, there was a world much deeper than the small bar he was confined to. An orchestra of thoughts, dreams, and silent prayers played inside, cloaked by his quiet demeanour, known only to those brave enough to venture beyond the surface.

Zack continued his diligent dance, unloading the drinks, creating a symphony of clinking glass and the hum of the refrigerator. His black clothing absorbed the cold that radiated from the fridge, acting as a stark reminder of the chilling solitude of his world. He continued to meticulously log each bottle, ensuring that nothing went missing and everything was accounted for. His focused expression hinted at a story untold. The two detectives made their way towards Zack, their footsteps barely audible amidst the commotion. Detective Soliman's eyes narrowed; his senses heightened as he studied the young man. The dimly lit room was filled with an eerie silence as the two detectives approached him.

"Hey," Shouted Detective Smith, taking out a photo out of his pockets and holding it up. Zack quickly looks at them in frustration. "There was a young girl in here a few months ago. Her name is Elisa. She was brutally assaulted, and we want to know if you've seen anything suspicious around that time."

"I'm busy, as you can clearly see," Zack retorted dismissively, his voice dripping with annoyance. "Come back another day."

Sergeant Soliman, glanced at Zack's name tag and responded firmly, "We won't be coming back another day, because you are going to stop what you're doing and answer the question, Zack."

With a mixture of defiance and frustration in his actions, Zack reluctantly turned to face the officers. His face, contorted with a deep frown, showed a hint of vulnerability hidden beneath his tough exterior.

"Look, I don't even remember what I ate for breakfast this morning," Zack muttered, his voice laced with frustration. "How am I supposed to remember something that happened months ago?"

The detectives exchanged a knowing glance, understanding the challenge they faced. But they weren't going to let Zack off the hook that easily.

"Look, we understand that it's been a while, and memories can fade. But a young woman's life hangs in the balance. Every small detail counts, every clue could lead us towards helping her."

Blinking his eyes hard, Zack slowly took the photo from Detective Smith's outstretched hand. As he stared at it for a few seconds, his mind drew a blank. He couldn't put a name or face to the person in the photograph.

"No, I've never seen her," Zack replied, his voice tinged with confusion. "Better yet, I can't remember."

Detective Smith exchanged a glance with Sergeant Soliman, a silent conversation passing between them.

"Do you have any security cameras?" Detective Smith inquired, his tone raising a glimmer of hope in his eyes.

"Yes, for every day of the week," Zack answered, his curiosity piqued as he walked the two officers into the back room.

As Sergeant Soliman and his partner approached the room, a sense of curiosity washed over them. The hallway leading to the room was cluttered with paperwork, but as they entered, they were surprised to find a certain order amidst the chaos. The room smelled of delicate flowers, creating a pleasant contrast to the colour scheme that mirrored the design of the bar. The detectives couldn't help but appreciate the attention to detail that exuded an aura of sophistication.

Large ornaments and statues adorned the side of the room, casting an enchanting glow that added to the mystique. Sergeant Soliman knew that this was not an ordinary place; it was a haven of elegance and refinement. As his eyes scanned the room, they landed on a computer tucked away in the back. It seemed to hold the secrets that would shed light on the peculiar events surrounding the bar. With purpose, Zack strode towards the computer table, settling himself into the chair. He swiftly logged into the computer, his fingers moving with practiced ease. The files, containing prerecorded tapes, were like pieces of an unsolved puzzle waiting to be unravelled. The detective's heart quickened with excitement as he opened the digital vault, revealing a treasure trove of information. Looking at the screen, the officers were happy to know that they were getting somewhere. The long hours spent on this case seems to finally be paying off. Sergeant Soliman leaned closer to the computer, with hope gleaming in his eyes.

"There are hundreds of files here, we'll never get through them all today. Work with my detective to get them sent over to the precinct." Said Sergeant Soliman.

"Do you have a warrant for it?" asked Zack, his voice filled with worry.

"No, but I have a warrant to open your files that's already on our records, and I'll make sure to pull up every information since the day you were born." Responded Detective Soliman calmly, his focus still on the ongoing conversation. He answered his phone and walked away, leaving Zack slightly bewildered.

Detective Smith joined Zack, and together they worked meticulously to gather all the necessary files and evidence. There was a sense of urgency in the air as they raced against time. Every minute counted, and they couldn't afford any more delays.

Seventeen

Moments Frozen in Time

In a maze of law and order, nestled within the heart of a functioning city, Charlene found herself once again in the belly of the beast. The precinct walls echoed with whispers of guilt and the clang of expectations, holding her captive in a room that felt far too small for her racing mind. The room lay barren, save for an ominous black table that occupied the centre, a cup of water and a box of tissues perched on top. It struck her as a twisted stage set, prepared meticulously for a drama of confession and sorrow, where tears of regret were the usual script. But Charlene wasn't the type to follow the script. The windows, dark as a moonless night, stood locked under the weight of past escape attempts. They stared at her, reflecting her anxiety back to her, their closed mouths suffocating the faintest whiff of freedom. The stark white walls bore down upon her, reverberating with her silent pleas, inching closer with every tick of the clock.

Charlene felt her heart race in her chest as she traced the worn edges of the table with her finger. The memories of her last visit came back to her, a hurtling comet that crashed into her soul, igniting a wildfire of regret and guilt. Her friend Elisa, the innocent victim, torn apart by brutality was the reason she was here. Finding Elisa still haunted Charlene, and it was all her fault.

A cacophony of 'what ifs' roared in her mind. What if she had not left Elisa alone that fateful night? What if she had detected the danger lurking just around the corner? What if... But the past was a ghost that refused to be exorcised, and the burden of her guilt was a shackle she must carry. Charlene took a deep breath. The room was cold, indifferent, yet dripping with anticipation. She knew what was expected of her, she knew the answer to their questions. But could she face the piercing eyes of interrogation, the relentless probing that would stab at her guilt-stricken conscience? She clenched her fists tightly, the sharp intake of breath echoing in the eerie silence. She was ready. And as the door creaked open, admitting a glimmer of harsh fluorescent light, Charlene braced herself. Detective Moony entered the room with a book in his hand. Placing the book on the table, he sat down on the hard silver chair. In the steel-grey hues of the investigating room, Charlene sat, a stark figure poised against the cold ambience. Detective Smith, sat opposite her, his eyes etched with a mixture of empathy and inquisitiveness. He leaned forward, his voice a comforting baritone.

"Charlene, thank you for coming in and seeing us again. I understand that you might not want to go over this again, but we need to take a closer look at Elisa's case. So please start from the beginning again and let me know what exactly went on that night." Said Detective Smith.

Charlene paused, her eyes glossing over as she relived the memories.

"As I told you guys previously, detective, me and Elisa went out that night. Elisa was not the social butterfly type. She was a workhorse, her nose always buried in a book or engrossed in a project. Socializing was foreign to her. But that day, after my incessant pleading, she finally conceded. After she said yes, I felt a wave of euphoria, like a child who had just been told they were going to Disneyland. She told me she'd meet me at my house. As punctual as a Swiss watch, she arrived, already garbed in a dress. It was clear she had taken pains to escape her comfort zone."

The room fell silent as Charlene spoke. Detective Smith, despite his years on the job, felt a lump in his throat. He was well-versed with Elisa's case but hearing it firsthand from Charlene made it more real. He watched as Charlene's eyes filled with tears, her hands trembling as she took a deep breath, preparing to plunge deeper into the harrowing account of that fateful night. The story stretched on, each word echoing in the stark void of the questioning room. As Charlene's tale ended, Moony was left with more questions than answers. Detective Moony, a seasoned professional with sharp eyes and an even sharper mind, scratched his grizzled chin, taking in the story presented by the vivacious woman before him.

"What was she wearing?" he quizzed, intrigued by the vague but complex canvas being painted.

"As I mentioned, she was wearing a dress when she arrived, but it was ugly, so I told her to change it," gushed Charlene, her eyes dancing with the vibrant memories of the night in question. She was a living contrast to the grim demeanour of the detective; her vivacity lent an air of surrealism to the otherwise sombre room.

"Elisa hadn't been out in years," Charlene continued, her usually lively voice taking on a hollow tone. "I wanted her to feel special, to remind her of the woman she used to be before... Well, you know, before life happened to her."

Charlene described their preparation for the night out, how they raided her wardrobe and selected something more suited to the radiating beauty that Elisa was. She spoke of how the mirror had reflected two women, glowing with anticipation and excitement, Elisa choosing a chic little skirt and top ensemble while Charlene herself slipped into an elegant dress.

"All eyes were on us when we stepped into the bar," Charlene said, her voice a mix of pride and sadness. "We were the shining stars, turning heads with our vivacity and confidence. As predicted, Elisa stole the show with her natural beauty. She was back, the woman I'd known and loved as my friend, at least for that night."

The story of their night unfolded beautifully, a tale of laughter, freedom, and rekindled youth. According to Charlene, it ended as pleasantly as it had begun, with both women returning to their respective homes alone, their hearts lighter than they had been in years. The tale was riveting, filled with vivid imagery and emotion. Yet, Detective Moony wasn't entirely satisfied; he sensed a missing link, a loose end that refused to tie up neatly.

Detective Moony, who was more used to untangling threads of deception than deciphering the webs of hazy recollections, was struggling to connect the dots. The discrepancy in Charlene's account was glaring.

"So, let me get this straight. Elisa arrives at your place, you guys go out, have a good time, how can you be sure Elisa made it home if you left alone?" he probed, his hazel eyes penetrating Charlene's confused state.

"I...I... I don't know," she stammered, confusion dripping from her words like melting ice. "We were drinking all night, by the time we hit the bar, I was barely myself. Two unfamiliar faces, two men, I remember them talking to us, Elisa might have left with one of them, but that's where my memory trails off."

In the eerie stillness of the night, Detective Moony stared at Charlene across the cold steel table. The harsh interrogation room light etched deep shadows on his face, creating an ominous aura.

"I don't recall you telling us about Elisa leaving the bar with anyone, did that slip your mind?" he asked, his tone laced with suspicion.

Charlene clenched her fists, her knuckles whitening under the pressure.

"Look, my head was probably messed up, okay. I was wasted that night...I completely blame myself for what happened to Elisa." Her voice was barely a whisper, quivering with guilt and regret.

Moony raised an eyebrow, leaning back on his chair as he crossed his arms over his chest.

"Well, that should give you every reason to ensure we had all the information we needed," he retorted, his icy blue gaze unwavering.

A single tear slipped from Charlene's eye, trailing a glistening path down her cheek as she buried her face in her hands. On the other side of the interview door, Detective Smith and Sergeant Soliman stood watching the interrogation, their expressions varying degrees of surprise and concern. The revelation of a mystery man who had left the bar with Elisa was a game-changing detail in the investigation. As the hours rolled on, Moony continued his relentless probing, each question a twisted dagger in Charlene's heart. She was trapped in a whirlpool of guilt and fear - a fear that was less about her impending doom and more about the truth behind Elisa's brutal attack. In the grim, dimly lit room outside the interview room, the towering figures of Detective Smith and Sergeant Soliman loomed, casting long shadows. They watched the interrogation through a one-way mirror, disbelief etching lines of confusion on their faces. The elusive mystery man, the missing puzzle piece in their investigation, was suddenly a tangible reality. Charlene had known all along, and she had kept quiet.

"Why on earth didn't she mention him before?" Sergeant Soliman grumbled, his brows furrowing like a storm on the horizon.

Detective Smith, his weathered face an unreadable mask, replied calmly.

"Fear. The poor woman found her best friend unconscious; she then fell into a coma for the last three months. It's a lot to bear."

A chill wind of realization swept through the room as they watched Charlene speaking with Detective Moony, her face etched with worry and regret. She was a victim too. The light in her eyes was lost in a sea of dread, trapped in a traumatic narrative she didn't ask for. Detective Moony left the investigation room and entered another room where the detectives were standing. His eyes homed in on the screen displaying Charlene's terrified face. The room fell silent, a barely audible gasp slipped from their lips as the reality of the situation sank in deeper.

"Well, we need to find out who this mystery man is. Moony, what's the update on the previous case you worked on?" Asked Sergeant Soliman, his gaze fixed on the photographs strewn across the table.

"I've got it right here, Sergeant," replied Detective Moony, stepping into the dim light. His voice was the only sign of life in the otherwise stagnant room. "I called in a favour from my buddy down in New York. This case... it's eerily similar to Elisa's."

His words hung in the air like a cold fog, casting a shadow over the room. He swallowed hard before he continued.

"A young woman, named Dakota Young, age twenty-eight, was found brutally beaten. Her body was thrown in the river. We only identified her through her dental records. Just like Elisa's case...she was sodomised, fingers broken. There was no evidence on her body, no trace of the merciless assailant. She was absolutely clean. No one had evidence of her going out that night."

His words stirred the echoes of countless unsolved cases that were stacked in the room, each carrying a tale of desperation and despair. Each a testament to the brutalities that lurked in the underbelly of the city. It was a chilling reminder of the realities they grappled with every day, but it was an integral part of their mission to mete out justice for the lost souls.

"My God, we need to check if there are any relatable cases like this in any other precinct. We need to know if these are isolated incidents or if it's a serial killer on the loose. Smith, did you check the security severance footage from the bar that night." Said Sergeant Soliman, his words, a testament to the gravity of the situation that was unfolding.

Detective Smith, a man of unwavering composure, shuffled in his seat slightly, his eyes revealing a twinge of uncertainty.

"Yes, I've combed through it with a fine-tooth comb, and guess what, there is every video on there before the day that Elisa was assaulted, until yesterday, but.... Listen to this"....

Soliman's heart pounded in his chest, his intuition already dreading the words that were about to leave Smith's mouth.

"Don't tell me that it has been erased." He muttered, praying for a different answer.

Smith's grim nod confirmed his fear.

"Exactly, gone. Now that's some bullshit. Something is definitely going on".

He left the sentence hanging in the air, the words as unsettling as the silence that swallowed them. The three men shared a sobering look, the weight of their responsibility setting in. This was more than a simple assault case. It was a sinister game, a hunt for a ghost lurking in the shadows.

"So let me get this straight," Sergeant Soliman began, his normally deep voice tinged with worry, his grey eyes reflecting the flickering neon sign encrusted outside their makeshift office. "Elisa and Charlene went out that night, Charlene now claims that Elisa left with some mystery man, but there is no evidence of this because all the CCTV footage has been mysteriously wiped out. Someone must have seen her that night; she didn't brutally attack herself."

Sergeant Soliman leaned back into his worn-out chair, flipping open the black-and-white images of battered Elisa.

"We need to pay a visit to the bar owners. There's got to be an explanation as to why the footage has been tampered with."

"One step ahead of you, Sergeant," said Detective Smith, Swift as a shadow, he pulled out another photograph and slid it across the cluttered table towards Soliman. "And guess who owns the bar?"

The name on the picture hit Soliman like the full force of a speeding train. His worn-out features hardened as he stared at the image.

"Who is it?" asked Detective Moony, his voice barely a whisper.

"The Prince family." Replied Detective Smith.

The night held a hint of foreboding as the name resonated in the dim-lit room. The Prince family - the untouchables, a family woven into the city's fabric as deeply as its subways and sky-kissing towers. They held reins of a massive empire thriving on untold riches and whispered rumours of darker deeds. The realization sank deep within Sergeant Soliman. Setting his jaw firm, he stared into the depths of the Cleveland night, the whirlwind of possibilities spinning wildly in his mind. Was Elisa just a pawn in the Prince's shady games? Or was there more to this story than what meets the eye? What did the erased footage and the Prince family's involvement mean?

"Well, fuck me from behind and call me a bitch" said Detective Moony as an astonished look washed over his face.

All three detectives sat in the dimly lit room, their faces etched with skepticism. They had seen it all, from petty thefts to high-profile murder cases, but this revelation had stunned them into silence.

Sergeant Soliman, the seasoned investigator and Sergeant of many years with eyes that seemed to possess an uncanny ability to read people, broke the silence.

"If this turns out to be true," he said, his voice filled with a mix of astonishment and trepidation, "we're dealing with a whole new level of danger, gentlemen."

Detective Smith, known for his unwavering determination and sharp instincts, leaned forward, his brow furrowed.

"This changes everything," he muttered, his voice barely audible above the distant sirens. "We can't afford to make a single misstep. Our lives, as well as the lives of countless others, hang in the balance."

The three detectives looked around at each other, saying nothing. The night fell silent, enveloping them in an eerie stillness.

Eighteen

The Path of Healing & Restoration

Each day Elisa awoke to a world that was suddenly familiar. Despite the regular hum of activity around her, a strange hollowness echoed in her room, as if the world of white walls and bustling nurses was now her new normal. Yet, there was a palpable energy of hope; a hope that stemmed from the persistent efforts of her saviours - the doctors who were relentlessly striving to restore her to the Elisa she once was. With every passing day, the distant memories of her former self grew a bit clearer, like a painter slowly recreating the masterpiece on a blank canvas. Her body was a battlefield, and every little movement was a battle won; each word was a merciful victory.

The smallest gestures- eating, talking, even a faltering step - became milestones in her road to becoming whole again. Every day, she met herself anew - her strength, discovered in fragments and pieced together by the unyielding determination of her doctors and nurses. Charlene, her beacon of support, would often feed her, her soft touch adding a gentle warmth to the sterile hospital atmosphere. The quiet strength she provided was an unspoken promise - a vow to never leave Elisa's side.

Elisa, once a carefree spirit, had been thrust into a world of syringes, medication, and rehabilitation. Yet, she clung to the essence of who she was - a fighter, a survivor. There were days when it seemed impossible, yet she often found herself reaching out to the little life living within her - a reminder of her purpose and will to march forward. Then there were the visits from the physician, the unseen hand guiding her recovery. The doctor was an artist, his deft touch guiding her from the precipice of despair towards hope. Each exercise, each therapy session was a stroke on the canvas of her recovery, slowly but surely bringing back the hues of health in her life. But the story of Elisa was not merely a tale of survival or recovery. It was an epic journey of a woman bracing against the tide with the spirit of a warrior. Rebirth in every sense, from the ashes of despair to the phoenix of hope, from a patient in a hospital bed to a mother-to-be. But as each day ended and the sun dipped below the hospital horizon, Elisa was alone with her thoughts.

She was left wondering - what next? Even as she felt the fluttering movements from within, a question left her lips, barely a whisper.

"What kind of world am I bringing you into, my little one?"

And then...in the quiet of the night, she could almost hear the faint echo of a heartbeat- a reminder of her unwavering resolve and her journey ahead. A journey filled with uncertainty, resilience and a love that transcended her circumstances. In the midst of a seemingly ordinary day, with the hum of mundane existence surrounding her, she was suddenly transported. Not to another place, but another time. Her mind, a restless time machine, was causing her to relive moments she had tucked away in the deepest corners of her soul. A haunting melody unravelled the thread of her meticulously shielded memories, dragging her into an abyss of angst and pain.

The music that was playing that fateful day, a melody that once brought her joy, now echoed derisively in her memories. Her own screams reverberated in her ears, a chilling reminder of the assault she had braved. A brutal, unasked for intrusion into her life that had shattered her spirit. She grimaced, her hands involuntarily balling into fists, a physical manifestation of her internal struggle to forget. No sooner had this painful memory started to fade, another one took its place. She saw herself standing amidst a sea of black-clad mourners, her tiny hands clutching onto the fresh lilies, their sweet smell failing to mask the stench of death. She shook with silent sobs as she watched her parents' coffins being lowered into the earth, doom pushing away her childhood innocence into a dark abyss.

Just as abruptly, her mind flitted to her college days, the euphoria of graduating and becoming a teacher, the joy of achieving a dream that her parents had seen for her. Then, came the flashes of her friends, people she had once trusted and loved, laughing and walking alongside her on paths that led nowhere and everywhere. Her memories were a kaleidoscope, fragments of her life brought to the surface by her sub-conscious. Each flashback was vivid, as if she was reliving her entire life since childhood. As a child of foster care, she'd learned to package away her past and focus on the present. But these memories, they were rampant, seeping into her present with a vengeance she couldn't combat.

The flashbacks were not sequential, they were jumbled and chaotic. They were sparks of a past life, revealing themselves in the most unexpected moments, making her feel like a spectator in her own life. Like a ghost who had lived a thousand lives and was forced again and again to walk through them. And with each passing day, they came back stronger, more persistent. The past was not a far-flung land anymore; it had become her tormenting companion, an uninvited guest who refused to leave. It was a vicious cycle, her waking hours filled with flashes of forgotten events and nights filled with shrouded dreams, all clawing at her, not letting her escape. As she let the weight of her past sink in, she understood. These were not just flashbacks, they were fragments of her, pieces that made her who she was. Scarred, yes, but also strong; broken, yet unyielding. She was a survivor, a warrior of her own battered past. Yet, deep in her heart, a question lingered, a whisper in the wind.

She wondered, will there ever come a day when these flashbacks would stop tormenting her and instead become powerful reminders of survival and strength? The silent nights would only hold the answer; until then, she remained caught in the web of her own reality, wrestling with the undertow of her past, waiting patiently for the dawn of a new day.

Nineteen

Consistency & Care

In the grand halls of St Mary's Hospital, beneath the unforgiving fluorescence and the constant hum of life-sustaining machines, a grizzled figure paused. The figure was none other than Sergeant Soliman. He was there to visit Elisa. As he ventured closer to Elisa's room, the silence of the corridor was broken by the sudden appearance of Dr. Washington. He emerged from her room, a medical clipboard in his hand and a surprised expression on his lined face.

His eyes widened as he spotted Sergeant Soliman. "Hey, how are you, Sergeant? I didn't know you were coming today." The doctor's voice echoed lightly in the hallway. He juggled his clipboard under his arm, making way towards an adjacent desk, the corners of his lips lifting into a gravely worn smile.

"I'm good, Doc. How's Elisa?" Soliman managed, his voice barely above a whisper, the stark concern evident in his tone.

"She's a fighter, that one," Dr. Washington began, flipping through several pages on the clipboard. "She's doing quite well. We've got a top-notch physician working with her. She's slated for discharge in a few weeks if everything continues on this positive trajectory."

The doctor paused, reflecting on the young woman he had just left behind in the room, battered but unbowed.

"That young lady... she's strong, Sergeant. Not many could survive the kind of brutality she did, and fewer would have the strength to recover as she has."

The words hung in the air, echoing in the sterile silence. Sergeant Soliman nodded, relief washing over him. His heart still ached for Elisa, for the scars, both physical and mental that she would carry, but for today, there was hope.

"That's wonderful to hear, Doc. She indeed is resilient. And the baby, has she made a decision?" asked Sergeant Soliman, a tall, broad-shouldered man with sharp but compassionate eyes. He had seen much in his years on the force, but it was cases like this that truly tested his mettle.

"Yeah, she's keeping it," answered the doctor, a brilliant but battle-weary man who had seen the best and worst of human spirit in his line of duty. "Most women wouldn't, considering the circumstances, but she's made her decision, and she's not changing her mind."

"Thanks for the update, Doc," says Sergeant Soliman, his voice full of admiration, as he gently taps the doctor on the shoulder. His gaze then followed the sombre, grey hallway leading to her room. He walked away, leaving the doctor with his own thoughts.

The hospital hallway echoed with the rhythmic thud of Sergeant Soliman's boots, keeping time with the ticking clock hanging precariously on the white-washed wall. A single knock on the door was met with a soft invitation from inside. A deep breath, and the Sergeant pushed the door open.

"Hello Elisa, how are you doing?" The words were habitual, flowing from countless past visits. The Sergeant smiled, his eyes taking in the sight of Elisa. She was sitting up, her skeletal frame draped in a hospital gown, arm extended with a certain determination to spoon the yogurt into her mouth. It was a small victory in the grand scheme of things, and yet, it was colossal.

"I'm better, thank you for asking, healing. Doctors says I can go home soon" Elisa's voice was quiet, almost a whisper, but her words pierced through the silence, echoing in the sterile room.

Sergeant Soliman couldn't help the swell of pride that enveloped him as he watched Elisa. It wasn't long ago that the young woman was teetering on the brink of life and death. The brutal attack had left Elisa shattered, her body a jigsaw puzzle of broken bones and spirit. It had flung her deep into the abyss of a coma, every moment uncertain. It was a nightmare from which Elisa was clawing her way out, painstakingly learning to live anew. To see her now, sitting up, eating unassisted, was nothing short of a miracle. With each visit, Elisa was blossoming, growing into a woman of resilience and strength. Her journey was an inspiring saga of human spirit, a tale that was being written with every breath she took, each word she uttered, and every step she managed.

"Yes, I heard. I am so very happy that you are doing better and healing well. Is there anyone who you will be staying with?" Sergeant Soliman's eyes bore into the young woman sitting across from him in the clean white room. His concern was genuine - it was more than a mere formality that his role demanded.

"Yes, I'll be staying with Charlene, at least until I heal and get better." Elisa's voice wavered a bit as she forced down the unease burgeoning inside her. With an effortful smile, she placed her yogurt on the table in front of her, as if to show she was following the doctor's orders.

"That's wonderful, Elisa. I don't want to rush you, but would you be comfortable with answering some questions? As we continue our investigation into who attacked you, we need to understand what happened that night." The Sergeant, aware of the territory he was stepping into, tread as lightly as he could.

Elisa swallowed hard. The thought of that night sent shivers down her spine and made her stomach churn.

"I'm not sure if I remember much, but I'll try," she said, her words a whisper in the tension-rich room.

As Elisa began recalling the fragments of her shattered memory, the room fell into a heavy silence. The questions flowed, and Elisa's answers painted a terrifying tale that began to take form. A tale brimming with fear, bravery, and an inexplicable mystery. Dropped into a spiral of uncertainty, they navigated through the labyrinth that was Elisa's memory of the fateful night.

"I remember the day starting as usual," she began, her voice barely more than a whisper. "I was running late, as I often am, yet somehow managed to arrive at work precisely on time. There was an ethereal magic to such ordinary moments, like the universe was conspiring to make the day seem just like any other. But it wasn't," she added, her voice trailing off as she recalled the memory of her friend, Charlene, bursting into her classroom with an impromptu invitation for a night out on the town.

"We met at her house, the scent of her lavender perfume mingling with the distinctive aroma of excitement and anticipation. We raided her wardrobe, each piece of clothing a promise of the night's potential. We laughed and drank until our sides ached, our toasts echoing around her penthouse apartment."

She could still taste the fruity tang of the cocktails they'd consumed, the liquid courage that had fuelled their journey to the pulsating heart of the city's nightlife.

"At the bar, we danced until our feet throbbed and the room swirled around us. We were the vibrant centres of our own world, oblivious to the increasingly blurry faces that swarmed around us."

"Men approached us, two of them." Her voice wavered as she delved into those muddled memories of faces blurred by alcohol and time. "Charlene, ever the social butterfly, buzzed around them. But something inside me wanted to retreat, to escape back to the comfort of my own cocoon."

"Okay, thank you, Elisa. That's great," said Sergeant Soliman, his voice a soothing balm on her frayed nerves. "Do you remember what the guy looked like?" The question hung in the air, heavy and charged, as Elisa let memories flood her mind.

She stared blankly at the far wall, her eyes lost in the maze of her recollections. "He was tall... white, and he seemed smart," she began hesitantly, her voice barely a whisper. "Green eyes, shoulder-length hair," she added, each word pushing her further into the labyrinth of the past.

A spark of interest lit in the Sergeant's eyes as he commanded, "Do you remember what he was wearing?" His voice echoed, aching for the tiniest speck of a clue.

With a thoughtful frown, Elisa ventured further into her memory.

"I think... a suit. Yes, a suit," she began, her frown deepening. "And I remembered his shoes... they were really nice and shiny. Or it might have been the floors that were shiny... I'm not too sure," she confessed, her voice dropping to a near inaudible murmur.

At the mention of shiny floors, Sergeant Soliman's mind involuntarily jumped back to the afternoon he entered the Oasis Bar. The lavish establishment shone brightly like a desert mirage, the oppressive gleam bouncing off the polished floors. He mulled over her words, rolling them in his mind as he picked at the pieces of the puzzle.

"Do you remember the bar you went to that night?" he asked, his voice dull. As the Sergeant continued to probe, he remained oblivious to the fact that far away, in the privacy of her own thoughts, Elisa was on a journey of her own.

"Yes, it was the Oasis Bar, beautiful place, I have never been there before but Charlene said they served the best margaritas, so we went there, it looked like a palace." Answered Elisa.

"That's wonderful Elisa. Is there anything else you remembered from that night?" asked Sergeant Soliman. His gruff tone softened slightly, a calculated attempt to create a safe space for her to release the cloud of haunting memories that had been looming over her.

"Not really, but I get flashbacks, you know," she paused, her voice brittle like thin ice over a deep winter lake. Her eyes, oceanic with sorrow, filled with tears that ran freely down her cheeks. "Sometimes I don't know if I'm dreaming or if it's real."

She swallowed hard, her throat constricting around the bitter pill of reality.

"I was tied up, beaten...," she trailed off, her hands trembling as she clenched them into fists. A soundtrack of relentless rock music echoed in her mind, a cruel score to her nightmare. "I was in this room, it was painted black. I keep seeing black and white walls. My skin... it was burning... I was numb."

Her confession crashed into the room like a devastating tidal wave, leaving no corner unscathed. She started to cry harder, the tears now a waterfall cascading down her face and landing on her hospital gown. Sergeant Soliman shifted uncomfortably in his chair. He was a seasoned professional with haunting cases under his belt - but Elisa's ordeal was something else altogether. He walked over to her, his heavy boots echoing ominously against the linoleum floors, and gently placed a comforting hand on her trembling shoulder.

"It's okay, Elisa," he said, the gruffness in his voice now replaced with a touch of humanity. "I know this must be so hard for you, but you have done so very well remembering all these details, it's truly remarkable."

There was a strange expression on Elisa's face.

"I'm pregnant too," she said, her voice trembling with disbelief. "After everything that has happened, I am pregnant too. I don't even know how that was possible, I haven't had intercourse for four years."

The sense of shock that hung in the air was palpable as she tried to comprehend the unexpected twist in her life.

"Have you decided on what you want to do with the baby?" Sergeant Soliman asked, even though he already knew what Elisa's decision was, his eyes brimming with a rare mix of empathy and curiosity.

Elisa shook her head, her eyes reflecting her internal turmoil.

"What can I do, I'm a Mormon, I don't believe in abortions. My faith has brought me through a lot in my life. Plus, what would my parents say," she whispered, as if the very idea of making a decision was too overwhelming.

Sergeant Soliman nodded, his face a mask of understanding.

"I understand Elisa, well if you do keep the baby, that would be great, we can get a DNA sample from the baby and see who the father is, maybe we can catch this guy sooner than we think."

Even amidst the symphony of shadows that played on her face, Elisa's beauty shone through like the beam from a lone lighthouse amidst a stormy sea, guiding lost sailors' home. The tear tracks adorning her cheeks highlighted her vulnerability, yet there was an undeniable strength in her ebony eyes. Glistening tears clung to her lashes as she shook her head, accepting the hand fate had dealt her with stoic grace. Intrigued yet cautious, Sergeant Soliman watched the play of emotions on her face, his experienced eyes missing not a single flicker. The room was filled with an aura of melancholy beauty that revolved solely around Elisa, making it seem as if time itself had slowed down to admire her resilience. Even in this room of cut-and-dry facts and logical deductions, her ethereal charm was undeniable.

"Elisa," Sergeant Soliman's voice was a gentle rumble. He presented his next words with an air of regret, akin to a surgeon slicing through healthy flesh to reach the infected part beneath, "I hate having to ask you this, but the toxicology report showed a high concentration of drugs in your system. Do you remember taking any drugs on the night in question?"

"Never," The word came out as a whisper, yet it echoed against the room's cold, white walls, filling the space with her adamant denial.

"Very well," Soliman responded, his eyes reflecting a mixture of sympathy and unwavering professionalism. He then reached into a folder, pulling out a series of photographs, "I have a few images here I would like you to take a look at."

Elisa lay in her hospital bed, a prisoner of her own failing memory. She was like a book with half its pages torn out, desperately trying to fill in the blanks. A stack of photos on her lap was her only hope, anonymous faces from her past hoping to unlock keys to her cloudy mind. She hovered over each picture, hopeful for a spark of recognition, a glimpse into the missing days, weeks and months of her life. But her efforts seemed futile as face after face blurred into one another. Just as she was about to surrender to despair, her gaze fell upon one photo, a man with captivating green eyes and shoulder-length hair. His aura radiated through the photo, his charming smile piercing the fog that clouded her memory. The instant her eyes met his, a flurry of emotions surged through her. Her heart raced like a runaway horse, her palms moistened, and a quiver ran down her legs. Something in those green eyes had triggered a primal fear that left her trembling. Sergeant Soliman who had been observing Elisa closely, noticed the change. The colour drained from her face replaced by a ghostly pallor and her eyes almost doubled in size, mirroring an unspoken fear. Alarm bells rang through his mind.

"Elisa, are you okay?" he inquired, his voice layered with concern.

A chilling silence hung in the air as Elisa continued to stare at the photo, her pupils dilating, as if she was trying to make sense of a terrifying revelation. In the deafening silence of the room, a story was taking shape. A story that started with the simple turning of a page but ended with a torrent of questions. Why did his photo spark such an intense reaction in Elisa? And what untold secrets lay between them, waiting to be unravelled? Like footprints in the sand waiting to be washed away, the answers lay silent and obscured.

"Okay, it's okay Elisa," reassured Sergeant Soliman, his voice soft and steady. The sterile walls of the hospital room echoed his words, a feeble attempt to cloak them in an air of normalcy.

Soliman's heart ached for the young woman. He had delivered grim news countless times over the years, each one leaving him with a haunting koan of human resilience. He had seen people shatter, crumble, and rise. But something about Elisa struck him differently. The sound of hurried footsteps brought him back to reality. Charlene had arrived, her face a cocktail of concern and confusion. She wasted no time in rushing over to her friend, her bags dropped carelessly on the hospital floor.

"What's going on, why is she crying?" Charlene asked, her voice trembling slightly as she embraced her friend. Soliman watched the scene unfold, sadness etched on his weather-beaten face.

"She's okay, she's just a bit emotional," he gently explained, hoping to provide Charlene some measure of comfort. Now was not the time to discuss the stark reality of what Elisa was facing. Soon, but not yet. "I am going to leave you guys. Elisa, if you ever need to talk to me, here is my card. Please don't hesitate to contact me." Soliman said, placing his card on the bare hospital table.

Quietly, he stepped out of the room, leaving the two women in their bubble of shared pain and consoling silence. The last image seared into his mind: Charlene, strong and steady, supporting her friend through the raging storm. Elisa, beautiful and brave in her sorrow, a testament of resilience he would carry with him. He had seen this scene play out many times, but there was something uniquely poignant about this one. As Sergeant Soliman stepped out of the bleak room, the disconcerting reality of the situation gripped him. The chill in the air seemed to thicken, wrapping around him like a second skin, as he took a shuddering breath. His heart pounded in his chest, a deafening echo in the silence. He couldn't get the image out of his mind, Elisa's wide, terrified eyes, he was almost scared for himself, but he was a man with a job to do. Reaching into his pocket, he pulled out his mobile phone with a grim determination. He dialled Detective Smith, his most trusted ally in these tumultuous times. He didn't want to involve others, but the gravity of the situation left him with no other choice.

"Smith, meet me at the station in an hour. I need all the manpower I can get," Sergeant Soliman said, his voice steady despite the storm raging within him.

Twenty

Return to Base

A certain energy buzzed through the corridors of the precinct, a hushed anticipation that whispered of a mystery on the brink of being unravelled. Sergeant Soliman had just set foot in the station, carrying with him the key that could unlock the answers – a name, Elisa, and a story waiting to be told. The echo of his boots against the linoleum floor reverberated through the precinct.

"Smith, Moony, my office now please," he called out, his voice a blend of determination and intrigue, the blazer he draped over his office chair a symbol of the unyielding commitment to justice that it held.

Detectives Smith and Moony, two of the finest men under his charge, instantly fell in step, their curiosity piqued at their superior's serious demeanour.

"What's up, Sarge?" Moony inquired, his eyes reflecting the smouldering anticipation of a detective faced with a promising lead.

Soliman paused, gesturing for Smith to close the door behind them. As the faint echo of the latch clicking into place filled the room, he began,

"I went to visit Elisa an hour ago. She was able to remember fragments of her ordeal and what happened to her."

The room was suddenly filled with a tangible silence, the air thick with suspense. Smith and Moony hung onto their superior's every word, their minds racing to piece together the enigma that was Elisa's story. Soliman paused, studying the faces of his detectives before he spoke again. Then, he narrated the bits and pieces of Elisa's traumatic ordeal. It was a haunting tale of a woman who had faced the worst of humanity and lived to talk about it.

"Well, that's wonderful Sarge, what did she remember?" asked Detective Moony, his eyes ever watchful and mind racing through a labyrinth of possibilities.

"She remembered going to work, then going to her friend Charlene's house. They were drinking before they went to the bar. Which corroborates with Charlene's statement. They then went to the bar and the next thing she remembered was she woke up in the hospital," replied Sergeant Soliman. His voice was steady, providing a firm anchor within the storm of uncertainty they found themselves in.

Detective Smith chewed on his lower lip, a sign of quiet contemplation.

"Well, that doesn't give us much to go off, that gives us about as much as a haystack gives a needle" he finally said, frustration simmering just beneath the surface of his words.

Sergeant Soliman offered a reassuring nod. "Well, she is getting flashbacks, remember this girl suffered a brutal assault. So slowly, her memory will start to come back. But she said she remembers being in a dark room, being tied up, her skin was burning too," Sergeant

Soliman's voice broke the silence, a grim reminder of the horror the young girl had experienced.

The air thick with the weight of a story yet to be told, they found themselves on the precipice of an unfolding revelation – a dance with truth and memory, tangled in the complexity of human resilience and fear.

"Well, that adds up to the whip marks that we saw in the photos of her skin after the assault," Detective Moony responded. His fingers ran over the grainy images that captured the harrowing aftermath of the inhumane incident.

Nodding solemnly, Sergeant Soliman continued.

"Right, then I asked her to look through some photos. At first, she didn't say anything, but then her eyes picked someone." There was a pause, an air of suspense filled the room as the Sergeant slowly opened a photo book, sliding it across the table to the two officers.

"Who did she pick out of these photos?" begged Detective Smith, his eyes filled with a strange mixture of hope and terror.

Their eyes widened as they saw the face the girl had identified. A crushing silence hung in the room like a thousand unsaid words. The perfect picture of betrayal, disbelief, and shock painted across the faces of the officers.

"Donald." Answered Sergeant Soliman.

"Donald Prince?" Detective Moony asked incredulously. "From the Prince family, the real estate moguls? Are you suggesting he was involved in this? How reliable is she? The poor girl has survived a traumatic event. She was in a coma, for God's sake."

"Look here, Moony," retorted Soliman, his tone gruff, "if you had seen terror manifest itself on a person's face, it was on hers when she saw his photo. It was raw and visceral. She is telling the truth."

A gasp echoed around the room - reverberating off the steel grey walls, heightening the surrealism of the situation. Stunned silence followed, the collective disbelief was visible. They were law enforcers, hardened by years of confronting the city's underbelly, yet nothing had prepared them for this.

"But... this is...," Moony stammered, grappling for words that seemed to have evaporated. "This is fucking unbelievable! The Prince family are one of the wealthiest property development families in the entire country. Why would..."

His words trailed off, hanging in the air like a question mark. The room seemed to close in on them, the reality of the situation gnawing at their senses. A heavy pause crippled the atmosphere as they all tried to digest what this could mean.

Detective Smith let out a weary sigh. "Why do men with power feel the need to abuse it?" He pondered aloud.

"Well, clearly Elisa didn't want the fucking guy. So he decided to take it from her. Men like that, with power, don't like the word no. And plus, we expected this would happen, just not one of them directly, maybe one of his men, but not him." Muttered Sergeant Soliman. His words a stark reminder of the grim reality they were perpetually entangled with.

Looming over the cluttered table, strewn with half-empty coffee cups and timeworn case files, the weary Sergeant barked his orders, "I'll get a search warrant for his address, in the meantime, Smith, Moony,

I need you two to drive over to see Mr. Donald Prince and arrest him. Bring him in for questioning. I want his house torn to pieces, bring me evidence - anything. CCTV footage, clothing, everything. I don't care who he is, we are not sparing him, as a matter of fact tear his fucking house down, burn the mother fucker down if you have too."

"Copy that, Sergeant," Moony retorted, his voice laced with focused dedication. He glanced at Smith, who nodded, their eyes reflecting a singular purpose. They grabbed their coats, badges shining in the evening light, and stepped out into the cold dawn.

The room fell silent again. Satisfied yet burdened, Sergeant Soliman leaned back in his worn-out chair, his gaze lingering on the empty doorway. His mind was a whirlwind of thoughts, fragments of past cases, similar but so different. He could still feel the echo of Moony's firm reply, and deep inside, a spark of hope kindled.

Twenty-One

The Long Arm of the Law

The pounding on the door echoed through the grand halls of the mansion like the drumbeat of an impending storm. A sea of uniformed bodies swarmed the house of Donald Prince, their stern faces radiating an unspoken tension. At the helm of this wave of justice stood two figures, Detective Moony and Detective Smith, their badges catching the first rays of dawn as they banged on the ornate door. The mansion door creaked open to reveal Donald Prince. His piercing gaze fell upon the detectives.

"Are you Donald Prince?" asked Detective Moony, standing outside on the steps of the grand mansion. A swarm of officers stood behind him, their eyes fixed on the ornate entrance.

A sly smile creeping across Donald's face as he asked.

"Who's asking?"

"Donald Prince," Detective Moony replied, holding his badge inches from Donald's face. His voice was curt, his tone steely. "My name is Detective Moony, and I'm the man who's about to arrest you."

A split-second silence followed, so stark it echoed in the hearts of the assembled officers.

"Put your hands behind your back, bastard," growled Moony, his anger barely veiled, his eyes boring daggers into Donald.

The tension in the air thickened, the sea of officers behind the detectives shifting uneasily as they waited for Donald's response.

But Donald merely laughed, the sound reverberating through the still morning air, his smile never leaving his face.

"Is that so?" he retorted, his voice dripping with arrogance. His gaze swept over the sea of officers, taking in their uneasy faces, their fingers twitching towards their holstered guns.

"Do tell me, Detective... What makes you think you can arrest me?" His smirk widened, revealing a row of perfect white teeth.

The question hung in the air, a ticking bomb waiting to explode. The officers exchanged glances, a thread of confusion weaving through them. Moony's determined glare never wavered, his hand reaching out to grab Donald's arm.

"What, what is this about?" Donald yelled as Detective Moony, cornered him. "You're making the biggest mistake of your life, buddy, you will regret this. Do you know who I am. Do you?" His voice echoed against the high ceilings, filling the vast empty space with a palpable tension.

Detective Moony, showed no signs of intimidation.

"Of course I know who you are, Donald Prince," Moony retorted, his voice charged with stoic resolve. "You're not a real Prince, even though I know you wish you were. But theatrical titles won't help you here."

The detective stepped closer, the outlines of his large firearm casting ominous shadows on the marble floor.

"Donald, you have the right to remain silent. Anything you say can be used against you in a court of law. You also have the right to have an attorney present. If you cannot afford an attorney, one will be appointed to you."

The seriousness of the situation finally sinking into Donald. The once invincible mogul, now just another suspect in the unyielding eyes of the law, swallowed hard. As the detective tightened the handcuffs around Donald's wrists, the city outside blinked obliviously. In the world of extravagance and power, where the scales of justice were often tipped by wealth, Detective Moony was an unyielding force of integrity and dedication. He didn't care about Donald's status, his threat, or influence. To him, crime was a crime, no matter who committed it. As the grating sound of the metal cuffs locking echoed in the silence, it was as if the city held its breath. What would become of Donald Prince? Would the Tycoon be toppled, or would this just be another chapter in the saga of his invulnerability?

The grim spectacle of armed officers descending upon the palatial residence of Donald had turned the quiet street into a theatre of the absurd. Their large guns glinted menacingly in the dimming light as they began to methodically tear his world apart. Donald watched from the backseat of a patrol car as the officers rifled through his life. His neatly curated existence was being meticulously disassembled by the very authorities he had once entrusted with his protection. Yet, in the midst of the chaos, a small, defiant grin began to carve itself onto his face. The sight of this was grotesquely out of place, like a splash of vibrant paint on a blank monochrome canvas. As the search matured, a crowd of onlookers began to form. Hushed whispers of speculation from his neighbours cut through the pervading silence, their fear-tinged voices unable to mask their morbid curiosity. The comforting monotony of their once serene neighbourhood had been brutally shattered, replaced by an atmosphere electrified with tension and uncertainty.

Detective Smith, a man known more for his stoic demeanour than his bedside manner, cast a sidelong glance at Donald. His piercing gaze met Donald's smirk with an icy indifference. Something about Smith's silence gnawed at Donald, making his grin waver for a moment. Unfazed by the subtle power play, Smith turned away, joining his partner in the passenger side of the car. As they began to leave the scene, pulling away from the now ruined vestige of Donald's life, the grin returned to his face, more pronounced than before. The convoy of patrol cars moved like a serpent through the suburban jungle, swallowing the distance towards the police station. In the rearview mirror, the reflection of Donald's house grew smaller, soon disappearing altogether, swallowed by the encroaching night. The mystery of what the search would yield remained hanging in the air, much like the dust left unsettled in Donald's deserted home. What secrets lay within those opulent walls? Only time would tell.

Twenty-Two

In-depth Coverage

The streets buzzed with whispers and murmurs, the words "Donald Prince" echoed everywhere. Is he arrested? Did the real-estate magnate actually assault a young woman? The news had spilled over the airwaves like an unleashed torrent, leaving everyone in a state of utter bewilderment. As the clock struck six, the echoes of the evening news filled the quiet streets of Cleveland Ohio. The news about the arrest of Donald Prince, an estate tycoon renowned for his grandeur and wealth, rocketed through the town like a cannonball. Everyone glued to their television screens, listening to the reporter on CCW News. The intrigue was palpable.

"Good evening, this is CCW News at 6pm," began a confident voice on the television, the calm before the storm so to speak. He adjusted his glasses, arranged his papers and with a deep breath, he plunged into the shocking headline, "We bring you the exclusive news of the arrest of the estate tycoon, Donald Prince."

The world seemed to reel at that. Donald Prince, the eminent big shot whose shadow loomed over not just the real-estate market but also the high-profile social circles, was now getting acquainted with the iron bars of a prison cell.

The broadcaster continued.

"Prince was arrested earlier today on charges of sexual assault and attempted murder against a young woman." As the details unfolded, it was like a glossy façade was being stripped away, revealing the grim truth beneath. The victim, only named as Ms. Elisa, had endured a brutal assault. She'd been left in a coma, her life teetering on the brink for four long months. The fact that she had only recently awakened was nothing short of a miracle. The specifics of the arrest weren't yet fully disclosed."

The air was thick with suspense and unanswered questions. The moment the broadcast ended, Sergeant Soliman snapped the television off leaving the room wrapped in a deafening silence. The news of Donald's detention echoed in the station's bare walls and a palpable tension permeated the air. It took a string of favours, and some old contacts to make sure the city heard the news of Donald's arrest. Justice was slow, but Sergeant Soliman was patient. Soliman was not a man who meddled in games of chance. Every move he made, every favour he called in, was meticulously calculated. He was a tightly coiled spring, waiting for the right moment to pounce.

Sergeant Soliman did not allow himself to linger in this vortex of conjecture. Instead, he ran his fingers across the worn-out keyboard. His eyes anchored on the screen, reading and re-reading the report, as if trying to coax secrets from the words. His focus was unwavering. The now cold room thrummed with his resolve to crack the case wide open. Meanwhile, in the heart of the city, the sun began to sink, casting long shadows that shrouded the entrance of the police station. Suddenly, the quiet evening erupted into orchestrated chaos as a navy sedan maneuverer its way slowly through a maelstrom of flashing camera lights. The air buzzed with anticipation, thick enough to slice through.

"He's here," someone murmured, and the swarm of reporters tightened.

Donald, a man whose name echoed louder in that moment than ever before, stepped out from the backseat, guided by the firm hand of Officer Smith. His face was unreadable as he straightened up, his broad shoulders tipping back to avoid a poorly placed camera boom.

"Donald! Donald!" The voices came at him in a cacophonous wave, each reporter hoping to be the one to penetrate his indomitable demeanour.

"Is it true that you brutally assaulted a victim, Donald?" a sharp-voiced woman reporter asked, thrusting her microphone towards him. Her eyes, eager for a sensational scoop, bore into him.

"Are the rumours true, Donald?" Another reporter chimed in, his camera catching the flicker of vulnerability that fleetingly crossed Donald's face.

Yet, Donald said nothing. His silence was as thunderous as the questions hurled at him. The reporters jostled for attention, their voices blending into a wall of noise that underscored the gravity of the situation. As swiftly as the storm had stirred, the police and detectives fell into formation, creating a human shield around Donald. Like an ocean parting, the reporters were pushed back, the unanswered questions hanging heavily in the air. Then together, they walked into the station, the door closing behind them with an echoing finality.

The street fell into a silence that was almost deafening in its suddenness. Donald, now out of sight, left a vacuum in his wake. The reporters, left empty-handed, could only stare at where he had been, their recording devices whirring into the void. As the police station swallowed the man who held the city's collective breath, one couldn't help but wonder: Who was Donald, truly? The answer, shrouded in ambiguity, was now a captive of the station's cold, grey walls.

Twenty-Three

The Dynamics of Interrogation

Donald sat in the glaringly lit interview room, the clicking hum of the fluorescent lights above the only sound in this boxed theatre of justice. His lips curled into a smirk as he surveyed the cold, grey walls, his eyes glowing with a defiant emerald spark that could light up the darkest corner of any room. They had the audacity to arrest him, Donald? It was nothing short of preposterous! Swathed in his overpriced suit, bespoke to the last stitch, his serpent cufflinks glinting in the artificial light, he reclined - a picture of nonchalance, Donald, a man born with a silver spoon and bathed in privilege, was in the harsh grasp of the law now. Whoever dared to put Donald in such a lowly setting surely didn't know who he was, or who his parents were. Or maybe they did, and this was their cheap shot at him. Either way, he thought, they will regret their decision.

A flicker of malicious amusement twinkled in his eyes as he fantasized about the downfall of this arrogant police department. The walls of this precinct would crumble, bricks and mortar reduced to nothing but dust, when his parents came to know of this travesty. He shifted his gaze to the two-way mirror, knowing full well behind the reflective glass were hawk-eyed detectives, their curious gaze boring into him, scrutinizing every twitch, every blink. Should they want a show, a show they would get. Donald tilted his head up, an air of theatrical supremacy about him, and flashed his most charming, devil-may-care grin towards the mirror.

This would be their biggest regret, he mused to himself, the corner of his lips curling even more at the thought of the impending storm his arrest would bring. In the smoky shadows of the police station, Sergeant Soliman and Detectives Moony and Smith kept a close eye on Donald through the cold, one-way mirror. His grubby figure sat hunched unceremoniously in the interrogation room, the fluorescent buzzing of the lone light making him squirm uncomfortably. His face, a canvas of time-hardened lines and calculated innocence, exuded a villainous charm that repulsed them equally.

"Moony, I want you to drill him with the ferocity of a jury in hell's courtroom," commanded Sergeant Soliman, his voice barely carrying over the antiseptic coolness of the room. "Has that rat squealed for a lawyer yet?"

Snorting contemptuously, Moony hitched a thumb towards the interrogation room.

"Just as you'd expect from that coward, Sergeant. He's clamoured for his lawyer quicker than a roach scuttles in the light. As for the search, is it still underway?"

Sergeant Soliman nodded grimly.

"Oh yes, we have our hounds ripping apart his fortress. If there's anything to find, they'll sniff it out."

But as Sergeant Soliman continued, a sudden interruption throbbed into the scene. The door creaked open, and in sauntered a man with a presence as commanding as a king entering his court. It was Donald's lawyer, Craig Boxall. Slim, tall, and impeccably groomed, Boxall was the epitome of legal prowess. His sleek, black suit hugged his lean body, while his freshly shaved head reflected the room's dim fluorescent light. His beard, manicured to perfection, added an aura of sophistication to his persona. He looked as out of place in that dingy station as a Rolex watch in a second-hand store.

"Detectives," Boxall drawled with the faintest hint of annoyance, his voice echoing around the room like a judgmental gavel, "why did I have to leave my new page seven model to deal with this rubbish?" His steely grey eyes then scanned the room for his client. "I hope you haven't started questioning him without a lawyer?"

Sergeant Soliman, a seasoned officer with an uncanny instinct for lies, turned to face the intruder.

"Boxall," he said, with a hint of a smirk, "they hired you, must be desperate, huh?"

As the words reverberated through the room, Boxall merely smiled back, the corners of his lips curling into a confident smirk. The battle lines were drawn; it wasn't just about this case anymore. It was a war of wits between the steadfast law enforcement officer and the top lawyer of the state.

"No need for desperation when money's abundant Sergeant, who else would the rich hire? As far as anyone is concerned, I'm the only player in this game. Only a few moments with my client," Boxall said, brushing past them with an air of entitlement.

"Before you decide to apply your creative license to his story, that is." He then promptly disappeared into the adjacent room, leaving the detectives gaping after him.

Smith pointed towards the room, where Boxall's silhouette could be seen in deep conversation with Donald. All the while, the detectives with their disbelieving faces continued their observation from outside. They were in the presence of the man who was notoriously known for transforming narratives - and not just in the digital realm.

"They've sought Boxall's help," Detective Moony murmured, staring at the now closed door. "This is going to make things a lot more...interesting."

"There's always something peculiar about a box that hasn't been opened," mused Detective Moony, as they looked on at Boxall.

Sergeant Soliman, a tower of a man, chuckled darkly.

"Well, they have the money, and this is a high-profile investigation," he rumbled, his gaze steady on Moony. "I'm sure they wanted to hire the biggest con man in conman history."

Soliman's words echoed in the ornate hallway as he strode away, his polished boots clacking rhythmically against the marble floor.

"Moony," he called over his shoulder, a note of stern authority in his voice, "give them a few minutes before you talk to Donald, but don't ease up, I don't care how rich he is."

Left alone, Moony turned back to gaze at the enigmatic door. Boxall was notorious, known for manipulating evidence and witnesses alike. The challenge was as intriguing as it was daunting. Smoothing his tweed jacket, Mooney steeled himself, waiting for the ticking gold Rolex on his wrist to hit the five-minute mark.

....

The second hand on the wall clock ticked its way around with a slow, agonizing inevitability. Detective Moony paused at the cold steel door leading to the interrogation chamber, hypnotized momentarily by the ticking, each beat a cruel reminder of the pressing seconds slipping away. Inside, the suspect Donald, draped in a coat more expensive than Moony's annual salary, sat with all the arrogance wealth could afford. His lawyer, Boxall, a man as sleek as an oil spill, settled in the corner, his hawk-like eyes missing nothing. Moony took a deep breath, straightened his tie, and made his entrance, his shoes echoing authoritatively on the linoleum floor. The door echoed as he shut it, the sound hanging in the air, carrying the weight of steel and justice.

"Good afternoon, Donald," his voice rang out clear and cool as he took a seat across from the smirking billionaire. He placed a thin, brownish file on the table. The file, though mundane looking, held the secrets of a case that had kept the city on edge.

Moony let his gaze linger on Donald, making sure the man understood the gravity of his situation. His piercing gaze was met with a nonchalant shrug, but he noticed Donald's eyes flicker slightly - a hint of worry creeping in.

"Okay Donald, do you know why you are here?" asked Detective Moony, his experienced eyes penetrating deep into the soul of the man sitting across the table.

"Well, no, you decided that it was in your best interest to arrest me, moany."

Donald replied with a smirk, deliberately mispronouncing the detective's name. He slightly arched his brow, attempting to assert control over a situation that was slipping through his fingers.

Detective Moony, unaffected by the insolence, coolly retorted.

"Can you tell me what you were doing on the night of July 29th?"

"How the hell should I know? That was four months ago, are you kidding me? Why are you asking me this?" Donald growled back, his frustration starting to bubble over.

In the dead silent room, the whispers of the unspeakable hung heavy in the air. Donald's lawyer, Boxall, interrupted the unbearable silence.

"Calm down, Donald. Okay, detectives, where are you going with this?" His voice was steady but the beads of sweat on his forehead betrayed his anxiety.

Detective Moony, with the calm of a seasoned professional, flipped open a folder.

"Well, a young girl was brutally attacked after leaving your bar. She was raped, beaten and assaulted in the most horrible way you could imagine." He spread out a series of horrifying photos across the table. The images, stark and bleak, radiated an eerie silence that echoed in the room, landing with a catastrophic thud in the hearts of those present.

Shock and disbelief adorned Donald's face as he took in the dreadful sight. His hands unconsciously uncrossed, and a faint smirk crept onto his face. A smirk that seeped out the insufferable darkness residing within him. He leaned forward, as if intrigued by the grotesque masterpiece laid out in front of him. The bruises, the vicious marks of a whip, etched into her once flawless skin like a twisted canvas. A chill ran down Boxall's spine as he watched Donald, his client, seeming to relish in the sight. The room fell into a haunting silence once more, the only sound being the quiet hum of the overhead lights. Donald's unsettling joy was juxtaposed with the hideous, black-and-white reality sprawled out on the pristine table. His eerie fascination was met with a stony silence from the detectives, their expressionless faces guarded their thoughts.

Was Donald reminiscing or was he merely an onlooker, appreciating the savage artistry of a deranged mind? The question hung in the air, unanswered, feeding the already heavy atmosphere with more dreadful anticipation. Time seemed to slow, each tick echoing through Donald's mind, further amplifying the silence and amplifying his anticipation. His heart thumped audibly in his chest, like a secret drum echoing the rhythm of his unfathomable thoughts. Studying the photos, Donald's face was a mask of confusion and disbelief. The pictures showcased a woman of unparalleled beauty, her features sculpted by angels, her eyes harbouring a universe of innocence. Inexplicably, her face stirred a storm of emotions within him. He felt as if he had been plunged into a tempest of unexplainable thoughts. He was certain he had never seen her before, yet a primal part of him seemed to awaken in her presence.

"Detective, I swear to you, I've never seen this woman in my life." Donald's voice was steady, but his body language betrayed him; his gaze was nervously darting around the room, avoiding any contact with the photos now.

His mind was engaged in a relentless battle between guilt and innocence, accusations, and denials. He was no saint, he admitted it. He was a man of earthly pleasures. A man who had shared his bed with countless women, each of them willing and desirous. He oozed charm, his charisma undeniable, his confidence irresistible. Jealousy, the putrid green monster, had never found a place in his life. He had enough and more to attract women to him, he didn't need to use force.

Yet, the images before him sparked a flame of jealousy that he had never known. He was jealous of the photographer who had captured her beauty, jealous of the artist who managed to present her in such a divine light.

"So why did a witness identify your photo?" Detective Moony broke the silence with his grating voice, laden with skepticism.

"I don't know, she probably wanted me and I refused, or this might be a setup, look I'm rich people do this... all the time." Donald retorted, his arms now crossed in a false display of indifference.

"Then you wouldn't mind us taking a DNA test then, would you?" Detective Moony countered swiftly, the corners of his mouth curling into a sarcastic grin.

"Look, you can do whatever you want." Donald shot back, annoyance seeping through his forced smile.

"Not without a warrant, you fucking won't" a new voice interjected. The voice belonged to Boxall, Donald's shark of a lawyer, who now stood in the doorway, arms folded and eyes narrowed.

Detective Moony met Boxall's gaze, his jaw set in defiance.

"Well, we have reasons to believe that your client was involved in this," he said, his tone firm and determined. "And we will be arresting him."

"Where is the evidence? You have one alleged person who claimed to identify my client for this bullshit, that's not enough evidence to even take this shit to trial is it detective Moony?" Asked Boxall, his voice echoing through the stark, empty room.

"The witness identified him. He'll be arraigned, take it up with the judge," Detective Moony's voice was as cold as his gaze. His calculating eyes never left the man walking ahead of him - Donald.

As if on cue, Detective Smith walked into the room. Reluctantly, he placed handcuffs on Donald. The metallic clink against Donald's wrist seemed to echo eerily around the room. Yet, the man showed no sign of discomfort. Instead, he smiled. In the midst of the tension, his smile was jarringly out of place.

"I'll be out in an hour, and I will make sure that you never get another job in the city or anywhere again," Donald's voice was calm and assured, the smile never fading from his face.

Detective Moony watched as the man confidently exited the interrogation room. Moony noticed the unwavering smirk on Donald's face and felt a tingle of unease. The audacity, the arrogance, and the eeriness of the situation all combined to send a chill down his spine. Was this just another case, or was it the beginning of their end? Was Donald just an arrogant accused, or a mastermind setting his plan in motion?

"Another case cracked too late for a satisfactory dinner," Boxall, Donald's lawyer, muttered under his breath. He sulkily watched his firm's clock hands mock him past his scheduled reservation time at the city's finest steakhouse. "You're making me miss dinner with Miss page 4 now, detective. Now I'm getting annoyed," he griped, lifting his designer briefcase off the mahogany table. With one last contemptuous gaze at the unfolding proceedings, he exited the buzzing scene, leaving in his wake a room bristling with tension.

The space seemed to tighten when the door closed behind Boxall, but it quickly deflated as Sergeant Soliman entered. His towering figure filled the room, an intimidating presence that matched his reputation. He walked with a grace that belied his size, which was a testament to his years spent on the beat. His piercing gaze shifted onto Moody, his fellow detective, and they shared a nod that spoke volumes of their shared history. As he looked on, a curious figure entered the scene. It was a Caucasian woman, her short grey hair framing a face that exuded confidence and authority. Dressed impeccably in the finest brand of clothing, she strutted with elegance in her low-heeled heels, her black Gucci sunglasses adding an air of mystery to her presence. All eyes turned towards her as she approached the detectives, her two-piece shirt and blazer accentuating her slim form. This was no ordinary woman; this was Mrs. Prince, a force to be reckoned with. Her reputation preceded her, and no one dared challenge her when it came to her son's well-being. As she approached, detectives Moony and detective Smith walked away.

"Sergeant Soliman, now, you know better than to arrest my son without informing me. Where are your morals?" Mrs. Prince interrogated, her voice firm and unyielding.

Sergeant Soliman maintained his composure in the face of Mrs. Prince's assertiveness. He greeted her with a polite smile, although a tinge of apprehension danced in his eyes.

"Well, hello Mrs. Prince. It's lovely to see you too," he replied, attempting to diffuse the tension.

Mrs. Prince's gaze remained fixed, her eyes piercing through Soliman's facade.

"Well, I can't relate," she said with a hint of desperation in her voice. "Where is my boy? Did his lawyer arrive? I hope you weren't foolish enough to question him without a lawyer, Mr. Soliman."

Sergeant Soliman looked on, trying to maintain a professional demeanour.

"Well, I wouldn't be that dumb now, would I, Mrs. Prince?" he replied calmly. "Your son has been arrested due to the amount of evidence we have against him. He will be appearing in court in the next few hours."

Mrs. Prince's eyes widened in disbelief.

"You know very well that my boy would never do anything to hurt a soul," she exclaimed. "I have two boys, one is disabled and in a nursing home, a very expensive one too may I add, and the other is a businessman. Now rape and attempted murder? How disgusting! We are too rich for that sort of nonsense, my boys can get as many women as they want."

Soliman could see the pain in Mrs. Prince's eyes and the genuine belief she held for her son's innocence. He had seen this countless times before – the desperate denial of reality when it came crashing down on someone's life. But he also knew that sometimes, appearances could be deceiving.

"Well, I can understand, Mrs. Prince," Sergeant Soliman began, his voice calm and steady. "I'm sorry you feel that way."

A hint of a smirk played on Mrs. Prince's lips as she crossed her arms.

"We both know that this will never stick, Mr. Soliman. Your department is trash and only wants to find a reason to harass my family."

Sergeant Soliman raised an eyebrow, genuinely confused.

"Now why would we want to do that, Mrs. Prince?" he asked, his voice laced with intrigue.

A mischievous glimmer danced in Mrs. Prince's eyes as she leaned forward slightly.

"Enjoy your little crusade now, Mr. Soliman," she said, her words dripping with sarcasm. "We'll see who will be laughing in the end."

With a final flick of her wrist, Mrs. Prince turned and began to walk away. But before she disappeared into the shadows, she looked back at Sergeant Soliman, a sly smile playing on her lips.

"Aren't you up for retirement soon?" she said, her voice low and taunting. "I hope you enjoy that."

She slipped on her glasses, the glint of a hidden agenda shimmering behind the lenses. With each step, she seemed to melt away, leaving Sergeant Soliman standing there, his mind spinning with questions. The precinct was abuzz with activity as Detective Moony and Detective Smith approached Sergeant Soliman, who was observing Mrs. Prince as she walked away. The air hung with an unspoken tension, and the three detectives exchanged smirks, their camaraderie evident.

"Bitch," Detective Moony muttered under his breath, a hint of amusement colouring his voice. His words were met with stifled laughter from his companions, the sound echoing in the otherwise noisy room.

Sergeant Soliman raised an eyebrow as he crossed his arms over his chest. His piercing dark eyes never wavered from the scene unfolding before them. He knew there was something more to this.

"Well, here we go," Soliman murmured, folding his arms across his chest. His dark eyes focused on the scene unfolding before them.

Twenty-Four

The Rights of the Accused

The courtroom was filled with an air of anticipation. While not packed, it housed a collection of individuals awaiting their turn to face the judge's discerning gaze. The brown chairs and white walls stood as silent witnesses to years of legal battles and the weight of justice. It was in this solemn setting that Donald, accompanied by his lawyer, found himself standing at the front behind the defendant table. With a smug look on his face, Donald exuded an air of confidence that bordered on arrogance, as if he knew something the rest of the room did not. The judge, known for her no-nonsense approach, couldn't help but acknowledge the strangeness of the situation.

"Oh wow, Mr. Donald Prince, I'm surprised to see you here," she began, her eyes narrowing ever so slightly.

"I'm surprised to be here too, judge," Donald replied, a mischievous smile tugging at the corners of his lips.

The murmur of curiosity filled the room, everyone wondering what could have led Donald to this courtroom. The prosecuting lawyer, Melissa, stepped forward with purpose. She requested for the accused to be remanded in prison, citing a brutal assault on a young woman that had taken place just a few months prior.

"Judge, we request for this criminal to be remanded in prison, as he is being indicted for the brutal assault on a young woman a few months ago," Melissa stated firmly, her eyes never wavering from the accused.

Donald's lawyer, Boxall, had a calm demeanour masking the intensity within.

"There is no evidence of this, Your Honor," he countered, his voice steady.

Feeling the weight of the moment, Melissa gathered her thoughts and continued.

"The victim picked his photo out and was very sure he was the one who assaulted her."

A skeptical murmur rippled through the courtroom, doubts lingering in the minds of those present. But Boxall had his own card to play.

"Yeah, after waking up from a coma after four months, there is no way that she could remember him, if it allegedly was him," he argued, his tone laced with subtle indignation. "Judge, my client is an estate model, and very wealthy. His family depends on him to run the family business."

As the arguments spiralled back and forth, the courtroom swirled with an aura of uncertainty. The judge's expression was inscrutable, carefully considering each word presented before her. And just when it seemed that the scales of justice could tip either way, a flicker of curiosity sparked within her. Melissa voice was unwavering as she presented her argument to the judge.

"Your Honor," Melissa began, her voice carrying an air of certainty, "we believe that Donald might be a flight risk. His passport needs to be taken and he should be remanded."

The judge, stern yet fair, listened intently, her gaze shifting between Melissa and Donald. Though it was only the arraignment, the atmosphere resonated with tension. The judge raised her hand, signalling for Melissa to pause.

"Okay, stop," the judge interjected, her voice commanding attention. "This is not a trial. Save the details until then." She leaned forward, clasping her hands together.

The judge, stern and composed, cleared her throat before addressing the accused.

"Mr. Prince, how do you plead?" she inquired, her voice resonating through the room.

A small smile crept onto Donald's face as he looked up, meeting the judge's gaze.

"Not guilty, your Honor," he replied, his voice unwavering.

The gallery murmured with surprise, whispering amongst themselves. Voices filled with doubt and suspicion echoed, surrounding Donald like a never-ending chorus. The room was filled with curious eyes, desperately seeking answers to the questions that lingered in their minds. But Donald remained calm, unwavering in his assertion of innocence. The courtroom walls reverberated with his confidence, captivating the attention of everyone present. Each person was sucked into a web of intrigue, wondering what secrets lay hidden beneath that confident facade.

"The defendant's passport will be revoked until after the court case. He will be released and placed on house arrest." Said the judge.

The air grew thick as the judge's words hung in the room, leaving everyone to ponder the implications of her ruling. Melissa eyes narrowed, her mind racing with questions. How would they ensure Donald's compliance with the house arrest? What secrets might he hold that would prompt such caution? Donald, however, remained unfazed, his eyes fixed on the floor. His silence only deepened the enigma surrounding him. What was he hiding? Why did he seem so indifferent to the gravity of the situation? As the judge swiftly moved on to the next case, the spectators exchanged curious glances. The courtroom's occupants were left to wonder about the intriguing dynamics at play. The unexpected ruling had sparked a chain of unanswered questions, each thread intertwining with the others in a web of mystery.

Twenty-Five

Timely Resolution

Ever since Donald's high-profile arrest, the media had been relentless in their pursuit of the truth. As he stood at the top of the courthouse steps, he maintained his composure, carefully choosing his words with each query that came his way. The crowd of reporters pushed and jostled, desperate for a piece of the story that had captivated the nation. Donald stood at the top of the courthouse steps, his eyes squinting against the bright sunlight as news reporters surrounded him. Cameras flashed, microphones were thrust in his direction, and questions flew at him from every angle. It was a whirlwind of confusion and chaos, but Donald remained composed.

"I don't know what this is all about," he said, his voice steady and resolute. "But I am innocent, and I can't wait for the trial to start so that everyone can understand the truth. That's all I have to say."

The reporters scribbled furiously in their notebooks and shouted follow-up questions, but Donald turned and walked towards his waiting car, leaving the crowd behind. As the engine roared to life, he couldn't help but feel a mix of anxiety and anticipation. As he slid into the plush leather seat of the sleek black vehicle, a flicker of determination sparked in Donald Prince's eyes. The fire within him burned brightly, fuelled by a thirst for retribution and a desire to prove himself as the legend he knew he could be. Leaning back against the seat, a sly smile crept across Donald's face. They had underestimated him, those who thought they could manipulate and deceive. They had no idea who they were dealing with. Donald Prince was not just a name; he was a force to be reckoned with, a shadow in the night, and an embodiment of unwavering determination. As the chaotic crowd slowly faded into the distance through the rear-view mirror, Donald glanced at his trusted driver, who awaited his command. The resolute gleam in his eyes was mirrored by the unspoken understanding between the two.

Donald spoke, his voice laced with an air of quiet intensity.

"I'm hungry. Take me somewhere nice to eat."

The driver nodded, his stoic demeanour revealing a shared determination to stand by his employer's side. Without a word, the sleek vehicle glided through the city streets, its engine purring like an obedient beast. As they passed the familiar landmarks, anticipation coursed through Donald's veins. This was only the beginning - a mere taste of the enigmatic puzzle he was determined to unravel. But first, he needed sustenance to fuel both body and mind. The rain drizzled down gently, transforming the city streets into a shimmering symphony of reflections. Sergeant Soliman and Detective Smith stood outside their patrol car, their eyes fixed on the figure of Donald, who was being driven away. As the vehicle disappeared around the corner, Sergeant Soliman couldn't help but feel an overwhelming curiosity gnawing at him. There was something about Donald that didn't sit right, something that tugged at his instincts. Sergeant Soliman had a reputation for his intuition and his knack for unravelling the truth. He prided himself on being able to spot the tiniest details that others might overlook. As he stared at the spot where Donald's vehicle had vanished, he knew he couldn't just let it go. He had to dig deeper, to uncover the truth that lingered in the shadows.

Twenty-Six

A Safe Haven of Health

Back at St. Mary's Hospital, Sergeant Soliman arrived to visit Elisa. There was a certain air of curiosity in his eyes. He made his way down the familiar corridor towards Elisa's room. It had been a while since he had last seen her, and he couldn't help but feel a sense of anticipation as he approached the door. He had heard stories about Elisa's miraculous recovery and couldn't help but wonder how it had all happened. As he knocked on her door, he could hear the muffled sounds of conversation from inside. The door swung open, revealing a petite woman physician standing beside Elisa's bed. She was delicately massaging Elisa's hands, determined to bring back the sensation that had long eluded her. Months of rigorous therapy sessions had led to this moment, and Elisa was finally starting to feel hopeful. Her touch gentle yet purposeful. Elisa, with her eyes closed, was clearly lost in the moment. The physician's hands seemed to bring life back into Elisa's once immobile fingers, and a sense of hope flickered in the room. The door slowly opened, revealing Elisa's radiant smile as she caught sight of Sergeant Soliman.

"Well, someone looks better, wow," he exclaimed, genuinely amazed at her progress. Stepping into the room, he couldn't help but notice the determination etched on the physician's face.

140

Both the physician and Elisa looked up as the doctor gently placed Elisa's hands on the bed. The room was filled with a mix of relief and anticipation. They knew that soon, Elisa would be able to leave the hospital and start her life anew. As the physician walked out of the room, she gave Sergeant Soliman a smile. He returned the gesture, relieved to see Elisa's recovery. The room was filled with a sense of hope and gratitude.

"Hello Elisa, how are you doing?" asked Sergeant Soliman, genuinely concerned.

"Much better actually," Elisa replied, her eyes shining with happiness. "I heard that you caught the guy who assaulted me."

Sergeant Soliman nodded, his expression filled with a mix of satisfaction and determination.

"Yes, that is why I came here to let you know. This is a big breakthrough in the case."

Elisa's smile widened, but she couldn't help but feel a pang of curiosity. She had been through a traumatic ordeal, and the thought of closure brought her a sense of relief. However, there was something about the Sergeant's tone that hinted at more than just a solved case. As Sergeant Soliman settled into the chair next to Elisa's bed, he couldn't help but ask the question burning in his mind.

"Elisa, I hope you don't mind me asking, but how did this all happen? How were you able to make such amazing progress in such a short period of time?"

Elisa's eyes sparkled with a hint of mischief. She paused for a moment, relishing the curiosity in the Sergeant's eyes.

"Well, Sergeant Soliman, it all started with a dream," she began, her voice filled with a sense of wonder.

She went on to recount how one night, as she lay in her hospital bed, she had a vivid dream. In this dream, she saw herself completely healed, her hands moving with grace and ease. Upon waking up, she couldn't shake the feeling that the dream held a deeper meaning.

The room was filled with tension as Elisa sat across from Sergeant Soliman, her eyes filled with worry and fear. The question hung in the air.

"Where is he now?"

"He has been released on bail," replied Sergeant Soliman, his voice laced with determination. "But we are doing our very best to make sure that we send this guy to prison for life. As we are preparing for the trial, our detectives are working harder than ever to bring you justice, but we will need you to testify in court too Elisa".

Elisa's heart sank. She knew that justice needed to be served, but the mere thought of facing her attacker in court made her stomach churn. She mustered the strength to voice her concerns.

"Oh no, I won't be able to do that, I'm sorry."

Detective Soliman leaned forward, his eyes filled with empathy.

"I know this must be hard for you, Elisa, but we need you on the stand. Your testimony is crucial in ensuring that this man faces the consequences of his actions."

Tears welled up in Elisa's eyes as she whispered.

"There is no way that I would be able to face him again. What if he comes after me?"

Detective Soliman paused, understanding the gravity of Elisa's fear. He took a deep breath and gently replied.

"Elisa, we have taken every precaution necessary to ensure your safety. Our team will be by your side every step of the way. Your testimony will not only secure justice for you but for others who have suffered at his hands."

Elisa's mind raced, torn between her need for justice and her fear of the unknown. She knew that facing her attacker would be an act of bravery, a step towards closure. But the thought of reopening old wounds and exposing herself once again left her paralyzed with fear.

"Elisa, I promise you that we are here to protect you, we will not allow him to do anything to you. We won't let him hurt you anymore," Detective Soliman reassured Elisa, his voice filled with determination and empathy. "What that man did to you was abhorrent. You were in a coma for four months, but you are a fighter. The fight doesn't end there, Elisa. You have to keep fighting. We will get this guy, I promise you. At least think about it, please."

"Okay," Elisa replied softly, her voice filled with a mix of uncertainty and hope.

As Detective Soliman walked out of the room, Elisa was left alone with her thoughts and the haunting memories of her brutal attack. Each scene flashed back to that fateful day, engraving itself deep within her mind. She couldn't shake the image of being tied up, the sound of the whip lashing against her fragile body, and the feeling of losing consciousness. Days turned into weeks, and Elisa found herself attending therapy sessions to cope with the aftermath of the trauma. Her therapist, Dr. Michaels, gave her tools to face her fears, helping her rebuild her shattered confidence and find the strength to move forward. Elisa's determination grew stronger with each passing day. She refused to let the darkness consume her. As she embarked on her journey towards healing, she discovered a newfound sense of resilience within herself. The support from her loved ones and the unwavering dedication of Detective Soliman gave her the courage to confront her past head-on. Together, Elisa, Detective Soliman, and the police department worked tirelessly to gather evidence against her attacker. Their efforts led to a breakthrough when they uncovered a series of similar cases, all linked to the same man. It was a race against time to bring him to justice before he could harm another innocent soul.

Eternal Sisterhood

In a quaint little town, where dreams intertwine,
There lived a girl with a smile, so divine.
Her laughter would echo through the bustling streets,
As she danced with grace to a melody, so sweet.

~

Her smile was something only God could make,
It radiated love, never to forsake.
But hidden beneath her joyful facade,
Lay a heart that was broken, scarred and flawed.

~

We were more than just friends, we were like sisters,
Bound by a love that nothing could blister.
Through highs and lows, we stood side by side,
Our souls intertwined, like an unbreakable tide.

~

But one fateful day, darkness veiled the sun,
A tragedy struck, leaving us undone.
Her heart shattered into a million pieces,
Leaving her soul in a state of ceaseless greases.

~

Why did this tragedy have to occur?
For goodness sake, life's cruel spur?
Questions unanswered, doubts in my mind,
Searching for solace, a reason to find.

~

Days turned into weeks, and weeks into years,
But her memory still etched within my tears.

I longed to hear her whisper, to feel her grace,
To see her smile light up this desolate space.

~

For now, I must wait, until we meet again,
In a different realm, where life won't remain.
But until that day, I'll hold onto our love,
A bond unbreakable, forged from above.

Twenty-Seven

Shattered Bonds

Charlene had just arrived home from another exhausting day at work. All those hospital visits had drained her both physically and emotionally, and all she wanted was to collapse on her bed and shut out the world for a while. As she parked her car in the dimly lit parking space, she couldn't help but let out a deep sigh of relief. Her body felt heavy as she rested her head on the steering wheel, cherishing these few moments of tranquillity before facing the chaos of her daily routine once again. The weight of responsibility pressed down on her shoulders, a burden she carried with unwavering dedication.

But something felt off tonight. The air was thick with an eerie silence, and the usual sounds of the neighbourhood were absent. Charlene's instincts went on high alert, and her heart raced with an unfamiliar panic. She had never experienced this kind of unease before, and a cold shiver ran down her spine. Elisa, her once vibrant friend, had been through a tumultuous journey of pain and struggle. She had endured countless surgeries, endless therapy sessions, and the relentless weight of a court case that loomed over her like a dark cloud. Charlene had been there every step of the way, supporting Elisa through the darkest moments of her recovery. She would arrive early in the morning, armed with a cheerful smile, ready to face whatever challenges lay ahead. With unwavering determination, she became Elisa's pillar of strength, her voice of reason, and her beacon of hope. Their friendship was forged in the crucible of adversity, and through it all, Charlene never let Elisa's spirits' waver. She would regale her with stories, crack jokes, and find the silver lining in every setback. Charlene's infectious optimism helped Elisa find the courage to push through the pain and keep moving forward.

But amidst the therapy sessions and the hospital visits, there was always the shadow of the court case that gnawed at their peace of mind. The prospect of justice seemed distant, as if it were a mirage mocking their hopes. Each day, as Charlene sat by Elisa's side, she couldn't help but fantasize about the day when it would all be over. The day when the final verdict would be delivered, and Elisa could finally put the past behind her. It became a mantra in her mind, a whispered prayer in the depths of her soul. Slowly, Charlene mustered the strength to unbuckle her seat belt and reach for her bags on the passenger side of the vehicle. It had been a long day, and all she wanted was to get home and sink into the comfort of her bed. Her tired eyes glanced towards her surroundings, ensuring her safety in the familiar neighbourhood. The street was eerily quiet, with only the dim streetlights casting long shadows on the pavement.

As she prepared her belongings, out of nowhere, a chilling figure emerged from the shadows in the back of her car. Startled, Charlene turned around to face this unexpected presence. Her heart raced as panic gripped her entire being. Her eyes widened in horror as she came face to face with a man, his face hidden behind a shadowy mask. In his hand, he held an object that sent shivers down her spine. It glinted ominously under the pale moonlight, catching her attention. Charlene's mind raced, desperately searching for a way out of this terrifying situation. With each passing second, her fear intensified, her breath coming in short, shallow gasps. Charlene's mind was racing, thoughts of escape becoming increasingly desperate. The neighbourhood she had once considered safe now felt like a prison. Her surroundings seemed to close in on her, suffocating her with their cold, oppressive grip. As the moon cast an eerie glow upon the deserted road, Charlene found herself in a situation she never could have imagined. Without a second thought, she was being strangled by a rope wrapped tightly around her delicate neck. Panic coursed through her veins, her instincts urging her to fight for her very existence.

Desperately, Charlene clutched at the rope, her trembling fingers frantically attempting to loosen its deadly grip. But the more she struggled, the tighter it seemed to become, as if the very fabric of the universe conspired against her. The air grew thin, her vision blurred, and with each passing second, her life slipped further away. In the confined space of the car, her surroundings felt suffocating, closing in on her as she fought for survival. Her legs kicked wildly, desperation fuelling her movements, but her screams for help were met with only silence. The night seemed to hold its breath, as if it too were waiting for her demise. Time ceased to exist as Charlene battled against an invisible adversary, her body growing weaker with each laboured breath. Her mind raced, trying to make sense of the cruel fate that had befallen her. Was this a random act of violence, or was there something more sinister at play? With her last ounce of strength, Charlene resolved to leave her mark upon the world. She etched a name into her consciousness, determined to uncover the truth and ensure her tormentor would not go unpunished. It was a race against time, a quest for justice that would haunt her until her last breath.

Charlene found herself gasping for breath as she desperately fought off her attacker. The person in her car, their face concealed by shadows, exerted an overpowering force, strangling her with an unyielding grip. Her heart raced, pounding against her chest like a desperate plea for salvation. Charlene's strength diminished with each passing second, as her very life slipped away. It was a battle she couldn't win, a fight against an unknown adversary who seemed fuelled by darkness itself.

As her vision blurred, Charlene's eyes closed involuntarily, surrendering to the cruel fate that awaited her. Her grip on the rope, an embodiment of her determination, began to loosen. In that fleeting moment, she made peace with her impending demise, acknowledging that her struggles were in vain.

The mysterious man, a cold-blooded killer, continued to tighten his grip, his eyes devoid of any remorse. He knew the end was near for Charlene, and he relished in the knowledge that he was the one who held the power of life and death. With a swift precision, he released the rope, letting Charlene's lifeless body slump against the seat. Time seemed to stand still as the stranger, devoid of any emotion, slowly reached towards Charlene with the gleaming knife. He then quickly grabbed a handful of Charlene's hair and pulled her head up, forcing her lifeless body to meet his cold, calculating gaze. The sharpness of his eyes pierced through her now lost soul. Seconds later, he penetrated Charlene's neck with the knife. As Charlene lay lifeless in the car, blood gushing from her open wound, a feeling of dread filled the air. The once beautiful car, now a twisted wreck, was like a river flowing with blood. The **metallic** smell of blood hung heavy in the night as the mystery man stood silently, his eyes fixed on the wonderful results of his work.

But as he gathered his wits and looked around, a sense of urgency washed over him. He needed to leave, to erase any trace of his presence. His hands moved swiftly, wiping away any evidence he might have left behind. There was no room for mistakes in his twisted game. With the evidence carefully concealed, the mystery man hastily exited the vehicle. As he leaned against the car, overlooking Charlene's lifeless figure, something unexpected happened. Her eyes, were open in surrender, gazing at the world with an unyielding intensity. He looked on at the beautiful sight before him, the vibrant colours dancing in the moonlight. It was as though nature itself had painted this masterpiece. He couldn't help but feel a twinge of pride. He stepped back, his knife still in hand, and marvelled at the scene he had crafted. The canvas before him was splattered with vibrant reds, a chaotic array of emotions captured in one moment. It was a bloody scene, yes, but it held a deeper meaning - a story waiting to be unravelled.

As he admired his creation, a smile spread across his face. The job was well done. He had successfully portrayed the rawness, the intensity, and the beauty of life in all its forms. He was an artist, not in the conventional sense, but in a way that allowed him to create something extraordinary. His canvas was not made of paint and brushes, but of carefully planned and executed actions. He was a master of his craft, and his work was his art. The next observer's eyes would be drawn to the vivid contrast, drawn into the emotions that dripped from every knife stroke. As he gazed around his tranquil surroundings, memories of his latest creation flooded his mind. The scene he had left behind was now stained with red, a testament to his skill and precision. It was a bloody scene, but for him, it was a work of art. A masterpiece crafted with meticulous detail.

A soft breeze rustled the leaves, carrying away any traces of his presence. He took a step back, admiring his handiwork once again. The smile that tugged at the corners of his lips was not that of a psychopath revelling in bloodshed, but rather the contentment of an artist who had achieved perfection. With a sense of satisfaction, he turned away from the sight, leaving it behind like a signature on a masterpiece. He walked away, his footsteps echoing in the silence of the evening, confident in his abilities. The night fell, casting a shroud of darkness over the parking lot. The moon peeked out from behind the clouds, illuminating the blood-stained scene he had left behind. It was a secret, hidden in plain sight. The beauty of it all was that no one would suspect him. For he, himself, was a work of art, a master of deception.

Twenty-Eight

In the Eye of the Storm

It was the morning of the first day of court, and as the jury walked into the room, anticipation hung heavy in the air. Twelve individuals, chosen to decide the fate of the defendant, Donald, took their seats, their eyes brimming with determination. Beside them, Donald and his lawyer sat at the stable, their expressions a mix of anxiety and hope. Melissa, the prosecutor, sat at the table, her eyes darting nervously between her mobile phone and the entrance of the courtroom.

Time seemed to stretch as she waited for her first witness, Charlene, to arrive. A sinking feeling settled in her stomach as she received no missed calls. Something was off. Unable to ignore her growing unease, Melissa excused herself and swiftly left the solemn atmosphere of the courtroom. As she stepped out into the corridor, she reached for her mobile phone and dialled Charlene's number. The sound of the ringing filled the empty hallway, but no answer came. A knot of worry tightened in Melissa's chest. She paced back and forth, her mind racing with questions. Where could Charlene be? Was she running late, or had something happened? Melissa's heart sank with each passing second, her desperation growing. She needed Charlene's testimony to start building her case, to prove Donald's guilt beyond a reasonable doubt. Just as Melissa contemplated her next move, a familiar figure caught her eye. Sergeant Soliman, a veteran of the force, strode purposefully towards the courtroom. Sergeant Soliman looked at his watch, his brows furrowing in concern. Melissa, the prosecutor, stood beside him in the courthouse hallway, her eyes scanning the busy corridor.

"Sergeant, have you seen Charlene?" she asked, her voice filled with urgency.

"She will be my first witness on the stand today, but she is not answering her phone, and she hasn't arrived."

Sergeant Soliman rubbed his chin thoughtfully.

"Maybe she's running late," he suggested, trying to calm Melissa's growing anxiety.

But Melissa shook her head.

"No, I spoke with her a few days ago. She promised to be here on time. Something doesn't feel right."

The Sergeant sighed, realizing the gravity of the situation.

"Okay, try to make an excuse with the judge. I will send someone over to her house to check if she's there."

"Thanks, Sarge," Melissa said gratefully as she turned and hurried back into the courtroom.

As Sergeant Soliman dialled a number in his phone, his mind raced with worry. Charlene had always been reliable, and her sudden disappearance sent shivers down his spine. He knew he had to act quickly to find answers before it was too late.

Meanwhile, inside the courtroom, the judge looked at Melissa with a mix of curiosity and impatience.

"Where is your witness, Ms Melissa Thompson?" he asked sternly.

Melissa bit her lip, searching for the right words.

"Your Honor, I apologize for the delay. Unfortunately, there seems to be an unexpected situation with my witness. I believe she's encountering some personal issues, but I assure you, we're doing everything we can to locate her."

The judge's expression softened slightly as he leaned back in his chair.

"Very well, Ms Thompson. I will grant you a brief recess to sort out this matter. But I expect your witness to be present when we reconvene."

Melissa nodded, grateful for the judge's understanding. As the courtroom emptied, she took a deep breath, her mind racing with worry for Charlene's safety. She couldn't shake off the feeling that something was seriously wrong. Outside the courthouse, Sergeant Soliman paced back and forth, his phone pressed to his ear.

"Smith, I need you and Moony to go over to Charlene's apartment," Sergeant Soliman said urgently over the phone. "She hasn't shown up for court, and she's the first witness to testify at the trial today." The panic in his voice was palpable as he hung up, leaving Smith with a million questions racing through his mind.

Twenty-Nine

In Pursuit of Hope

Smith's heart pounded in his chest as he listened to Sergeant Soliman's urgent request. The missing witness, Charlene, held the key to an important trial, and her absence threatened to jeopardize the entire case. Without hesitation, Smith grabbed his coat and called for Moony, his trusted partner, to join him on a race against time.

"Moony, let's go, we have to rush over to Charlene's apartment," Smith urged, his voice filled with concern. "She hasn't showed up for court today."

Moony glanced at his watch and raised an eyebrow.

"Maybe she's running late," he suggested optimistically.

Smith's gaze hardened as he shook his head.

"Well, the Sergeant doesn't seem to think so, and neither do I," he replied, his tone revealing a hidden worry.

They both knew the gravity of the situation as they hurriedly made their way to Charlene's last known whereabouts. The streets were dimly lit, eerily quiet, but their determination pushed them forward. The two detectives hurriedly made their way up the stairs, arriving outside Charlene's apartment door. Smith knocked loudly, his impatience mingling with the growing tension in his chest. There was no answer. The detectives exchanged a glance, their shared concern deepening.

"Charlene!" Smith called out, his voice echoing through the empty hallway. Still, there was no response. Without hesitation, he reached for his pocket, pulling out a set of lockpicks. Moony watched as his partner expertly and quickly unlocked the door.

As they stepped inside, the detectives were met with an eerie silence. The apartment seemed frozen in time. The sound of their footsteps echoed through the empty rooms, amplifying their growing unease. They cautiously entered, Their eyes scanning the room for any signs of her. The place seemed undisturbed, as if Charlene had simply vanished into thin air. Moony, sensing his partner's distress, softly barked. Smith turned towards him, finding solace in his loyal companion's presence. Together, they explored every nook and cranny, searching for any clue that might lead them closer to Charlene. The apartment was empty, with no signs of a struggle or forced entry. Smith's mind raced, wondering where Charlene could have gone. Why had she disappeared on such a critical day? Questions piled up, but the answers remained elusive. Smith's eyes scanned the room, searching for any clue that might lead him to answers. But there was no sign of a struggle or forced entry. The apartment appeared untouched, as if Charlene had never been there. Confusion mingled with worry as the unanswered questions piled up.

Moony's voice broke the silence.

"Do you think she left willingly?" he asked, his eyes narrowing with suspicion.

Smith shook his head, his mind grappling with possible explanations.

"I don't know, Moony. It doesn't make sense. Why would she disappear right when we need her the most?"

They combed through Charlene's belongings, hoping for any hint of her whereabouts. Letters, photographs, and personal belongings offered no insight into her sudden disappearance. The apartment remained an enigma, refusing to divulge its secrets. Walking back downstairs, he couldn't shake off the feeling that something was off. The parking lot seemed eerily quiet and deserted. His heart raced as he scanned the area, desperately searching for any clues that would explain the unsettling atmosphere. As he made his way through the rows of parked vehicles, his eyes locked onto a familiar shape. Charlene's car. The sight of it brought a flicker of hope, but also a surge of anxiety. What was her car doing here at this hour?

Approaching cautiously, he peered through the window, hoping to catch a glimpse of Charlene inside. A figure slumped over the wheel instantly caught his attention, sending a chill down his spine. Panic gripped him, as he desperately tried to identify the lifeless form. Knocking on the window, he called out Charlene's name, his voice trembling with fear. Silence filled the air, leaving him feeling more unsettled than ever. Time seemed to stand still as he wrestled with the terrifying thought that Charlene might be in danger. Detective Smith was no stranger to crime scenes. He had seen it all, or so he thought. But as he cautiously approached the abandoned car in the deserted parking lot, he had no idea what awaited him inside. With a gloved hand, he carefully opened the car door. The scene that unfolded before him was unlike anything he had ever encountered. Blood splattered the seat, staining it a deep crimson, and it pooled on the car's floor, forming a macabre reflection of the chaos that had ensued. Astonishment took over him, his eyes widening in disbelief. As a seasoned detective, Smith prided himself on his ability to maintain composure in the face of gruesome sights. But this crime scene rattled him to the core. Who would do such a thing? And why? These questions burned in his mind as he took a step back, trying to make sense of the horrifying tableau before him. With a deep breath, Smith regained his composure and approached the car once more.

As the weight of the situation sank in, he knew he had to gather his wits and contact the authorities. But deep down, a nagging curiosity gnawed at him. He couldn't ignore the burning need to unveil the truth, to uncover the hidden secrets that led Charlene to this grim fate. As the rain poured heavily outside, Charlene lay motionless in the backseat of the car. Detective Smith's heart pounded as he reached out to check for Charlene's pulse. Panic consumed him as he realized there was no sign of life. He screamed for Detective Moony, who was tirelessly searching for any trace of information regarding Charlene's whereabouts. Hearing the desperation in his partner's voice, Detective Moony abandoned his search and rushed downstairs. The sight that awaited them was chilling. Charlene, once full of life, now lay dead with her throat slit in the car. It was a horrifying scene that sent shivers down their spines.

"Oh fuck, her head, it's hanging off her body, my fucking goodness" Detective Moony muttered, his voice trembling as he removed a cloth from his pockets and covered his mouth. "Who could have done this?" The weight of the tragedy hung heavily in the air as they stood in silence, their minds racing for answers.

Detective Moony's instinct kicked in. He knew he had to call for backup. He pulled out his phone and dialled Sergeant Soliman's number. Each ring felt like an eternity, as if time itself was mocking their despair.

"Moony," a gruff voice finally answered.

"Sir, it's Moony," the detective's voice betrayed his distress. "We've got a murder. Charlene is dead, we just found her in her car, it looks like someone cut her throat, it's so bad Sergeant, she's gone."

The silence on the other end of the line was deafening. The gravity of the situation sank in. In that moment, Detective Moony realized that their lives would never be the same. The rain poured down relentlessly, mimicking the turmoil inside his head. His mind raced, desperately trying to make sense of the chaos and find the missing pieces to this dark puzzle. Why would someone do this? Why would they silence Charlene, just as she was about to testify? The questions burned in his mind like embers, fuelling an insatiable need for answers. The hunt for the killer had begun, and justice would be their only solace.

Thirty

Back in the Dock

Sergeant Soliman stood outside the courtroom, his mind reeling from the shocking news he had just received. Detective Smith had just informed him that Charlene, the witness set to testify that day, had been brutally murdered. The weight of the information sent heatwaves through Soliman's body, and his heart sank as he struggled to make sense of it all. Curiosity consumed him as he thought about the mysterious perpetrator responsible for Charlene's untimely demise. Who would want to silence her, and why? As Soliman's mind raced with questions, he took a deep breath and composed himself before stepping back into the courtroom. Making his way towards prosecutor Melissa, Soliman beckoned her outside, needing to share the devastating news. Melissa, sensing the gravity of the situation, followed him without hesitation.

"It's Charlene," Soliman said, his voice heavy with sorrow.

Melissa's eyes widened, her heart racing as she anxiously asked.

"What happened? Where is she?"

Soliman's words caught in his throat, unable to bring himself to say the words out loud. He sighed deeply, gathering his thoughts before continuing.

"She's gone, Melissa. Someone... someone killed her."

Melissa gasped, her hands instinctively covering her mouth as tears welled up in her eyes. The air around them suddenly grew heavy with grief and an overwhelming sense of injustice. They stood outside the courtroom, two dedicated individuals connected by a shared determination for justice. As the reality of the situation sank in, Soliman's mind raced with countless theories and suspects. The need to find the truth and bring the culprits to justice consumed him. He knew that unravelling the mystery behind Charlene's murder would not only provide closure for her grieving family but also ensure that no one else would suffer the same fate.

"Oh my God, why? Who could have done this?" Melissa muttered under her breath, her mind racing with questions.

She had been counting on Charlene, her main witness, to testify against a powerful criminal who had wreaked havoc on Elisa. Charlene's testimony was crucial to ensure justice was served, and now, everything hung in the balance. Unable to contain her growing unease, Melissa interrupted herself mid-thought and turned to Sergeant Soliman, her trusted ally.

"Elisa is in the hospital. We need to get her into protective custody immediately," she said, her voice shaking with urgency. "Call the hospital and make sure she's okay. I'll have to inform the judge about this unfortunate development."

Sergeant Soliman's eyes widened with concern as he realized the gravity of the situation. Without wasting a moment, he picked up his phone and dialled the hospital's number. As he made the call, his mind was already racing ahead, strategizing to ensure Elisa's safety. Simultaneously, Melissa hurriedly made her way back into the courtroom, her heart pounding. She knew she had to deliver the disheartening news to the judge, who had entrusted her with the responsibility of seeking justice in this complex case. Every step felt heavier than the last as she approached the judge's bench. The courtroom was packed as the air buzzed with excitement. Melissa, the determined prosecutor, hurriedly stepped into the room, her heart pounding in her chest. She walked over to the Judge's bench, where the judge and jury waited expectantly. Something wasn't right. She had just received some shocking news that threatened to unravel her meticulously built case, like a carefully woven tapestry being pulled apart. As she stood in front of the judge, Melissa struggled to compose herself. The weight of the situation bore down on her, and a wave of panic washed over her. This case had consumed her life for months, the countless hours of preparation, the sleepless nights pouring over evidence, and the tenacity she had displayed, all now hanging precariously by a thread.

She glanced at the defense attorney, a smug smile playing on his lips, unaware of the storm brewing within her. Melissa knew she couldn't afford any missteps, not after the countless hours she had spent building the case brick by brick. Every detail had been thoughtfully put together, every witness interviewed, every evidence analysed. But now, a single piece of information had the potential to shatter it all. In the midst of this tense battle, Melisa's mind raced, desperately seeking a solution. She couldn't let everything she had worked for slip away. Taking a deep breath, Melissa addressed the court. Her voice was steady, masking the turmoil inside her. Her heart raced as she stood before the judge, her mind swirling with a thousand thoughts. The courtroom was hushed, waiting for her next words. Taking another deep breath, she mustered the courage to speak.

"Judge, erm, I have just been informed that our main witness has just been murdered," she stammered, her voice trembling.

"Murdered? What do you mean, murdered?" the judge questioned, his eyes wide with disbelief.

Melissa nodded, her voice growing more steady.

"Yes, Judge. She was our main witness, and I believe that the defendant has something to do with it. We need to hold off on the case until we are able to find out more."

A wave of tension flooded the courtroom as the judge contemplated the gravity of the situation. Before he could respond, Boxall, Donald's lawyer, erupted in a fury.

"Judge, there is nowhere that they can pin this on my client!" Boxall shouted, his face turning red with anger. "He has been on house arrest! He cannot be responsible for this!"

Melissa's eyes locked with Boxall's, her determination unwavering.

"I understand your concerns, Mr. Boxall, but we cannot ignore the possibility that Donald may have orchestrated this in order to secure his freedom."

As the courtroom filled with tension, Boxall, and Melissa, engaged in a heated battle of words. The air crackled with their arguments, each one trying to outwit the other. Boxall vehemently defended his client's innocence, ensuring to emphasize that Donald had no involvement in the recent murder.

The judge, growing weary of their constant bickering, abruptly boomed.

"Enough! In my chambers, now!" His authoritative voice echoed throughout the room, demanding their immediate compliance.

Boxall, a confident and composed man, took the lead and made his way into the judge's chambers. As he passed by Melissa, a chilling smirk crept across his face. The look in his eyes was both enigmatic and sinister, leaving Melissa with an unsettling feeling. Deep down, she knew that he held the key to unravelling the truth behind Charlene's untimely demise. Inside the private chambers, the atmosphere didn't change. The tension thickened, and the stakes grew higher. The judge, known for his strict demeanour, slammed the door behind him, locking the outside world away. The room seemed to shrink, engulfing them in an intimate setting that intensified their silent confrontation. Boxall, quick on his feet, unfolded a series of compelling arguments, presenting a web of evidence that aimed to exonerate Donald. His words were calculated, every sentence crafted to cast doubt on the prosecution's case. Meanwhile, Melisa, determined to bring justice to Charlene, refused to waver.

"Look, Your Honor, I don't know what the prosecution is playing at, but there is no way that they can accuse my client of such atrocities," Boxall asserted, his voice brimming with conviction. "As I mentioned, he's been on house arrest for months."

Melissa, the determined prosecutor, shot back with a venomous tone.

"Well, that doesn't stop him from sending his little goons to do his dirty work, does it? We all know what that family is capable of."

Boxall smirked, a glimmer of confidence shining in his eyes.

"But can you prove these terrible accusations, Ms. Thompson?"

Melissa's face turned beet red with anger. Veins protruded from her temples as she shouted.

"Not now, but I sure will!"

The tension reached its peak, and it seemed as though the walls themselves were ready to burst. However, the judge, sitting in his chambers, observed the chaos with a sense of detachment. As the two attorneys continued their heated exchange, the judge sighed and ran his fingers through his thinning hair. He had seen countless trials, but this one seemed to be unlike any other. The accused, a member of a wealthy and influential family, seemed to be untouchable. The evidence was circumstantial, and now the witness was dead. As time ticked by, the voices in the chamber grew louder, echoing through the walls. The debate escalated into a battle of wits, each side presenting their version of events, fighting tooth and nail for victory. The judge, a wise and experienced figure, listened intently, weighing every word with careful consideration.

"Okay, okay, quiet you two, that's enough," the judge finally spoke, his voice commanding attention.

Melissa took a deep breath, desperately trying to quell her nerves.

"I have read and listened to both your arguments," the judge continued, "Melissa, I'm sorry to hear that your main witness has died, but unfortunately, there is not enough evidence for a trial, and neither is there enough evidence to convict Donald Prince."

Melissa's heart sank. How could this be happening? She had believed in the strength of her case, in the power of the main witness who had bravely come forward.

"Judge, we still have the main witness who identified Donald," Melissa pleaded, desperation evident in her voice. "She remembers everything that had happened to her."

The judge sighed heavily, his brow furrowing with contemplation. He had heard countless cases throughout his career, but this one seemed to have taken a twisted turn. He knew the weight of his decision, and the consequences it would have for both the victim and the accused. After a moment of silence, the judge finally spoke again.

"Melissa, I understand your frustration, but without solid evidence to support the witness's claims, I cannot proceed with a trial. The burden of proof lies with the prosecution, and in this case, it falls short."

Melissa had always believed in the power of justice. She believed that no matter the circumstances, every person deserved their day in court. And she was determined to ensure that her victim, the one who was caused so much pain, got the justice she deserved.

"I understand, Judge," Melissa said, her voice filled with anger and determination. "But my victim deserves a trial, and I will not stop until she gets that."

Judge Slater knew the gravity of the situation, and he knew that he had to handle it carefully, so as not to raise any suspicions. He took a deep breath and looked at Melissa, trying to maintain a calm exterior.

"Okay," Judge Slater replied, his voice steady. "So this is what I can do. We will have a bench-only trial. Present all your evidence to me in a week, and we can get this trial started. For now, Boxall, your client is still on house arrest."

Melissa listened intently as the judge's words echoed through the room. Her heart sank as she once again realized that her main witness had been killed. The weight of the situation pressed heavily upon her, leaving her with a sense of uncertainty. The evidence she had gathered felt insufficient, and doubts crept into her mind. How could she convince the jury without a strong supporting witness? Despite the challenges ahead, Melissa clung to a glimmer of hope - a bench trial was on the horizon, offering a chance to present her case, albeit with limited resources.

"Thank you, Judge," Melissa responded, her voice filled with gratitude mixed with a hint of determination. She knew she had to make the most of this opportunity, no matter how slim the odds appeared.

Boxall, known for his brash and unconventional demeanour, raised an eyebrow.

"Well, to be honest, I don't see the point in all this," he remarked, a smirk etched on his face. His words hit Melissa like an unexpected blow, shattering her confidence for a moment. But she couldn't afford to let his skepticism deter her.

With a forced smile, she replied.

"Sure, I'll see you in a week." The room fell silent once again, leaving a lingering tension in the air as Melissa collected her thoughts and walked out of the room.

Leaving the chambers, Melisa's anger grew, fuelling her determination to uncover the truth. She couldn't let an unjust ruling prevail. Her footsteps echoed in the hallway as she hurried towards the detective's office, determined to share her suspicions. Meanwhile, Judge Slater, the man behind the desk, took a deep breath and slowly rose from his chair. His gaze fixed upon the vast cityscape beyond the window, he contemplated the consequences of his actions. He knew he was crossing a line, but it seemed there was no way out. Seated once again, his hand trembled as he opened the drawer. His eyes were drawn to a large envelope, neatly addressed to him. The weight of guilt pressed upon him, but there was something else too – a sense of desperation, of feeling trapped.

He had always prided himself on his unyielding integrity, yet circumstances had forced him into a web of deceit. The contents of the envelope held the key. With a hesitant hand, he unfolded the letter, revealing the dark secrets it contained. Each word etched into his consciousness, leaving him torn between the truth and his own predicament. Slater closed his eyes, torment gripping his heart. He knew the consequences of his actions would reverberate far beyond the confines of his office. But was there another way? Could he find a glimmer of redemption amidst the darkness that now consumed him? In that fateful moment, the judge knew he had to make a choice. A choice that would shape his legacy and determine the years that lay ahead. He thought about his impending retirement, just a few years away, and the dreams he had of spending his days basking in the sun on a tropical island, far away from the shadows of his conscience. It was then that a decision crystallized in the judge's mind. He would retire in the Bahamas, a place where he could escape the weight of his guilt and the haunting memories of his past. The thought of starting anew, surrounded by crystal-clear waters and endless white sands, offered solace in a way that nothing else could.

Thirty-One

Almost Lost

In the early veil of dawn, Elisa watched the sunlight creep over the horizon, casting long shadows in her hospital room. Cradling her budding belly, she relished the unfamiliar thrill of motherhood that fluttered within her. Today was the day she would bid farewell to her sterile confinement and take a leap into the world with two heartbeats drumming inside her. She would be moving in with her best friend, Charlene, who had stuck with her through the storm. A wave of gratitude washed over her at the thought.

Charlene, a beacon in the tempestuous sea of her life, was more than a friend; she was her saviour when everything around her crumbled. Charlene was testifying against a haunting past today, a testament of unwavering loyalty and resolute comfort. Elisa was busy arranging her belongings into her duffle bag. The sight of her worn-out sneakers and faded ripped jeans brought a cynical smile to her face - a stark contrast to the arid white hospital sheets. Over the past few months, Elisa had become a resident of this room, nestled amidst the beeping monitors and scent of sterilization. Today was the first day of the rest of her life, a triumphant march from the snare of death, after a series of surgeries and countless therapy sessions.

As Elisa was lost in her thoughts, she found herself caressing her pregnant belly, her heart bubbling with anticipation. She was ready to leap into the next chapter of her life - staying with her loyal friend, Charlene. Her unwavering rock, a fortress of solidarity and love, Charlene had been her life-saver, her guiding star in the darkest nights of her life. The door creaked softly, jerking her back to reality. The new doctor entered with a warm smile that crinkled at the corners of his eyes.

"Good morning, Elisa," he greeted, his voice soft, yet carrying a note of respect. Elisa returned the greeting with an eager smile, visibly excited about the prospect of a new beginning.

There was a charismatic dance in Dr. Adams' steps as he approached Elisa.

"Ready to leave this fortress, I see," he chuckled, recording her vitals, his eyes never leaving the screen. Elisa nodded, her gaze drifting towards the window. The world outside seemed to have moved on, while she felt like a character from an old book gathering dust; familiar, yet never forgotten.

"Yes, I can't wait to finally leave this place," Elisa said, her eyes shimmering with anticipation.

The doctor nodded in understanding, gently taking her hand, readying the needle for one last time. His acknowledgment of her journey, her bravery and resilience, brought a sense of closure Elisa desperately needed. As the door closed behind the doctor, Elisa looked out at the awakening city, her heart pounding with a newfound fervour. The next chapter of her life awaited her – a life that would be imprinted with her courage, her survival, and most importantly, her love for her unborn child and her best friend, Charlene.

At that moment, time stood still. The air held its breath, the walls closed in, and the Earth slowed its pace. As the doctor was about to inject the syringe, Elisa's heart fluttered with a cocktail of emotions - fear, hope, apprehension, and joy. She was on the precipice of a new life and, although fraught with uncertainty, she was ready to take the plunge. As the needle pricked her skin, she felt a rush of surreal calmness wash over her, as if she were floating in a tranquil sea under a sky adorned with stars. His hands, more calculating than comforting, moved in a synchronized dance between the syringe and the tightening grip on Elisa's hand. But it wasn't the hypodermic needle that was the harbinger of danger, it was the other object concealed in his pocket. As the doctor reached in, a metallic glint sparked ominously. It was a gun. His intentions were as deadly as the weapon he held. The pillow was not for comfort, but for something far more sinister. But as fate would have it, salvation was inching closer down the hallway.

Sergeant Soliman, Detective Smith, and Detective Moony, a trio well-versed with danger, sprinted down the corridors of the hospital, their hearts pounding a symphony of urgency. Their eyes caught sight of Elisa's usual doctor, a trusted figure, engrossed in his paperwork, oblivious to the danger brewing a few rooms away. The trio skidded to a stop just as the doctor looked up, startled by their sudden appearance. They huddled over, their words tumbling over in a chaotic frenzy, trying to get the truth out.

"Hey doc, where is Elisa? Is she okay?" demanded Sergeant Soliman, his fierce eyes seeking answers and his voice rippling with anxiety.

Doctor Washington, a silver-haired man with kindly eyes, looked up from his clipboard, surprised at the sudden intrusion.

"Yes, she's fine, there's a new doctor in her room giving her injections. What on earth is going on?" he asked, confusion warring with concern on his lined face.

His question hung in the air, a resonant note in the symphony of unease. The entrance of Detective Moony added to the clamour, his dark eyes a mirror to the sergeant's worry.

"A new doctor? What do you mean, Doc?"

"He started today. What's going on?" Doctor Washington repeated, his voice wavering on the edge of shock. He took off his glasses, cleaning them nervously, as though hoping that clarity in his vision might also bring clarity to the situation.

The very air seemed to vibrate with the energy of the unsaid, the unknown. A group of men, each heart pounding in sync with the other, moved swiftly towards a room at the end of the corridor. Their movements suggested a practiced discipline, a desperate urgency. A name resonated in the silence – Elisa. As they got closer, a chilling scene unfolded before their eyes. Elisa, frail and lifeless, was sprawled on the bed, and looming over her was a figure in a doctor's coat. A silencer-equipped gun, muffled under a pillow, pointed menacingly at her face. Time seemed to stand still, but the men were already in motion. Before any coherent thought could formulate, they burst into the room—glinting weapons met with a sharp retort. Amid the sudden chaos, a figure crumbled, blood spattering the sterile white floors like a horrifying abstract painting. The phony doctor lay still, his threat neutralized. Once the room was secured, they rushed over to Elisa. Her body was unnervingly still, an eerie contrast to the recently transpired chaos. Something wasn't right—Elisa wasn't waking up. The room fell into a deadly hush as the men waited for signs of life, their hope dwindling by the second.

Sergeant Soliman, a grizzled veteran whose gaze held stories of a thousand wars, cradled Elisa's fragile form in his calloused hands. His gruff exterior cracked as he let out an agonizing scream for a real doctor, his roar echoing through the sterile corridors. Desperation painted a grim picture in the room as they waited for the sound of hurried footsteps. Overhead, a storm was brewing, an ominous reflection of the turmoil within the white walls. The symphony of life and death played out, punctuated by the frantic footsteps of the medical team and the erratic beeping of the EKG. Without wasting a minute, the doctors and nurses swept into the room like a whirlwind. Every second was a battle against an invisible assailant - the poison coursing through Elisa's veins. One nurse quickly inserted an IV, pumping in lifesaving antidote in a desperate bid to cleanse the toxin from her body. They needed to protect not just Elisa but the tiny life burgeoning within her. Chaos reigned in the room. Orders were barked, procedures performed with breakneck speed. It was a war zone, their weapon of choice - knowledge, their enemy was - time.

"Sergeant Soliman, we need you to step out," a stern-faced doctor demanded, barely looking up from his work. Soliman reluctantly took one last look at Elisa, her face white against the crisp white hospital sheets, before being ushered out of the room.

Outside, the hospital corridor was ominously silent. The echo of each tick from the wall clock was a jarring reminder of the passing seconds, each one carrying the weight of a lifetime. Kneeling on the cold hospital floor, Sergeant Soliman cupped his face in his hands, the gravity of the situation finally sinking in. His mind raced back to their last conversation, the light in Elisa's eyes, the warmth of her laughter. How could things go wrong so fast?

As inexplicable fear gripped him, his hushed whisper echoed in the silence.

"Stay with me, Elisa." The empty corridor reverberated with the unspoken promise of a thousand tomorrows yet to unfold.

Thirty-Two

Inspiring Resurgence

Sergeant Soliman stared at the silent figure of Elisa. A myriad of machines beeped rhythmically, the slow cadence a testament to her dormant state. The last few months of her coma had been a test of his patience, a game of wait and see. He was a patient man, but even patience wore thin when someone was trying to kill the woman you swore to protect, not once but twice. Despite the odds, Elisa had survived a brutal assault that landed her in a coma. And now this. His heart sunk into an abyss every time he thought about it. His mind laid the cruel imagination like a looping tape in his brain - the assassin tiptoeing into the hospital, the cold steel of the weapon gleaming under the sterile hospital lights.

As these thoughts clouded his mind, a faint but distinct gasp broke his distraught reverie. Elisa's eyelids fluttered, her pale face twitching as her eyes flickered open. Surprised and elated, he rushed to her side, eager for any words she might speak, or clues she might spill.

"Elisa," he urged quietly, taking her hand in his, a comfort he hoped she would register.

Her eyes, though weak, locked with his, a flicker of recognition passing through them. She tried to speak, but all that came out were incoherent whispers.

"Elisa? Can you hear me?" a firm but caring voice pierced through the fog of her mind.

"Where am I? What happened?" she asked, her voice weak and her eyes scanning the drab hospital room.

"Elisa, we had an incident. You were poisoned, and we had to put you under surgery," explained Soliman, his tone steady but eyes betraying his concern.

"My baby... where is my baby?" she asked, her hand instinctively reaching for her stomach.

Without missing a beat, Soliman reassured her.

"The baby is fine, the doctors managed to get you both stable, and they removed all the poison out of your system. You are such an amazing fighter, Elisa."

A sigh of relief escaped from her lips as she felt her stomach, grateful that her unborn child was unharmed. Amidst her relief, a sudden realization dawned upon her.

"Charlene, where is Charlene?" she asked weakly, as she strained her eyes to see through the dim room.

Elisa lay there, her once vibrant eyes now dull and vacant, the shadowy remnants of battle scars adorning her face. But what struck him the most was her stomach, round and firm, a testament to the life burgeoning within her. It was a stark contrast to the frailty that seemed to be creeping over her like a slow-moving fog. He swallowed hard, the news he carried weighing heavy on his heart.

"Elisa," he began, his voice trembling with an unusual tremor. The room seemed to contract, the air thickening as he uttered the words.

"I'm very sorry to tell you this, but Charlene was murdered a few days ago."

The words hung in the air like a spectre, wrapping its cold fingers around the room. His words hit her like waves on a stormy night, pulling her under their dark currents. Her eyes widened in shock, her lips parting in a silent plea as she processed the news.

"Wh-what? Why... who would do this? Please... don't tell me that." Her voice was barely a whisper, carrying the weight of her anguish.

He pressed his lips into a thin line, the knuckles of his clasped hands turning white. This was the hardest part of his job – breaking bad news to loved ones. But it never got any easier, not for him, not for anyone.

"I'm so sorry Elisa," he reiterated, his heart aching for her.

"We're doing our best to find who's responsible, I promise you that."

A veil of silence descended upon them, the ticking of the wall clock the only reminder of the passing time. As the last remnants of the sun slithered away, tucking itself beneath the horizon, Soliman spoke with determination in his voice.

"I'm so sorry Elisa, we will be putting you in protective custody and make sure that you have around the clock care by some of our trusted men," said Sergeant Soliman, his face drawn with the weight of the news he'd just delivered.

Elisa's heart plunged into a deep abyss of sorrow. The room spun around her, her knees gave way, and she was engulfed in an ocean of agony and disbelief. Her best friend, her confidante, her pillar of strength had been cruelly taken away. The tears she'd been fighting so hard to hold back rushed forward, deciding it was time to stage a revolt against stoicism. The night was long and filled with echoing silence. Elisa could barely comprehend the reality. She was left all alone in this world, her best friend gone forever, and the only company she had now were her own echoes bouncing off the walls of this desolate hospital room.

Thirty-Three

The Bittersweet Nature of Goodbyes

The aged stained-glass windows of the St. Augustine church bore silent witness to the sea of mourners painted in monochrome that day. It was packed to the brim, the sad notes of "Cynthia Erivo, singing I'm here" weaving a haunting melody that echoed throughout the stone walls. The air bristled with grief, a palpable entity that gripped every heart. At the centre of it all was Charlene's glossed photo, perched above her casket, her radiant smile a stark contrast to the bleakness that filled the building.

The attendees, a mix of family, friends, and colleagues, celebrated her life even as the tears cascaded down their faces. They relished in stories of her kindness, her zest for life and her unyielding spirit. Yet, there was an underlying note of heaviness, the elephant in the room that no one dared to address- Charlene's life had been stolen away all too soon. Among the congregation, Elisa held a prominent spot, right at the front of the church. Tears were streaming down her face, each droplet holding a memory of Charlene, and as she rubbed her pregnant stomach, she felt a piercing pain of loss. Her best friend, her confidant, her sister by bond, was no more. Charlene's laughter would no longer fill her days, her advice would no longer guide her, and the thought sent fresh waves of tears trickling down her cheeks.

The news that Charlene was killed in cold blood had hit Elisa like a freight train. Days had turned into a blur of disbelief and despair. Guilt gnawed at her sanity. She blamed herself. Had she not asked Charlene to testify in court, Charlene would've been safe. Instead, she had walked right into the hands of her death. As the last echoes of the profound hymn danced off the stone, Elisa sat alone, gazing up at the image of her best friend Charlene. Her eyes shimmered with tears, reflecting the sorrow etched deeply into her soul.

"Forgive me," she whispered, her voice barely slicing through the silence, each word heavy with remorse that settled on the age-old walls of the chapel.

Elisa and Charlene, friends since childhood, had shared every life milestone, every joy, every sorrow, every tear, and laughter. Their bond was stronger than any blood relation, and now that sacred bond was ruptured, leaving Elisa in a whirlpool of sorrow and guilt. Charlene's untimely departure was a harsh reality to swallow, the rough edges scraping Elisa's heart with every breath she took. As the crowd started to disperse, the casket carrying Charlene was delicately guided towards its final resting place. Elisa clutched her swollen belly, a new life budding within her. In her womb, she carried the hope of a brighter tomorrow, the promise of a new dawn. She clung onto the thought that her unborn child would carry a part of Charlene within them, a spark ignited by the memory of their dearly departed.

Elisa held on to this lifesaving hope, like a woman lost at sea clutching desperately onto a wooden plank. She dreamt of seeing Charlene's brilliance reflected in her child's eyes, her unyielding spirit in their laughter, and her fierce determination in their every action.

Thirty-Four

O'Brien's

In the dimly lit corner of O'Brien's, a bar that had seen its share of fracas and frolic, sat three weary figures. Their badges discreetly tucked away, Sergeant Soliman and Detectives Smith and Moony were a fine sight of law enforcement fatigue. The cracks deepening on their faces, mirroring the ones on the green painted wall behind the bar, told of a case that was eating them alive, much more than the sting of the hard liquor they sipped. Elisa's case hadn't been just another file in their stack of unsolved mysteries. It was a throbbing thorn in their conscience, a constant reminder of the darkness lurking in the heart of the city they've sworn to protect. Elisa, a soon to be single mother, was set to testify against the kingpin.

She was a brave soul, about to face the unknown, all for the hope of a safer world for her and her baby. As the night deepened, the bar filled with a raucous crowd, all numbing their frustrations of the day with gallons of intoxicating relief. But amidst the noise, the trio couldn't shake off the stinging silence of the unanswered questions hanging over them. Who was protecting Donald? And why wasn't anyone willing to come forward? They had their heads together, their conversation an inaudible hum against the background of clinking glasses and slurred words. Soliman pulled out a photo, placing it in the centre of the table. The innocence in the eyes of Elisa's baby gnawed at their hardened hearts. Justice wasn't just a duty anymore. It was a personal mission. Even as they downed their drinks, their minds raced, trying to piece together the scattered breadcrumbs of the case. The bar around them blurred to a mere backdrop as the urgency of the situation beat in rhythm with their heightened heartbeats. They needed a breakthrough, and they needed it soon.

Detective Moony's whisky shimmered in the glass and Detective Smith took a long draw from his half-empty beer.

"This is an absolute shit show at this point," grouched Detective Moony, his voice hoarse and his eyes as weary as his spirit. His fingers traced the rim of his whisky glass, the ice clinking softly in the mournful silence.

Smith grunted in agreement.

"Out of my fifteen years of being a detective, I have never felt so defeated." His gaze became distant, memories of the countless faces he had seen flash of grief and relief replaying in his mind. "Elisa deserves justice," he added, downing his beer.

The silence returned, often punctuated by the clinking of glass and low murmurs of other patrons. The bar had seen better days, much like the detectives themselves.

"I feel that this case has been a buyout from the beginning," Soliman finally broke the silence, voice barely above a whisper. His reflection mirrored in the liquid amber of his drink, a shadow of the tenacious investigator he once was. "I was talking to Melissa and she saw the look on Judge Slater's face when she tried to continue the case for Elisa. Something has been going on from the very beginning."

His words sank deep into the loud ambiance of the bar. The detectives, bound by their mission for justice, felt the weight of the world on their shoulders. The silence returned once again, heavier and burdened with a story that had to be unfolded, a mystery that begged to be unravelled. As they ordered another round, the night aged around them. The tale of Elisa's injustice was not meant to be buried in the annals of forgotten cases. It was a story that had taken a life of its own, and as the night grew darker, it was clear that this was merely the beginning. The search for justice for Elisa was far from over, and the underbelly of the city was yet to reveal its darkest secrets. The grim figure of Sergeant Soliman cast elongated shadows against the peeling wallpaper. His eyes, hardened by years of battling the city's underbelly, mirrored an unspoken storm.

"You are definitely right, Sergeant, there's some bullshit going on and I won't let up until we figure this out," Detective Smith declared, his voice echoing off the room's dank, musty walls. Smith held a reputation for ferreting out the truth, no matter how deeply it was buried.

"Any leads on Charlene's murder?" Moony inquired, the question punctuating the heavy silence. His face remained impassive, yet his clenched fists betrayed his concealed anxiety. Charlene's case had become personal.

"Not yet, but we are working on it. Let's get this court case out of the way first, then we will make a start on this. Right now, we need to get justice for Elisa," Sergeant Soliman pushed back, the tension in his voice revealing the ticking time bomb in his heart. Elisa's frail body haunted the team, her unfulfilled dreams woven into the fabric of their mission.

His words cut the men deep, a stark reminder of the gravity of the situation. Their minds churned with the disturbing images of Elisa, each detail etched into their memory. The room grew thick with the weight of their responsibility, the impending court case looming like an eager spectre. The unsolved cases were not just numbers on a file – they were a physical embodiment of their duty to serve and protect.

"Guys, I'll see you tomorrow," Sergeant Soliman broke the silence, his voice echoing the silent promise of retribution in the air. His eyes carried a glimmer of determination, a fire that refused to be extinguished. "I need to get some rest."

"Leaving already, Sarge?" asked Detective Smith, his voice tinged with disappointment.

"This case has taken the best of me," the sergeant replied, his voice heavy with frustration.

"The more I think about it, the more I get pissed off. See you tomorrow, guys."

"Alright, Sergeant," responded Detective Moony, his expression mirroring the exhaustion that enveloped them all. "Rest well."

He placed his half-drunk glass on the wooden table, his fingers cautiously tracing the rim. With a final glance at his team, he picked up his hat, its shadow merging with his own. Leaving the bar, he bid farewell to the detective and expressed his gratitude to the bartender. Stepping outside and closing the doors behind him, he paused for a moment, closing his eyes to savour the calm of the night. As he opened his eyes, he found himself captivated by the brilliance of the stars scattered across the dark sky. They twinkled with a radiance that seemed to match the determination in his heart. Drawing in a deep breath, he yearned for something more. He wished he possessed the elusive leads that would shatter this perplexing case wide open. The mystery had consumed him, and he couldn't rest until justice prevailed. Thoughts of the victims, their families, and the truth tugged at his conscience. He was determined to uncover what lay hidden beneath the shadows.

Among the countless stars, one particular star caught his attention. It shimmered brighter than the rest, as if urging him to believe in the possibility of finding the breakthrough he sought. Its ethereal glow ignited a flicker of hope within him, reminding him not to give up the pursuit. With renewed determination, he set off into the night, driven by an insatiable curiosity and an unwavering sense of justice. The path ahead was uncertain, but he refused to be deterred. Each twist and turn in this intricate puzzle only fuelled his resolve to solve it. Taking a leisurely stroll through the park, the warm sun kissed his face as he observed the vibrant scene unfolding before him. Young people, seemingly without a care in the world, roamed around, their laughter filling the air. Their joyous freedom reminded him of the life he wished for Elisa, a life she truly deserved. Elisa, a spirited young girl, had been through more than anyone her age should ever endure. The cruelty of fate had dealt her a difficult hand, and it pained him to witness the injustice she had faced. But today, as he took in the youthful exuberance surrounding him, he couldn't help but dream of a brighter future for her.

However, as he continued his walk, his heart sank at the sight of a homeless man being targeted by a group of unruly teenagers. Their callousness struck a nerve within him, igniting a fire of righteous anger. No one deserved to be treated with such disrespect, just as Elisa and Charlene did not deserve the hardship they had endured. Summoning his courage, he marched over to the scene, his voice firm and unwavering as he demanded the teenagers to cease their torment. Startled at his intervention, they hesitated before begrudgingly backing away, leaving the homeless man to reclaim his dignity.

"Hey, leave him the fuck alone!" Sergeant Soliman's authoritative voice boomed, cutting through the air like thunder. The crowd fell silent, their attention now directed toward this unexpected interruption.

Sergeant Soliman rushed over to the scene, his heart pounding in his chest. Kneeling beside the homeless man, he placed a gentle hand on his shoulder and asked, "Are you okay?"

The homeless man looked up, his eyes filled with weariness and resignation.

"I'm okay, thanks. People are always fucking with me, and I haven't even done anything to them," he replied, his voice tinged with both sadness and frustration.

"Yeah, people can be assholes sometimes," Sergeant Soliman empathized, his gaze piercing into the depths of the man's soul. "Don't worry about them. Here you go." With a compassionate gesture, he helped the homeless man gather his scattered belongings from the ground.

The man, grateful for his intervention, extended a weathered hand in gratitude. As their eyes met, an unspoken understanding passed between them. This encounter would forever change both their lives.

"Thank you so much, see, it's people like you who make life just a little easier." The homeless man's voice quivered with gratitude as he clutched the warm cup of soup in his hands. The autumn wind howled down the desolate alley, but his heart was touched by the kindness he had received. "You remind me of that young girl on the television who helped me."

Detective Soliman, intrigued by this unexpected mention of a young girl, furrowed his brow.

"What young girl?" he asked, leaning closer to hear the homeless man's response.

"You know, that young girl, Elsa," the homeless man replied, his eyes clouded with sorrow. "She was assaulted. She's all over TV and the radio."

Sergeant Soliman's heart sank as he realized who the man was referring to. Elsa? Elisa? He couldn't be sure, but the resonance of the name sent a shiver down his spine. His mind raced, trying to connect the dots. Could this homeless man hold the key to solving the case? Or was he merely recounting a tragic news story he had heard? Determined to find out, Soliman mustered all his courage.

"Wait, do you mean Elisa, the girl who was in a coma?" Soliman asked cautiously, his voice almost trembling.

The homeless man's eyes widened, an expression of recognition crossing his face. "Yes, that's her," he confirmed, his voice strained with emotion. "She helped me, you know. Before all this happened."

Heart pounding, Soliman leaned in closer, eager to unravel the mystery.

"Tell me, please. Tell me everything you know about Elisa."

The homeless man hesitated, his gaze fixed on some distant memory. Then he began to speak, his voice barely above a whisper. As he struggled to remember the name of someone who had shown him an act of kindness, he turned to a kind-hearted police Sergeant named Soliman for help.

"Yeah, that one, sorry I'm not very good with names," Jack muttered, his fingers trembling slightly as he continued to organize his meagre possessions.

Curiosity stirred, Soliman leaned in closer and asked.

"When did you see her? Or when did she help you?"

With a deep sigh, Jack's eyes wandered into the distance as he recollected the memory.

"A few months ago, she was in the oasis bar," he began, his voice filled with a blend of gratitude and frustration. "These teenagers were fucking with me as always, throwing my stuff out of my trolley. The trolley that I bought, actually. Young kids these days are so fucking disrespectful, you know? They have no respect, I tell you."

Empathy welled up within Soliman as he listened to Jack's tale of relentless torment. He imagined the pain and humiliation that Jack must have endured day after day. Eager to learn more about this mysterious act of kindness and hoping to lift Jack's spirits, Soliman gently interrupted,

"Please, go on. How did this woman help you?"

Jack's weary eyes met Soliman's and his voice softened.

"You know, amidst all the chaos, she approached me with a genuine smile on her face. She didn't judge me or look down on me like most people do. Instead, she extended a helping hand and started picking up my scattered belongings. Her kindness took me by surprise."

Okay, hold on," Detective Soliman said, his curiosity piqued. "What's your name, I'm sorry."

"Oh, my name is Jack, but you can call me David," replied Jack.

Detective Soliman raised an eyebrow.

"So is your name Jack or David? Your mother gave you two first names as a first name?"

"Technically," Jack answered, a hint of sadness in his voice. "See, my mama was a crackhead. She didn't know what the hell she was doing. She had me at 19, she..."

Once again, Jack's story was interrupted by Sergeant Soliman, who was determined to unravel the truth.

"Okay, sit down here for me, Jack. Let me understand this. So, you're saying you met a lady called Elisa at the bar a few months ago?"

"No, not at the bar outside the bar," Jack exclaimed, his voice trembling. "Have you seen the Oasis Bar? It's the most lavish bar in town, they wouldn't let me go in looking like this. Or smelling like this for that matter."

Sergeant Soliman raised an eyebrow, intrigued. "Okay, so you saw her outside the bar," he said, leaning forward attentively.

"Yes," Jack nodded, his eyes filled with a mix of awe and admiration. "And she helped me, Sergeant. She was such a nice girl, very pretty too."

Sergeant Soliman leaned back, his curiosity piqued once again. "Who was she with, Jack?"

Jack shifted uncomfortably, a flicker of doubt crossing his face.

"She was with that billionaire guy," he hesitated, "the owner of the bar. But I must say, sometimes I felt like I was seeing two of them."

Sergeant Soliman furrowed his brow, puzzled. "What do you mean?" he asked, sensing that there was more to this tale than met the eye.

"I don't know, maybe it's the crack," said Jack, his voice raspy and filled with uncertainty. He glanced around nervously, as if expecting someone to jump out from the darkness.

Sergeant Soliman approached Jack cautiously. Concern etched his face, knowing that he had to act quickly.

"Look, Jack, would you like a shelter for tonight?" he asked, his mind racing with thoughts of protecting this crucial witness. "I can get you safely tucked away, clean you up."

Jack's eyes widened with surprise. He hadn't expected such an offer. He paused for a moment, contemplating his options. The allure of a warm bed and a meal was enticing, but he couldn't help his addiction.

"Sure, can I get a meal and some crack too?" Jack asked, his desperation evident in his voice as he absentmindedly scratched his face.

Sergeant Soliman sighed, realizing the depth of Jack's struggle. He knew that cracking down on crime meant dealing with individuals trapped in the vicious cycle of addiction.

"Food, yes. Crack, no," he firmly responded, his tone filled with empathy. "You don't need any crack, Jack. Let's go."

As they walked towards the shelter, Sergeant Soliman couldn't help but wonder about Jack's story. How had he ended up in this dark place?

What had driven him to the addiction that consumed him? Taking out his phone, he called Detective Smith. His voice trembled with a mix of excitement and nervousness.

"Smith, meet me in an hour, with Moony." Soliman then hung up his phone, his mind racing as he took the homeless man to a shelter before rushing over to meet his two colleagues.

Thirty-Five

Collective Intelligence

Sergeant Soliman was in a state of unease, his mind consumed by the new details on the case. There was something about the information he had stumbled upon that sparked a sense of curiosity within him, a nagging feeling that the truth was just within reach. With a sense of urgency, Soliman rushed into the police station, his steps echoing through the corridors. Detective Smith and Detective Moony, the two most trusted members of his team, were summoned immediately. They entered his office with expressions of concern etched across their faces.

"Hey Sarge, what's going on?" asked Detective Smith, his brow furrowed with curiosity.

Soliman took a deep breath, his eyes locked with theirs.

"Thanks for coming guys. Sit down," he said, gesturing towards the worn-out chairs that lined his cluttered office. "I've just found out some information, and I'm not sure if it's someone from beyond helping us, but it's crucial that we look into this."

Detective Moony's eyes widened, his interest piqued.

"Okay, what is it?" he asked, an eager tone colouring his voice.

"I was walking home after leaving you guys at the bar, and I met this homeless man, Jack, no, actually his name was David," said Sergeant Soliman, his voice filled with intrigue.

Detective Moony furrowed his brow.

"So was his name Jack or David?" he asked, genuinely puzzled.

"It was both," replied Sergeant Soliman, a hint of mystery in his voice.

"Both? So he has two first names as a first name," joked Detective Smith, trying to lighten the mood.

Sergeant Soliman's eyes glimmered with anticipation as he began recounting the peculiar encounter.

"Well yeah, apparently, his mother was a crack addict and she named him both names, but that's not the point here," Sergeant Soliman shared. As he continued his tale, he spoke with compassion and understanding, fully aware of the challenges Jack faced.

"I was helping him with his stuff because there were these young children constantly messing with him," the Sergeant explained, his voice tinged with sympathy. "I felt sorry for the guy, you know, young kids can be real shitty these days."

Taking a deep breath, Soliman continued.

"As I was helping him, he says I reminded him of someone, some girl called Elsa. I asked, Who is that? Then Jack said, that girl who is all over TV, the one who was assaulted. Then I said, Do you mean Elisa."

"Wait, how would he know who she is?" Detective Moony asked aloud. "She's been in a coma for four months, then in hospital recovery for two additional months. That's six months!" Said detective Mooney, his eyes reflecting the perplexity of the situation.

"That's what I thought, like what was this guy saying, you know. Then he said he met her outside of the bar, the Oasis bar, a few months ago." Added Sergeant Soliman, his tone indicating the gravity of the revelation.

In that moment, the room was consumed with a palpable shock. A surprise borne of a reality they had not anticipated. Both detective Smith and Moony exchanged perplexed glances. The enigma sank its claws deeper into the fabric of the case, seeping uncertainty into the minds of those in the room.

"Wait, so he met Elisa at the bar? What else did he say?" Detective Mooney asked, desperation crawling into his voice.

The answer to that question could either be a breakthrough or merely lead them down another convoluted path. The suspense hung in the air like a thick fog, each detective holding their breath, anxiously awaiting the response. Sergeant Soliman cleared his throat, the grimace on his face echoed the gravity of the information he was about to disclose.

"He said she was helping him, with a few things, just like I did today, he was being picked on, these teenagers threw his stuff everywhere, and guess who she was with that night?" He paused, creating an atmosphere of anticipation within the room.

"Who?" Detective Smith asked, the intrigue reflected in his wide, questioning eyes.

"Donald, Donald Prince," answered sergeant Soliman with a gravity that hung heavy in the room.

The name, 'Donald Prince', ricocheted off the precinct walls like a bullet. A momentary silence ensued. His name was known to all, a notorious figure whose reputation needed no introduction.

"So this means that she was at the bar that night, this witness puts her there and she was with our prime suspect," Smith concluded, his eyes narrowing as he connected the dots.

"Exactly," said Soliman, his tone grim.

"But how can we take the testimony of a crackhead? He could be making this up," Detective Moony interjected, always the cynic, his words slicing the tense atmosphere in the room.

The endless cycle of questions, suspicions, and uncertainties continued to spin. The truth was elusive, as if hiding in the shadows, mocking their frustrated efforts. The story that started out so simple now had more layers than an onion. It was like being caught in a web of lies, deceit, and enigmatic characters. With every peeled layer, the plot thickened, leaving them more entangled than before.

"Well, I don't think he is. He seems to recognize her face very well," said Sergeant Soliman, breaking the silence. His voice, low and serious, echoed against the walls, encapsulating the gravity of their investigation.

Detective Smith furrowed his brows, lost in his thoughts, then turned to Soliman.

"Where is he now?"

"He's at a homeless shelter," responded Soliman, "I'll get him cleaned up and ready for the trial in the next few days. We just need to work on this case and dig a little deeper."

Days turned into nights as the three men delved into the labyrinth of the case, climbing the mountain of evidence, and analyzing each thread meticulously. Their determination, akin to a lighthouse in the storm, didn't waver even when the odds were stacked against them.

Thirty-Six

Accepting the Devil Within

In the city, tucked away within the towering skyscrapers, was a man's secret refuge. Amid the deafening music and the numbing highs of the white powder, he found solace, an escape from the menial trials of the world. It was his peculiar sanctum, a haven where he could safely retreat, where he could be his raw and unabashed self. The notes of the music faded in and out, leaving in their wake a mosaic of memories that were as vivid as they were varied. Bathed in the electric neon glow of his perfectly furnished penthouse, the man swirled around, his head filled with the melodious cacophony of his favourite rock song and the intoxicating invincibility of white powder. This was his sanctuary, his fortress of solitude, where he hid from the prying eyes of a judgmental world. He yearned for these moments of liberty, moments where he could truly be himself.

The apartment was more than just four walls; it was a tangible manifestation of his memories, each object triggering a flashback. The Italian leather couch bore witness to the nights of celebration, the grand piano under the lustrous chandelier, a testament to his mother's love. Yet, amidst all the joy, a pang of melancholy pervaded his thoughts.

He himself, like any man, was ruled by his desires, his addictions. They gave him pleasure; they also brought pain. But he couldn't help but feel bound to them, a moth drawn to a flame, even if it meant getting burned. His addiction wasn't just hedonistic; it was existential. He was a prisoner to his passion, a puppet to his predilections. But he also believed, rather fervently, that his devil wasn't a unique entity.

The devil, he believed, was merely a companion, a shadow that lurked in every soul. It didn't matter what form it took - alcohol, sex, esoteric fetishes - it was always there, always watching, always waiting. The realization was liberating, but it also brought sadness. The thought that he couldn't continue to give in to his devil was akin to clipping a bird's wings. But soon, he knew, he would have to let his demon out. The devil within was a demanding entity, always yearning for release. The music crescendo, pulling him back from the labyrinth of his introspections. He drowned himself in the music, distracting himself from the inevitable showdown with his inner demon.

As the last notes died away, he found himself standing in front of the large panoramic window. The city's skyline sprawled out before him, bustling with life, unaware of the turmoil boiling within him. And in that moment, he made a promise to himself – to never leave his devil, he will finally allow it to control him. He sat alone, sipping his whiskey with a devilish grin etched on his face. Engulfed by the pulsating rhythm of the hypnotic music, his thoughts drifted back to his old sinister life. A nostalgic wave washed over him, whispering the intoxicating promise of returning back to his wicked ways: a life of thrill, danger, and an insatiable hunger for power. Out of the cacophony, his phone started vibrating. The bass was so deafening that it took him a few seconds to realize the harsh buzzing was actually his phone ringing. As though waking from a trance, he shot a glance at his device. Seeing an unknown number flashing on the screen, he curiously lifted the phone to his ear.

"Yes," he answered briskly, his voice getting swallowed amidst the chaotic symphony around him.

"It's done," replied a cryptic voice from the other end, audibly struggling against the backdrop of blasting music.

Without uttering another word, he hung up, letting the phone slip from his hand onto the table. The enigmatic call had left him intrigued, but it didn't seem to faze him. Instead, a victorious smile curled up on his lips as his eyes gleamed wickedly under the neon lights. He was one step closer to reclaiming his old life. The man descended his gamboge spiral staircase, eyes roaming the gilded frames of his lavish paintings. Shadows danced on the ornate furniture, their soft flicker a stark contrast to the icy chill that had begun to creep into the room. His eyes, cold as his gold-rimmed champagne flute, sparkled with a morbid fascination.

He stepped onto the marble floor, echoing the emptiness of his fortress. His well decorated apartment was as ostentatious as his reputation - an oasis in a concrete jungle, untouched by humility. A loft built on the currency of power, a place where secrets were bared over whiskey underpours and soft jazz. There was another room, though – a secret room. A space where his macabre hobby gave birth to stories that would never see the light of day. As he entered, a young girl met his gaze. Drugged, tied up, caught in the snarl of his killing machine. Her eyes, dulled with narcotics, still held an echo of defiance. He smiled, a predator baring its teeth. The thrill that his toys brought him left a bittersweet aftertaste. His heart pounded with the rhythm of the jazz reverberating through the mansion, the notes whispering secrets into the night, their melody turning into a dark waltz. He savoured the confused fear that rolled off of her. The girl stared back at him. The drugs were supposed to make her docile, an easy prey. Yet, there was an irritating spark in her eyes that challenged him. A spark that questioned her fate. Her destiny, it seemed, hung in the balance, held by a man who had never known the meaning of mercy. The night dragged on, each tick of the clock an ominous reminder of the inevitable horror that awaited. The moon hid behind the clouds, casting a gloomy shadow around the apartment. The notes of the jazz died down, leaving nothing but the cold silence of their aftermath.

Thirty-Seven

Nurturing Reality

In the hushed tranquillity of the morning, Elisa sat immersed in the comforting warmth of the bathwater. With her rounded belly breaking the surface, a symbol of a life burgeoning within for nearly six months, she yearned for a peaceful future for her unborn child. Her life, once an orchestration of mundane normalcy, had abruptly somersaulted into an uninviting abyss of turmoil. An abyss she felt herself drawn into, with little she could do but wait.

Once, she had walked the halls of an ivy-covered school, her voice echoing the lessons of history, math, and English. She fondly remembered the laughter that ricocheted off the classroom walls, the smudged little faces lighting up with curiosity at every new concept, every clever joke. She was a teacher, a beacon of knowledge and nurturer of young minds. But that was then—a past life, it seemed. Elisa looked down at her hands, submerged under the bathwater. The soft ripples distorted her fingers, but she could still see the imprints of chalk dust, the echo of a life she had cherished. The question arose from the silence - would she ever return to teaching? She yearned for it, yearned for the normalcy, the cheer, the everyday routine. But the question floated unanswered in the quiet of the bathroom, a silent ripple spreading out endlessly. Suddenly, a face imposed itself over the moment of solitude, invading her thoughts—Charlene. Charlene with her infectious laughter, her beaming smile, her unwavering support. Charlene, her confidante, her shoulder to lean on, the kindest soul in her life. The murder had ripped her friend away, the brutal reality leaving a gaping hole in Elisa's heart. It was a cruel joke of fate, an unbearable loss that seemed impossibly unjust. A single tear escaped Elisa's eye, breaking the surface of the water, creating a tiny ripple. She clutched at her belly, as if seeking solace from the life within. The warm water held her, the bathroom walls echoed her sigh, and the silence closed in around her, swallowing her grief.

As the drops of water slid down the bath, Elisa felt a strange sensation, a stir within her. She watched as her belly made a roll, a tiny bump appearing. A soft smile touched her lips. Here, within her, was a sliver of hope, a spark of life. It was a moment of poignant transition, a secret shared in the enveloping silence. It left a question hanging in the air — would this silent witness of her grief grow up to fill the void left by Charlene's departure? Just like the unanswered question about her return to teaching, this too remained suspended in the misty morning, an enigma that would unfold with time. Elisa's eyes fluttered open to a bathroom that was not her own. Each porcelain fixture, the odd scent of the unknown soap, even the peculiar hue of the wall was a painful reminder of her distorted reality. The once unassuming life of Elisa had become an element of espionage more complicated than any thriller novels she'd read.

In a world that had grown too familiar, too monotonous, she craved the exhilarating allure of the unknown. A desire to sever the ties to her yesteryears and chart a fresh course, a course so vast and liberating that it dwarfed her past and consumed her. She yearned for a new life, far removed from the grey familiarity of this place. Draped in the comforting blanket of solitude, she drowned deeper and deeper into her thoughts. Once her eyes fluttered shut, a myriad of memories unfolded, washing over her like a violent, turbulent wave. The sea of her subconscious was no longer calm and tranquil but teeming with vivid recollections. Her senses were awash with a strange blend of fear and excitement, her heart pounding wild and her hormones coursing like a torrential river.

In the distant, an enigmatic figure emerged from the labyrinth of her memories, a shadowy figure with piercing light eyes. The figure was ephemeral, a fleeting silhouette darting at the edge of her consciousness. She strained to ascertain whether it was a figment of her imagination or a spectre from her past. Yet, its presence, real or imagined, conjured inexplicable feelings of happiness, setting her heart aflutter. This ethereal entity, with its mesmerizing light eyes, seemed to beckon her, inviting her to embark on a voyage into the unknown. The figure was both a mystery and a promise, a symbol of the uncharted life that awaited her, a life full of promise and potential. The more she focused on the figure, the more it solidified, becoming a beacon guiding her towards her destiny. The memories were potent, untamed, like wild horses galloping in the prairies of her mind. Her heart pounded relentlessly against the cage of her ribs, her breasts hardening in response to the adrenaline that twisted and twirled within her. Her hormones flooded in, an emotional tsunami that left her breathless.

In the palpable darkness of her closed eyes, she saw it, a shadowy figure with luminescent eyes. It was indistinct, an enigmatic silhouette, simultaneously ethereal and profound. She didn't know if she was imagining it, or if it was real, but its presence was evident, so close she could almost reach out and touch it. An innocent smile crept up her face as she bathed in the warmth of this shadow. It was an unlikely source of happiness; an anonymous phantom that somehow ignited an inexplicable joy within her. In the desolate quiet of the bathroom, she began to explore the depths within herself. Her slender fingers started to weave a tale of their own, gently tracing the contours of her stomach, creating a story that had never been told before. Her slender fingers began to dance upon the canvas of her body, orchestrating a symphony of a tale untold.

With each stroke, they composed a narrative that had remained hidden in the shadows of oblivion. Her eyes, once windows to the world, closed into obsidian orbs, becoming the cinema of her dreams. The black and white film of her imagination metamorphosed into a spectrum of vivid colours, as a figure emerged out of the depths of her subconscious. Tall, mysterious, his aura held a blend of mystery and magnetism that was irresistible. His touch was gentle yet authoritative, like a maestro conducting an orchestra, awakening a symphony within her that had never been heard before.

He charted new territories within her, his fingers etching a path like an explorer unearthing an untouched civilization. Every touch, every whisper breathed life into the landscapes of her existence that had stayed dormant, unexplored. It was as if he was healing her wounds, reading her, one word, one sentence at a time, turning the pages of a novel that only they shared. Her heart began to pound against the cage of her chest, a drum echoing in the silence of the night. The rhythm quickened, keeping pace with the crescendo of their story. As each note of this melody of touch and emotion echoed through her veins, it felt like a dance - intricate, intimate and intoxicating. And then, just as the climax was within reach, the majestic figure vanished like a wisp of smoke, leaving her alone in the infinite chambers of her imagination. she immersed in the tranquillity of her bubble-infused bath, jumped at the sudden interruption. The echo still lingered in the room, bouncing off the marble tiles, invading her private sanctuary. Seconds later, she heard it again, this time followed by a deep, concerned voice.

"Elisa, is everything okay?" inquired the police officer from the other side of the door. It was a voice distinct with authority yet laced with a touch of worry. A voice that seemed completely out of place in the serene ambiance of her bathroom, like a clash of cymbals in a silent movie.

Jolted back to reality, Elisa hastily wrapped herself in a cotton robe, her heart pounding in her chest. Her eyes searched the room.

With a deep breath, she replied, trying to sound as normal as she possibly could.

"Yes, yes, I'm fine, thank you."

After a few more terse exchanges and reassurances from behind the door, the policeman's footsteps receded down the hallway. With a sigh of relief, Elisa leaned against the bathroom, her heart rate finally slowing down. She glanced out of the window at the sky, her eyes tracing the wispy trails of the passing clouds. A sense of calm washing over her.

Thirty-Eight

"Don't Miss Me Too Much"

S ergeant Soliman stared at the pile of files on his desk, exhaustion
etched across his face. Detective Moony and Detective Smith sat
across from him, their eyes bloodshot and their hands trembling with
fatigue. The walls of their small office seemed to close in on them,
suffocating the last remnants of their hope. The case of Elisa had consumed their every waking moment. Night after night, they had combed
through every piece of evidence, desperate to find a breakthrough. But
the answers they sought remained elusive, vanishing like smoke in the
wind. With a heavy sigh, Soliman reached for the file labelled 'Elisa'.
His tired eyes scanned the pages of witness statements, forensic reports,
and the details of the night Elisa went missing. As he delved deeper
into the case, frustration tangled with despair within him.

"This can't be it," Moony muttered, his voice laced with defeat.
"There must be something we're missing."

Smith nodded in agreement, a glimmer of determination flickering
in his tired eyes.

"We can't give up now. We owe it to Elisa and her child to find
the truth."

Soliman closed his eyes, trying to silence the chaos in his mind. How could they proceed without any substantial evidence? The killer had left no trace, no DNA behind. The bar's surveillance cameras had captured nothing and the only evidence they had was a crackhead. They were trapped in a maze of dead-ends, their search leading them nowhere. But as Soliman's mind wandered, a faint memory tugged at his thoughts. Elisa had always been known for her exceptional memory, capable of recalling even the tiniest of details. Perhaps, just maybe, she had left them a clue, a breadcrumb to follow. The air in the dimly lit room was thick with exhaustion. Smith sat at his desk, his stomach growling loudly. He hadn't eaten a proper meal in what felt like ages. His body was weak, dehydrated, and he couldn't remember the last time he had a good night's sleep. He longed for a night of uninterrupted rest, a chance to rejuvenate his weary soul. As the clock ticked away, Smith's hunger became unbearable. He couldn't focus on anything else until he satisfied the gnawing void in his stomach. With a determination fuelled by desperation, he stood up and removed his jacket from the back of his chair. His colleague, Detective Moony, looked up from his own pile of paperwork, sensing Smith's restlessness.

"I'm hungry. Anyone up for some Chinese?" Smith's voice broke the silence, his words betraying his craving.

Detective Moony blinked away the weariness from his eyes and felt a pang of hunger himself. The thought of egg rolls danced in his mind, a tantalizing temptation. He stood up, keys in hand, ready to accompany Smith on this impromptu food adventure.

"Yes, please. I could do with some egg rolls. I'll come with you," Detective Moony responded, his voice carrying a mix of exhaustion and eagerness.

Detective Smith glanced at Sergeant Soliman, his curiosity piqued.

"Anything for you Sarge?" he asked, hoping to pry some information from his colleague.

"No, I'm okay," replied Sergeant Soliman, his eyes fixed on the pile of documents in front of him. He was immersed in his work, determined to crack the case that had consumed his thoughts. "I'll grab another coffee though, please," he added, finally acknowledging his basic need for sustenance.

"Okay Sarge, we'll be back soon, don't miss me too much," Smith said teasingly, flashing a mischievous smile before stepping out of the office. Sergeant Soliman lifted his head and watched his trusted colleague leave the station. Smith could be a handful at times, but deep down, Soliman knew he was one of the most reliable men in the department.

Once alone, Sergeant Soliman allowed himself a moment of respite. He sipped on his steaming coffee, the warmth seeping into his tired body. But even in his rare moments of relaxation, his mind remained fixated on the case. He reviewed the evidence, connecting the dots in his mind, determined to find the missing piece that had eluded him thus far. The two men made their way towards the exit, ready to take a much-needed break. As they approached the door, Detective Smith realized he had forgotten his keys to the police cruiser. A pang of frustration ignited within him as he rummaged through his pockets, desperately searching for the missing keys.

"Damn it," he muttered, his brows furrowing. "I left my car keys. Let me go get them."

As they stood outside the police department, Detective Moony reached into his pocket and tossed his car keys to Detective Smith.

"It's fine, you can take my keys," he said nonchalantly, "but let me go for a piss first. I'm dying over here."

Detective Smith rolled his eyes and replied.

"Alright. Don't be too long. I'm fucking hungry, I have about five more minutes left in me, and I'll pass out." He grabbed the keys and made his way towards Detective Moony's car, closing the door behind him.

With a sense of urgency, Detective Smith approached the vehicle. He clicked the unlock button, expecting the familiar sound of the doors unlocking. To his surprise, nothing happened. Confusion washed over him. Had Detective Moony given him the wrong keys? Determined to figure it out, Detective Smith tried again. This time, the car's lights briefly blinked, indicating that it had indeed unlocked. Puzzled, he jumped into the driver's seat and glanced at the rear-view mirror to see if Detective Moony was almost finished. After a few minutes, Detective Moony stepped out of the police station. He couldn't help but wear a smile on his face, a slight twinkle of mischief in his eyes. His partner, Detective Smith, sat in the driver's seat of their sleek black car, seemingly lost in thought. Moony knew that when Smith was hungry, wasting time was the last thing on his mind. With an amused smirk, Moony strolled over to the vehicle, waving at his partner through the open window. Smith's face lit up with a smile in response, a silent acknowledgment of their long-standing bond. As Moony watched Smith insert the key into the ignition, something caught his attention.

A faint unease crept up Moony's spine, a niggling feeling that something was not quite right. Before he could voice his concerns, however, a deafening explosion shattered the peaceful surroundings. The force of the blast sent Moony sprawling backward, his world spinning into chaos. The car, once their trusted ally, was now a mangled heap of metal, smoke billowing up into the sky like an ominous warning. Panic rippled through the crowd that had gathered nearby, their eyes wide with shock and disbelief. Moony's heart pounded in his chest as he desperately scanned the scene for any sign of life. Amidst the chaos, Moony's mind raced to make sense of the tragedy. How could this have happened? Who would want to target them, two dedicated detectives on a mission to bring justice to the city? As the smoke slowly dissipated, the realization dawned on Moony - this was no accident. Startled, the police officers inside the building scrambled to their feet, their hearts racing with adrenaline. Guns in hand, they rushed outside, fearing the worst. Was it an ambush? What the hell was going on? Sergeant Soliman, their quick-thinking leader, emerged from the chaos, his eyes scanning the scene before him. Shattered glass covered the ground, sparking a sense of panic in his chest.

Frantically, he pushed open the precinct doors and his worst fears were confirmed. Detective Moony's car, ablaze with furious flames, illuminated the night sky. Instantly, he knew that the two men might be trapped inside. Worried for their safety, he scoured the area, desperate to locate his missing comrades. Detective Moony lay motionless on the ground, a twisted figure of pain and confusion. The heat from the inferno licked at his clothes, threatening to consume him. The air was thick with smoke and turmoil. The deafening blast had left a trail of destruction in its wake, and Sergeant Soliman's heart pounded in his chest as he surveyed the aftermath. Bodies lay scattered amidst the rubble, and the stench of fear hung heavy in the air. But it was Mooney's face that caught the Sergeant's attention. Etched with torment, Mooney's expression was a haunting reflection of the horror they had just witnessed. Without a moment's hesitation, Sergeant Soliman rushed over to his colleague, his heart sinking with worry. He had to make sure Moony was okay.

"Are you okay? What happened?" he pleaded, his voice laced with concern. He searched Moony's body for any signs of injury, a glimmer of relief washing over him as he realized that Moony was unharmed physically.

But where was Detective Smith? The Sergeant's eyes darted around in a desperate attempt to locate his missing colleague and friend. Panic started to creep into his voice as he turned to Moony, seeking answers. Moony, still in a state of shock, was unable to form coherent words. His eyes were wide, his ears were ringing and his breathing shallow. It was as if he had witnessed something so unimaginable that his mind had shut down, refusing to process the trauma. Sergeant Soliman's mind raced with possibilities, each one more terrifying than the last. What had happened in that moment of chaos? Where was Detective Smith? The Sergeant's determination fuelled his resolve as he vowed to uncover the truth. His eyes darted around, searching for any sign of his trusted colleague. Surrounded by chaos and the realization of impending danger, Sergeant Soliman's thoughts raced. Was Smith caught in the explosion? Or had he managed to escape?

As he looked around, time seemed to stand still. The chaos of the burning vehicle was a stark contrast to the eerie silence that surrounded him. Smoke billowed up into the night sky, casting an ominous shadow over the scene. The fire was still ablaze, dancing wildly with a malevolent energy. Soliman's eyes darted anxiously, desperately searching for any sign of his missing detective. Every second that passed felt like an eternity, each heartbeat an agonizing reminder of the uncertainty and fear that gripped his soul. Images of devastation and loss flashed through his mind, threatening to overwhelm him. And then, in the midst of the inferno, he saw it. A figure lying motionless inside the vehicle, its silhouette faintly visible through the flames. Soliman's heart sank as he realized it was Smith. The gravity of the situation hit him with a force he could scarcely comprehend. With a mix of desperation and determination, Soliman fought against the overwhelming heat and approached the burning car. His eyes were fixed on the figure, its head turned away, as if in defiance of the raging fire. It was a surreal sight—one he would never forget. As Soliman reached out, ready to pull his friend from the clutches of the flames, something inexplicable happened. The figure, engulfed in fire and brimstone, seemed to melt away, unravelling like a mirage in the desert. Soliman's tears blended with the smoke, his heart heavy with grief and disbelief.

He stood there, frozen in time, unable to process what he had just witnessed. A mix of sorrow, confusion, and anger coursed through his veins. How could this be? How could Smith, a person so full of life and vigor, simply melt away in the midst of chaos? The flames continued to dance, their crackling whispers mingling with Soliman's thoughts. The night swallowed his cries of despair, leaving him alone with unanswered questions, his mind forever haunted by the enigma of Detective Smith's mysterious fate.

His Last Words

In a small town where dreams were woven,
Lived a man whose heart was golden.
Not just an officer, but a beacon of hope,
He worked tirelessly so others could cope.

~

From children's laughter to the Pope's embrace,
He was loved by all, his kindness left a trace.
Every day he'd patrol the streets with a smile,
Bringing comfort and safety, going the extra mile.

~

But fate had a plan, it was something he couldn't foresee,
Death knocked on his door, leaving him and us feeling empty.
Broken and torn, his absence left a void,
Leaving us with unanswered questions, feeling annoyed.

~

Yet in the midst of our sorrow, a message he did send,
"Don't miss me too much, my dear beloved friends.
In the rustling wind, you'll feel my presence near,
I'll watch over my children, my kin, those I hold dear."

~

And so, the wind whispered secrets of his love,
His spirit dancing through the skies above.
Though physically he was gone, his essence lingered,
Guiding us through darkness, his soul never withered.

~

The town carried on, his memory alive,
The stories of his heroism continued to thrive.
But deep inside, we couldn't help but wonder,

What mysteries did he witness, torn asunder?

~

His final words left us with a curious itch,
What did he see, beyond life's final stitch?
In the realm beyond, where souls intertwine,
We're left to ponder, until our own time.

~

Curiosity lingers in the air, like a playful tease,
Leaving us wondering about life's mysteries.
For in his absence, we've learned to cope,
And we'll cherish the memory of this beacon of hope.

Thirty-Nine

Echo Chambers & Filter Bubbles

As the clock struck six, the world was abruptly interrupted by the piercing sound of breaking news. The chaotic melody of urgent voices filled the airwaves, capturing the attention of millions who anxiously awaited the latest updates. The face of the news reporter appeared on the television screen, her expression fraught with panic and disbelief. Her trembling hands clutched the rumpled papers in front of her as she struggled to gather her composure. Just hours before, Detective Smith, a seasoned investigator known for his unwavering dedication to justice, had met an untimely demise.

The news of his murder was shocking, leaving the entire community stunned and mourning. The reporter took a deep breath, attempting to summon the strength needed to convey the devastating news. Crushing her papers in a desperate attempt to quell her rising emotions, the reporter fixed her gaze on the camera, her eyes filled with a strange mix of sorrow and shock. It was in that moment that a wave of silent curiosity washed over the audience, compelling them to lean in closer, desperate for answers to the countless questions swirling in their minds. Who could have wanted Detective Smith dead? Was it a case gone awry, one where the lines between right and wrong had blurred? Or was there a darker force at play, lurking in the shadows, waiting to strike those who dared to challenge it?

"Welcome to CCW News at 6pm. I am your host," the anchor began, struggling to compose herself. "It is with great sadness that I have to announce a tragic incident that has shaken our community to its core."

A heavy silence hung in the room as the anchor continued.

"Detective Smith, a revered member of our police force, met a horrifying fate last night. As he entered his vehicle at the precinct in Cleveland, it was engulfed in a rapid and deadly car fire. This has been declared a homicide."

Gasps filled living rooms across the nation as viewers tried to comprehend the shocking news. Detective Smith, a seasoned officer with over 15 years of service, was known for his unwavering commitment to justice. His untimely death sent shock-waves through the entire country. As the reporter continued her account, her voice began to unravel the twisted threads of the investigation. Clues emerged, painting a picture of a complex web of deceit, betrayal, and revenge. Each revelation punctuated by gasps of disbelief from the audience, as if the weight of the truth was too heavy to bear.

"The investigation into this heinous crime is still ongoing, with no arrests made thus far. But there is a chilling twist that has caught the attention of the nation. It appears that Detective Smith's tragic death may be connected to a haunting case he was working on – the assault of a young girl named Elisa. Elisa's brutal assault had left the community horrified, desperately seeking justice for the innocent victim. Detective Smith had dedicated countless hours to unravelling the truth behind this terrifying act. Now, with his untimely demise, the case seemed to take an even darker turn. We also reported that Elisa's Best Friend Charlene, who was also the main witness in her upcoming trial, was brutally murdered, she was found with her throat slit, dead outside her home." Read the News Reporter.

As the news spread, whispers filled the streets, and fear gripped the hearts of the people. Who could have committed such a vile act? Was there a sinister connection between Detective Smith's death and Elisa's assault? The nation waited anxiously for any updates, clinging to the hope that justice would prevail. The authorities were determined to bring the culprits to light, but the mysteries surrounding both cases seemed to deepen with each passing moment. Elisa watched the television with wide eyes, her heart pounding in her chest. The breaking news left her astonished and filled with a sense of dread. Detective Smith, the brilliant investigator who had helped her in the past, had been killed in a car fire. How could this have happened? Her mind raced with questions, desperately seeking answers that seemed to elude her. As she lay in bed, her thoughts were consumed by the tragic news. Memories of that fateful night resurfaced, sending shivers down her spine. If it wasn't for her own harrowing experience, none of this would have happened. The shadows of the past loomed over her, haunting her every waking moment.

Her best friend, taken away so cruelly, had been her beacon of light in the darkest of times. Together, they had struggled to overcome the trauma that had forever changed their lives. And now, with the news of Detective Smith's death, Elisa felt an overwhelming sense of loss and helplessness. Tears streamed down her face as she held her face in her trembling hands. The weight of her sorrow felt unbearable, suffocating her in a wave of despair. She had never felt so alone, so utterly abandoned by the world around her. But amidst the pain, Elisa found herself seeking solace in a glimmer of hope. She tenderly rubbed her growing pregnant stomach, feeling the life within her. The tiny kicks reminded her of the strength she possessed, the resilience she had developed in the face of adversity. Hoping for better days to come, Elisa yearned for justice. She knew that she couldn't let Detective Smith's death go unanswered, nor the assault she had endured. Determination burned within her, fuelling her resolve to seek the truth, to find the ones responsible.

Forty

Buried With Honor

The sky was heavy with the weight of sorrow as Detective Smith's funeral took place. Officers stood solemnly around his grave, their faces etched with grief. The sound of weeping filled the air as family, friends, and colleagues gathered to bid their final goodbyes. Sergeant Soliman and Detective Moony, both seasoned detectives, stood at the edge of the grave, their hearts heavy with pain. Detective Smith had been their most trusted man, a beacon of justice and integrity. To see him fall victim to such a heinous crime left them shaken to the core. Panic gripped their souls as they vowed to seek justice for their fallen comrade. As the pastor began reading from the sacred scriptures, the words seemed to echo with a chilling resonance. Each verse, once comforting, now held an eerie significance. The air grew thick with anticipation as the detective duo exchanged glances, silently vowing to avenge their friend's untimely death.

The rain fell like tears from the heavens, as if even the sky mourned the loss. As Sergeant Soliman stood among his fellow officers, he felt an indescribable weight on his chest. He tried to hold back his emotions, his face a stone mask of stoicism, but a single tear managed to escape, tracing a path down his weathered cheek. He made no move to wipe it away, allowing it to mix with the raindrops that cascaded down around him. Detective Smith had been a pillar of the force, admired and respected by all who had the privilege of working alongside him. His dedication and unwavering commitment to justice had earned him countless accolades, and his loss left a void that seemed impossible to fill. The ceremony unfolded with solemnity and reverence, officers standing shoulder to shoulder, their hearts heavy with grief. A montage of memories played in Sergeant Soliman's mind, flickering like old film reels. He recalled their adventures together, the countless hours spent unravelling mysteries and bringing criminals to justice. Minutes later, as if to punctuate the collective sorrow, officers blew trumpets in the air, their mournful notes cutting through the air like a lament. Guns were fired, their sound echoing through the sad atmosphere, a final salute to their fallen comrade.

The rain intensified, falling harder with each passing moment as if the heavens themselves wept for the loss of a hero. Sergeant Soliman couldn't help but feel a sense of surprise mingling with his grief. How could someone so full of life and determination be suddenly taken away? It was a reminder of the unpredictability and fragility of existence. As the ceremony came to an end, the officers slowly dispersed, their footsteps muffled by the rain-soaked ground. Each one carried a piece of Detective Smith's memory with them, forever changed by his impact. Sergeant Soliman stood alone for a moment, his heart heavy with a mixture of sadness and determination. He knew that life would continue, that new cases would arise, demanding their attention. But the loss of his dear friend reminded him of the importance of cherishing every moment, of embracing the capriciousness of life, and of the delicacy of the human spirit. And so, as the rain continued to fall, Sergeant Soliman made a silent vow to honour Detective Smith's memory. He would carry on with renewed purpose, fighting for justice, and ensuring that his fallen comrade's legacy would never be forgotten.

Forty-One

The Circle of Fate

The courtroom was ablaze with flashing lights as if Hollywood had displaced justice for a day. The air was thick with tension, murmured conversations buzzing like a disturbed hornet's nest. The man of the day, Donald, sat with an air of nonchalance that was at odds with the situation. In the sea of glum faces, his visage shone with the certainty of an Osprey focused on its prey. Not a bead of sweat on his brow, not a twitch at the corner of his mouth. All he wanted was to be home, not ensnared in this serpentine maze of law and its verbose manipulations.

He looked over towards the prosecutor, an eerie calm settling over him. He saw the cameras focusing on him, attempting to grasp the soul behind those unreadable eyes. Donald's family sat a few rows back, their faith as steadfast as ever, blissfully unaware of the layers of Donald's life which were yet to be unfolded. As the murmur in the courtroom gradually quieted down, a towering figure appeared at the entrance. The bailiff, standing at an awe-inducing 6'4", commanded attention without uttering a word. His chocolaty skin radiated under the courtroom's fluorescent lights, enhancing his stern yet graceful persona. His slicked-back hair and crisp uniform accentuated his aura of indomitable authority. The gun by his side was a silent promise of swift justice and order.

Detective Moony sat next to Sergeant Soliman in the courtroom, their eyes fixed on the unfolding case. They were both determined to bring justice to the victim, their curiosity piqued by the mysteries surrounding it.

"All rise," the bailiff commanded, and the room fell silent as the judge took his seat. It was clear that this would be a bench trial, with the fate of the accused resting solely in the judge's hands.

"Please be seated, Okay, let's make this case nice and smooth, you two," the judge addressed the courtroom, his tone firm. He turned to the prosecutor and instructed, "Call your first witness."

"Your Honor, I call Jack Hensley my first witness," Melissa announced confidently, her voice resonating in the air.

Detective Moony leaned forward, intrigued by the choice of witness. Jack Hensley was now a key figure in the case, his involvement shrouded in ambiguity. As he took his place on the stand, eyes darting nervously, the courtroom was filled with anticipation. In the bustling courtroom, all eyes turned towards Jack as he made his way through the hushed silence. Dressed impeccably in a tailored suit, he exuded an air of confidence and determination. As he approached the witness stand, the bailiff stepped forward, his voice echoing through the room.

"Please raise your right hand," the bailiff instructed, his tone authoritative. Jack obediently complied, his palm facing upwards, ready to take the oath. The weight of truth and responsibility hung heavily in the air.

"Do you swear to tell the truth, the whole truth, and nothing but the truth?" the bailiff demanded, his words resounding with importance. Jack took a deep breath, a mix of apprehension and resolve coursing through his veins.

"I do," Jack responded, his voice steady. Taking his place in the witness stand, he couldn't help but notice the flurry of activity surrounding him. Cameras clicked, capturing his every move, while photographers jostled for the perfect shot. The intensity of the moment made his heart race, his pulse pounding in his chest.

Melissa stood confidently, her eyes fixed on the man sitting in the witness stand. Jack looked back at her with a mixture of curiosity and apprehension. It was a high-profile case, and Melissa's reputation as a brilliant attorney had garnered attention from all corners.

"Thank you for being here today," Melissa began, her voice calm yet commanding. "Can you please state your name for the court?"

"Hi, I'm Jack David Hemsley," he replied, his voice echoing through the room. A small wave accompanied his introduction, adding an air of nonchalance that contrasted with the gravity of the situation.

"Thank you, Jack," Melissa said, her eyes never leaving him. "I appreciate you taking the time to be with us here today. Can you tell me how you've come to know Elisa, the victim in this case?"

A moment of silence hung in the air, as Jack's gaze shifted away momentarily, lost in thought. When he finally spoke, his voice held a touch of sadness mixed with nostalgia.

"I remember that day like it was yesterday. It was a balmy summer evening, and I found myself outside the Oasis Bar, minding my own business. As usual, the same old story repeated itself – kids picking on me, making fun of my situation. It wasn't easy being the constant target of their mockery. Just as I was about to retreat and find solace in a quieter corner, a voice called out, cutting through the noise and chaos. "Leave him alone!" It was a girl, not much older than the teenagers causing me grief. Her voice carried a sense of authority, yet kindness. I watched as the teenagers scattered. The girl approached me with a warm smile, her eyes sparkling with empathy. "Are you okay?" she asked, a genuine concern evident in her voice. I stuttered, trying to compose myself. "Yes, thank you. They were just being mean. I appreciate your help, I said to her." I could feel the weight of my belongings that had fallen to the ground as a result of the harassment. Without hesitation, she bent down to help me gather them, her grace and compassion shining through. As we picked up my scattered possessions, I couldn't help but notice how effortlessly we connected. It was as if we had known each other for years, despite this being our first encounter. And that was the first time I saw her." Answered Jack.

"So, prior to you meeting Elisa a few months ago, you knew nothing about her, am I right?" Melissa's eyes sparkled with intrigue.

"Nope, not at all, never met the poor girl. She was a complete stranger to me." Jack replied

Melissa leaned forward, her curiosity piqued, and asked, "And when you saw Elisa that day, and she was helping you, who was she with?"

Jack's mind travelled back to that fateful day.

"She was with Donald, Donald Prince," he recalled.

Melissa's eyebrows shot up in surprise.

"How do you know who Donald Prince is?" she asked.

Jack chuckled softly.

"Who doesn't know who Donald Prince is? They are the richest family in this town. Plus, they own every bar."

Melissa leaned in closer, her eyes shining with anticipation.

"Then what happened after that Jack," she urged.

Jack took a deep breath before continuing.

"Sometimes, Donald looks different. I would often sit outside the bar, begging for money to eat. On those days, his hair would grow really fast. It would always surprise me."

Melissa's mind spun with questions. Why did his appearance change near the bar? She couldn't help but wonder if there was a deeper secret hidden behind his ever-changing hair.

In that moment, Donald felt a huge lump in his throat, panic sweeping through him like a wildfire. But he knew that he had nothing to worry about. So he listened as Jack was being questioned, his mind racing with a million different thoughts. Melissa, the prosecutor, took a deep breath, ready to expose Donald's deceit. Clutching her notepad, she faced the witness, Jack, whose eyes darted nervously around the room. This was her chance to seek justice for a woman who had been pushed aside, forgotten by society.

"Can you see the defendant here today, Jack?" Melissa's voice resonated through the courtroom.

Jack hesitated for a moment, his gaze fixated on Donald, who squirmed uncomfortably in his chair.

"Yes," Jack finally answered, his voice shaking.

"Can you point to him, please?" Melissa asked, her voice steady but with a hint of determination.

As the room held its breath, Jack stretched his trembling arm and pointed directly at Donald Prince, the man who had caused irreparable damage to the victim's life. Donald's heart sank as he realized the gravity of the situation. The walls began closing in around him, suffocating him with the weight of his actions. He desperately searched for an escape route, a flicker of hope to hold onto.

"Okay, thank you Jack." Melissa acknowledged, her voice filled with gratitude. "No more questions Your Honor. She slowly made her way back to her chair, the evidence now mounting against Donald.

The courtroom buzzed with whispered conversations, as spectators struggled to comprehend the unfolding drama. Each word uttered had them on the edge of their seats, captivated by the unexpected twist. As the trial continued, Donald's mind raced, his thoughts intermingled with regrets and fears of what lay ahead. As the courtroom fell silent, Melissa's heart raced. She had spent countless hours preparing for this trial, and she was determined to make a powerful impact. The case was a high-profile one, and the stakes were incredibly high. Her client's future hung in the balance. Suddenly, a hush fell over the courtroom as the opposing attorney, Boxall, stood up. Adjusting his perfectly tailored suit, he walked over to the witness stand, his eyes fixed on the man who sat there nervously.

"You just testified that you always stand outside to beg for money to eat, do you mean you stand outside to beg for money for crack? Because you are indeed a crack feen."

Boxall asked, his words dripping with venom. It was clear that his vicious nature as a lawyer was coming through, seeking to discredit the witness in any way possible.

Immediately, Melissa's brow furrowed, sensing that Boxall's line of questioning was nothing more than a ploy to manipulate the judge's perception. Rising to her feet, she spoke up, her voice filled with confidence and conviction.

"I object, Your Honor. What's the relevance of this question, please?" she interjected, determined to protect her client's rights from Boxall's underhanded tactics.

Boxall smirked, revealing his true motives. "Okay, okay, withdrawn," he conceded, reluctantly relenting.

With a self-satisfied air, he strolled around the courtroom, his eyes scanning the faces of everyone around him. He knew he had made an impression, and he revelled in it. Unfazed, Melissa gathered herself, not allowing Boxall's theatrics to distract her.

"So, you are homeless, correct?" Boxall asked, trying to regain control of the narrative.

Melissa paused for a moment, her mind working at lightning speed. She knew that the answer to this question would be crucial to her case. Taking a deep breath, she glanced at her client. With steely determination, she locked eyes with Boxall and delivered her final blow.

"I object, Your Honor," she said firmly. "The relevance of my client's housing situation is irrelevant to the charges at hand. Rather than allowing Mr. Boxall to sway the jury's perception with ad hominem attacks, let us focus on the facts of the case."

"Overruled, you may answer the question Jack." Said the judge firmly, his voice echoing through the courtroom. The tension in the air was palpable as Mr. Boxall, the defense attorney, continued his aggressive line of questioning. Jack, a former homeless man, stood confidently on the witness stand, ready to share his story.

"I stay in a shelter now, and I will be given a home soon, but I was homeless before," Jack began, his voice steady but filled with a hint of vulnerability. His eyes scanned the room, as if searching for understanding, for someone to believe him.

Mr. Boxall leaned forward, his voice dripping with skepticism.

"So, let me get this straight," he sneered. "You randomly saw my client with the alleged victim in question, the same victim who allegedly helped you avoid bullying. But here's what I don't understand, Jack. You're on drugs, perhaps crack even. And yet, somehow, you remember every detail about that night. Are you sure you weren't paid to fabricate these stories just to secure a home?"

Jack's eyes widened, a mix of shock and indignation spreading across his face.

"No, no, absolutely not!" he exclaimed, his voice laced with determination. "Why would you say that? I saw them. You need to check the cameras, they always record everything!"

The courtroom fell into silence as Jack's words hung in the air. Mr. Boxall's confidence wavered for a moment, but he quickly regained composure. The defense attorney glanced at his client Donald, who sat in the defendant's chair, his face a mask of stoic indifference.

Surprised, Boxall began, his voice cutting through the silence like a sharp knife.

"There were no cameras on that day. No evidence to identify that my client saw the victim in question." He paused, his gaze unwavering as he continued, "Furthermore, he pointed out while walking to gather a yellow folder with papers inside."

All eyes turned to Jack as he fumbled with the folder, anxiety written across his face. The courtroom was on the edge of their seats, eager to discover what lay within those papers. Boxall's tone exuded confidence, as if he had an ace up his sleeve. As Boxall handed a photo to both the judge and Jack, the room held its collective breath once more. As Jack's eyes met the picture, his heart sank. The face in the photograph was undeniably his, but the circumstances surrounding the image puzzled him. He had never seen the photo before, and he couldn't recall any such incident in his recent memory. How could this be?

Boxall seized the opportunity to exploit Jack's moment of confusion. With a cunning smile on his face, Boxall began his relentless cross-examination.

"Is this not you, drunk in a parking lot a few weeks ago?" Boxall sneered, his tone dripping with disdain?"

Jack's mind raced, desperately trying to piece together the events that led to this incriminating image. Nothing made sense, but he had to defend himself. Gathering his thoughts, he mustered the courage to respond.

"Also, your mother was a crack whore, so technically it runs in your family, right?" Boxall asked, his tone laced with curiosity and a hint of accusation.

Jack felt a pang in his chest as the words sank in. He knew his past wasn't a secret, but to have it thrown back at him so casually felt like a punch to the gut. Jack took a deep breath, trying to regain his composure. The room fell silent, all eyes turning towards Jack. He felt a knot tighten in his stomach as he struggled to maintain his composure. The accusation hit him hard, and he knew that his response would be critical.

Interrupting the tense silence, Melissa, rose to her feet.

"Your Honor, may I object?" she said, her voice filled with urgency.

The judge, taken aback by the interruption, looked at Melissa with a mix of curiosity and annoyance.

"State your objection," he replied sternly.

Melissa took a deep breath and spoke, her voice filled with determination.

"Your Honor, the question posed by the prosecution is irrelevant and highly prejudiced. It has no bearing on the case and only serves to tarnish my client's character."

The judge considered Melissa's objection for a moment before making a decision.

"Objection overruled," he declared, turning his gaze towards Jack. "You may answer the question, Mr. Hensley."

Taking a moment to gather his thoughts, Jack realized that this trial was about more than just his own fate. It was less about the truth and justice prevailing over prejudice and assumptions.

With newfound determination, he looked up at the judge and began to speak, his voice steady.

"Your Honor, what happened in the past does not define who I am or what I am capable of. I am working hard to turn my life around and distance myself from the mistakes of my family. I deserve a chance to prove myself, everyone does."

The courtroom fell silent as Jack's words lingered in the air. Even the prosecution seemed taken aback by his unexpected response. The truth had a way of surprising everyone, even in the darkest of circumstances. Jack stood in the witness box, clutching onto the photograph as if it held the key to his redemption. The courtroom was hushed, the anticipation palpable. He took a deep breath, glanced at the judge, and once again began his testimony.

"Yes, Your Honor, my mother was an addict, and so was I," Jacked started, his voice steady and determined. "But I know what I saw that night, and I saw Mr. Prince here with Elisa."

The courtroom erupted into whispers and murmurs. Mr. Boxall, the defense attorney, scoffed dismissively and shot a smug glance in Jack's direction.

"How can anyone take the word of a crack addict to be true? It runs in your family, after all," he sneered, walking away confidently. "No more questions, Your Honor," Boxall stated smugly.

A flicker of hurt crossed Jack's eyes, but he remained resolute. He knew the truth, and he was determined to make everyone see it. Melissa couldn't ignore the nagging thought that had suddenly invaded her mind. She had one more question to ask, one that could potentially unravel the tightly woven web of lies in the courtroom.

"One more question, please, Your Honor," she spoke up, her voice strong and unwavering.

Without waiting for permission, Melissa walks purposefully towards Jack. She wanted to get to the bottom of this, to discover the truth hidden amongst the shadows. Jacked looked up, his eyes meeting Melissa's intense gaze. He could sense her determination and hoped that she would be the one to break through the wall of doubt.

"Jack, can you tell me," Melissa asked, her voice filled with suspense. "Do you remember what Elisa or Donald was wearing that night?"

The room fell silent once again, all eyes turning towards Jack. He closed his eyes, digging deep into his memory, trying to recall every detail from that fateful night.

As the seconds ticked by, a small smile tugged at the corners of Jack's lips. He could see it now, vivid as ever. Elisa, in her vibrant floral skirt, laughing as though she had not a care in the world. Donald, in his sharp black suit, exuding an air of confidence that couldn't be shaken.

Jack opened his eyes, locking them with Melissa's. "Yes," he whispered, and the room leaned in, captivated by his every word. "I remember."

Sergeant Soliman and Detective Moony sat in the courtroom, their eyes fixated on the witness stand. The air was thick with tension as Jack's words hung in the air.

"She was wearing a beautiful floral skirt and a very small top. She was also wearing high heels. She looked beautiful, but naturally beautiful, you could tell that she didn't need any makeup, you know." Responded Jack.

Sergeant Soliman and Detective Moony exchanged a quick glance. This information about Elisa's attire had not been disclosed to the public. It was only mentioned in the written testimony from Charlene and

Elisa themselves. How could Jack, a mere spectator, know these intimate details? The courtroom fell into another hushed silence as everyone processed this revelation. Whispers spread through the crowd like wildfire. How could Jack have seen what only the victims themselves knew? Detective Moony contemplated the situation, his mind racing to make sense of the puzzle before him. He couldn't shake the feeling that there was more to this case than what met the eye. Melissa took a deep breath, ready to call her next witness. The gaze of Detective Moony and Sergeant Soliman intensified as they locked eyes with Melissa, silently conveying their support. She nodded back, a determined smile playing on her lips.

"That's wonderful, thank you Jack," Melisa said to Jack as he walks away, his eyes filled with relief.

Turning her attention towards the judge, she heard him say, "You may step down, Jack." Jack nodded and was ushered out of the courtroom.

Melissa's heart raced as she prepared to introduce her next witness. The room fell into a hushed silence, waiting for her to reveal who would take the stand next. In that moment, all eyes were on her, waiting with bated breath.

"Your Honor," Melissa declared confidently, "I call our next witness, Elisa."

As the court room doors swung open, a hush fell upon the crowded space. The atmosphere was thick with anticipation as everyone turned their heads to catch a glimpse of the prime victim. The murmurs grew louder, creating a buzz of curiosity that permeated the room. Elisa, a young woman with an air of strength and determination, stepped into the spotlight. Her presence commanded attention as she made her way towards the stand. The onlookers could not help but be captivated by her aura of resilience. Sergeant Soliman and Detective Moony, the pillars of support for Elisa, exchanged encouraging smiles. They knew that this was a defining moment, not only for the case, but also for Elisa herself. She rubbed her pregnant stomach, a gentle gesture of comfort, as she prepared to face the trials that lay ahead.

Dressed in a flowing long dress that accentuated her natural beauty, Elisa exuded an ethereal elegance. Her long, lustrous hair cascaded down her back, framing her face with a soft glow. Even with her stomach visibly growing, she appeared to be the most beautiful girl in the room. As Elisa took her place on the witness stand, the tension in the courtroom became crucial. All eyes were fixed upon her, waiting for the words that would reveal the truth. The prosecution and defense held their breath, knowing that her testimony could shape the outcome of the trial. Donald couldn't tear his eyes away from her, a mix of awe and guilt welling up inside him. The memories of that fateful night resurfaced, haunting him with every passing thought. He remembered every detail - the sound of her voice and the sparkle in her eyes. Despite the darkness that consumed him, there was something undeniably beautiful about her, even as she lay on her deathbed. A flicker of regret flashed across Donald's face as he pondered the strange twist of fate that had spared her life not once, but twice.

But there was something else that gnawed at him, something that stirred a different kind of curiosity within his troubled mind. As he watched her, he couldn't help but wonder about the life growing within her, the baby she carried. A sudden wave of uncertainty washed over him, mingling with the bitter taste of regret. Lost in his thoughts, Donald barely noticed the bailiff's approach. The sound of his footsteps pulled him back to reality, forcing him to confront the consequences of his actions. The bailiff's stern expression matched the weight of the situation, a serious reminder of the impending judgment that awaited him.

"Please raise your right hand," said the bailiff, his voice echoing through the silence. "Do you swear to tell the truth, the whole truth, and nothing but the truth?" the bailiff questioned, his voice firm but laced with a hint of trepidation.

"I do," Elisa replied, her voice quivering yet resolute. As she uttered those words, a heavy silence descended upon the courtroom, the gravity of the situation sinking into every corner.

Sitting down on the witness stand, Elisa's heart pounded against her chest, her palms clammy with nerves. This was it—the moment she had been waiting for. Months of enduring a devastating ordeal had led her to this very spot. As she scanned the room, she noticed all eyes fixed upon her. Her testimony was being broadcast live to an audience scattered all over the world. The weight of the situation felt heavy upon her fragile shoulders, but she knew that she had to summon every ounce of courage within her to face this defining moment. Amidst the sea of onlookers, Elisa's gaze inadvertently found its way to Donald—the man who had forever changed her life. Memories of the assault flooded her mind, fragments of the traumatic experience flashing before her eyes. She could feel his presence penetrating her, his sinister face etched deeply into her soul. The mere sight of him ignited a surge of mixed emotions within her—fear, anger, and an unwavering determination to seek justice.

But, in that moment of torment, Elisa clung tightly to the memory of her best friend, Charlene. It was Charlene who had stood by her side throughout this harrowing journey, offering unwavering support and strength. Elisa drew inspiration from their bond, knowing that she needed to stay strong not just for herself, but for Charlene as well.

"Hello Elisa, thank you for coming today to give your testimony," said Melissa, with a sympathetic smile. "I understand that this must be very difficult for you. But can you please tell the court what you can remember that happened to you that night?"

Elisa glanced around the room, taking in the serious faces of the judge and the defendant. The weight of the room pressed down on her, but she knew she had to find the strength to speak.

"That night, I remember going to the bar. It was a typical Friday evening, and Charlene had convinced me to join her for a night out. I arrived at her house, dressed and ready to go. But, as always, Charlene hated what I was wearing. Being someone who doesn't often go out, I never know what to wear to these occasions, you know? Anyway, I quickly changed clothes, opting for a skirt and a stylish top. Charlene, on the other hand, was wearing a stunning dress that perfectly accentuated her curves. Together, we started pre-gaming at her place, sipping on our favourite cocktails. By the time we entered the bar, we were both already a little drunk. The bar was alive with music, laughter, and pulsating lights. It was as if the entire city had gathered there to celebrate the weekend, there were so many people. Charlene and I danced like there was no tomorrow, laughing and twirling around the dance floor. The energy was contagious, and we couldn't help but get caught up in the moment." Elisa Continued.

"Time seemed to be flying by as Charlene and I enjoyed our night out. We laughed, we danced, and we may have had a few too many drinks. But hey, it was a Friday night, and we were determined to have some fun. As we sat at the bar, I noticed two men across the room. They had been casting glances in our direction all night. I nudged Charlene and nodded towards them, but she merely shrugged it off. "It's just some guys checking us out, no big deal," she said. Still, I didn't want to ruin the evening by dwelling on it too much. Before I knew it, the two men had made their way over to us. They introduced themselves and their charm was undeniable. They seemed friendly enough, engaging us in delightful conversations and buying us more drinks. As the night grew darker, and my alcohol tolerance started to waver, I began to feel the exhaustion kick in. It was time to call it a night. I mentioned this to Charlene, but she had other plans. "Go on, just walk home with Donald," she suggested, pointing to one of the men. "He seems nice, and I'm sure he'd be happy to accompany you." It wasn't an entirely crazy idea. Donald had been polite and seemed harmless enough, I thought to myself.

"We bid our goodbyes to Charlene and the other guy, I'm sorry I don't remember his name, who were deep in conversation, and made our way out of the crowded bar. The cool night air hit my face, momentarily sobering me up. Donald and I walked side by side, making small talk along the way. As we were walking down the park, my eyes caught sight of a disturbing scene. A group of young kids, filled with mischief and cruelty, were tormenting a helpless homeless man. My heart ached with empathy, and without a second thought, I veered off my intended path and approached the commotion. I shouted at them. The kids turned their attention towards me, their eyes filled with surprise. Ignoring their insolence, I extended a hand towards the dishevelled man, offering him my assistance. His eyes held a glimmer of both gratitude and weariness as he accepted my gesture.

"Before I knew it, we were in Donald's house," Elisa recounted, her voice laden with unease. Memories of that night still haunted her, the unsettling feeling of being ensnared in a web she couldn't escape. Intriguingly, Elisa's recollection began with a seemingly mundane detail - Donald's request for a shower.

"I had a few more drinks," Elisa continued, her voice trembling slightly. "He went to take a shower, claiming he felt a bit smelly after a long day." As a teacher, Elisa empathized with the toll of exhausting days, understanding the desire for rejuvenation. Yet, a sinister undercurrent pulsed through her words, hinting at something far more sinister.

Donald's gaze fixated on Elisa as she spoke, relishing in every word she uttered. Unbeknownst to her, his mind wandered to a dark place, the cruel satisfaction of past transgressions resurfacing with a vengeance. His eyes closed, a chilling smile curling at his lips, as he vividly remembered the details of a courtroom spectacle. Sitting amidst the hushed whispers of the court, Donald felt an eerie sense of power. The gravity of his actions slowly unfolded a twisted tapestry of manipulation and violence. The courtroom became his theatre, his validation found in the horrified expressions of those who bore witness. Now, as Elisa recounted her ordeal, a sinister glimmer danced in his eyes.

"Anyway, he seemed different when he came out, his hair, the way he looked, maybe I was drunk, I don't know. The memories were hazy, as if they were playing hide and seek with my consciousness. But there are moments, like shards of broken glass, that still pierce my mind. I remembered waking up, my body bound tightly, in a room devoid of light. The darkness pressed against me, suffocating my very existence. Pain surged through my body, waves crashing against my fragile form. The whip lashed against my skin, leaving behind crimson imprints of torment. Time was elusive, slipping away between the muddled moments of consciousness and unconsciousness. Minutes blurred into hours, a twisted carousel of agony and despair. Each lash dug deeper into my soul, snuffing out the flickering flame of hope." Continued Elisa.

The courtroom fell silent, the air thick with anticipation as the woman sat before the judge, her eyes filled with anguish.

"Then there was the bottle," she began, her voice trembling with a mix of fear and desperation. "I could feel a sharp pain forcefully being injected inside of me, like a dagger piercing my very soul. I tried to scream for help, but no one came."

The gallery of spectators leaned forward, captivated by her words. Whispers of disbelief echoed through the room, mingling with gasps of shock. How could someone inflict such cruelty? Why didn't anyone come to her rescue?

"I then woke up after being in a coma for four months in the hospital," Elisa began, her voice barely above a whisper. "I had stitches in my anus, head, and all over my body."

Gasps echoed through the courtroom as people struggled to comprehend the extent of Elisa's injuries. The room was filled with a tangible tension as she continued her testimony.

"I was also pregnant," Elisa said, her voice cracking. "Which was a surprise because before this ordeal, I didn't have sex with anyone for four years."

Whispers and murmurs spread like wildfire among the spectators, their curiosity piqued by the enigmatic nature of Elisa's revelation. How could this be? What had happened to her during those lost months? As tears slowly streamed down her face, Elisa fought to regain her composure. She refused to allow the cruel man who had assaulted her and taken everything away from her to see her weak. Determination etched across her features, she wiped her tears away and continued her testimony.

"I had to learn how to walk and talk again," Elisa said, her voice filled with a mixture of anguish and resilience. "It was very hard for me."

The courtroom remained silent, captivated by Elisa's story. Each word she spoke added another layer of mystery to the already puzzling situation. Everyone looked around them in the courtroom, astonished by Elisa's testimony. Her words had left them in a state of disbelief, and even Donald, the accused, couldn't hide his surprise. Whispers filled the air as people tried to process what they had just heard. Donald leaned over to his lawyer, his eyes wide with a mix of shock and curiosity.

"I'm so sorry that this happened to you, Elisa. Thank you," whispered Melissa, her voice filled with compassion. She walked away and took her seat, wrapping her arms around herself tightly.

Donald's lawyer cleared his throat, breaking the silence that had settled over the room. He looked at Elisa, a slight smirk playing on his face.

"Yes, I am too... Well, everyone is sorry that this happened to you, Elisa," he said, his tone dripping with sarcasm. "Such a heartbreaking story."

The room held its breath, waiting for him to continue. Elisa's eyes narrowed, her gaze locked on the lawyer.

"I just have one question for you, if you don't mind," he continued, his voice now filled with intrigue. "If you're saying that my client assaulted you, how come the DNA of this baby came back negative to my client?"

The question hung in the air, a sudden twist that caught everyone off guard. Elisa's face paled, her eyes darting around the room. The tension in the courtroom became evident as the jurors leaned forward, their eyes fixed on Elisa. The silence stretched on, each second feeling like an eternity. Finally, Elisa's trembling voice broke through the stillness.

"I... I don't understand," she stammered, her words barely audible. "The DNA test... it has to be wrong. I saw Donald with my own eyes. He was there."

The lawyer's smile widened as he watched Elisa struggle to find an explanation. He knew he had struck a nerve, unravelling the carefully woven fabric of her story. The courtroom was alive with excitement. The air was thick with apprehension as everyone eagerly awaited the next revelation. The case had already taken unexpected turns, but nothing could have prepared them for what was about to unfold.

"Order! Order in the court!" the judge sternly commanded, trying to restore some semblance of control. The room slowly quieted down, all eyes fixated on the speaker's podium.

Melissa could hardly believe her ears. Her client's fate hung in the balance, and this new twist threw her meticulously crafted defense strategy into disarray. She stood up, her voice trembling with disbelief.

"Your Honor, this evidence was not passed by me. We knew nothing of this! How can it be presented at this stage?" Melissa implored, her eyes searching for answers.

The prosecutor, a confident and composed figure, stepped forward, a sly smile tugging at the corners of his lips. He sauntered over to his desk, picked up a neatly folded document, and approached the judge's bench. The sound of his footsteps echoed in the tense silence.

"Your Honor," he said, his voice dripping with self-assuredness, "we obtained a DNA sample for this child." He handed the paperwork to the judge, who studied it with a mix of bewilderment and intrigue.

Elisa, a witness in the case, watched in stunned silence. Her mind raced as she tried to comprehend the implications of this unexpected revelation. How could it be possible? Her heart pounded in her chest, her palms growing clammy with the weight of the truth that was about to be unveiled. The judge, his eyes filled with a mixture of curiosity and apprehension, examined the DNA report. With a deliberate pause, he looked up, scanning the room filled with anxious faces.

"Continue your line of questioning, Boxall. Answer the question, please, Elisa," the judge demanded, his voice cutting through the silence.

The room held its breath, awaiting Elisa's response. She hesitated, her voice trembling as she finally spoke up.

"I... I don't know, something must be wrong." Her words hung in the air, casting a perplexing cloud over the proceedings.

Boxall vehemently argued his client's innocence. With a fiery passion in his eyes, he pointed at Elisa, demanding answers.

"But how can it be wrong, Elisa?" Boxall's voice boomed across the room, his frustration evident. "Your statement clearly says that you did not have any sexual relationship for over four years, yet you suddenly wake up from a coma pregnant? Clearly, my client didn't assault you or have anything to do with this case."

The walls seemed to close in around Elisa as she sat silently, tears streaming down her face. The weight of the accusations pressed against her like an unforgiving boulder. She had never anticipated her life taking such a twisted turn. Boxall continued his tirade, his voice growing louder and more indignant.

"As a matter of fact, he wasn't even there that night because he was out of town on business. Why are you trying to get money out of my client? Because you're poor, and your parents died, is that it? You just see him as a rich man and want to extort him, is that it?"

Gasps reverberated across the courtroom as Mr. Boxall's words echoed. The jeers from the spectators created a chaotic ambiance, leaving Elisa feeling as though she were drowning in a sea of judgment.

The judge pounded the gavel, attempting to restore order.

"Order in the court!

Elisa's breath hitched as she tried to comprehend the gravity of the situation. Her eyes darted around the room, searching for answers, but all she found were skeptical faces staring back at her.

"There are no cameras or any witnesses, just one who claimed to have seen you out of nowhere," Boxall's voice echoed through the room.

"And may I add again, he is a crack addict, and not very believable. So why should we believe you, Elisa?"

Elisa felt her heart pounding in her chest over and over again, her palms growing sweaty. How did she end up in this nightmare? Her mind raced, desperately trying to come up with an explanation that would convince everyone of her innocence. The weight of the accusations pressed down on her, threatening to suffocate her. As the pressure mounted, Elisa's eyes instinctively lowered to her belly, where her unborn child rested. She could feel the baby's movements, as if sensing the turmoil that surrounded them. The stress was taking its toll, threatening the safety of both mother and child.

Feeling overwhelmed, Elisa's vision blurred, and darkness encroached on her consciousness. The stress had pushed her to the brink, and her body gave in, slipping into a state of shock. The courtroom erupted into chaos as Melissa rushed to her side. Sergeant Soliman and Detective Moony joined in, their urgent voices blending with the commotion as they called for an ambulance. Time seemed to stand still as the medical team arrived, their expertise taking charge of the situation. They carefully attended to Elisa, ensuring her well-being and that of her unborn child. The courtroom fell silent as the realization dawned on everyone that this was more than just a trial; it was a delicate and fragile moment of life hanging in the balance. As the trial continued without Elisa's physical presence, the absence of a credible witness began to chip away at the prosecution's case. Doubts crept into the minds of everyone in the courtroom, causing them to question their initial assumptions. They scrutinized the evidence, the testimonies, and the motives, searching for the truth that seemed to elude them.

Forty-Two

Decoding the Verdict

It was a day that the entire nation had been waiting for. The headlines screamed with prediction as news stations everywhere published the biggest court case of the century. The courtroom had been buzzing with tension ever since Elisa, the victim of a brutal assault, took the witness stand and shared her harrowing story. The accused, Donald Prince, stood trial for violently assaulting her. People from all walks of life held their breath, waiting for justice to be served. Elisa, still recovering from the emotional trauma of her testimony, had fainted in the courtroom just a few days ago. It was a moment that had left everyone stunned and concerned for her well-being. In the midst of the media frenzy, a sense of unease settled over the courtroom. The judge, a solemn figure in his black robe, had reached a decision. The room fell into complete silence as all eyes turned towards him. The weight of the moment was palpable, as the fate of both Elisa and Donald Prince hung in the balance.

"It's the final day of the verdict today as Donald Prince stands trial accused of violently assaulting the victim Elisa," the news anchor's voice crackled through the television screen. The anticipation was palpable, even for those watching from afar. The entire nation seemed to hold its breath, waiting for justice to be served.

Elisa, the victim, had taken the witness stand just days before. She had recounted her harrowing tale, the details of which sent shivers down the spines of all who listened. But tragedy had struck when she fainted in the courtroom. The trial had come to a halt, leaving everyone in suspense. As the news anchor continued his commentary, the judge emerged from the courtroom doors. The hushed murmurs of the reporters faded into silence as the judge took his place behind the bench. His gaze swept across the room, settling on the defendant. Outside the courtroom, a hushed crowd gathered, their cameras capturing every moment. Reporters from various news stations stood eagerly, waiting for the judge's verdict. The news anchor, solemn and composed, reported the latest development.

"News has just come in," he announced, his voice tinged with a mix of suspense and curiosity, "the judge has reached a verdict."

The judge entered the courtroom, his steps echoing in the tense silence. Sergeant Soliman and Detective Mooney exchanged nervous glances, their eyes filled with hope and trepidation. They both believed that Elisa was telling the truth, but the outcome of today's trial was uncertain. Fear gnawed at their insides, but they knew they had to stay strong and see it through. Meanwhile, Donald sat at the defendant's table, his lawyer Boxall by his side. They exchanged smug smiles, oozing with confidence that seemed to reverberate throughout the courtroom. They were sure that they had the upper hand, that justice would favour them this day. As the proceedings ensued, Melissa, watched intently. Her heart pounded in her chest as she silently prayed for justice to prevail. The weight of the truth rested heavily on her shoulders, and she yearned for a resolution that would bring closure to the injustice that had befallen Elisa.

Unable to contain her anxiety any longer, Melissa leaned towards her assistant and whispered.

"This could be the turning point, the moment that decides it all."

The assistant nodded, equally captivated by the unfolding drama. The words hung in the air, as the courtroom held its breath.

"All rise," said the bailiff as everyone stood up. The tension in the courtroom was clear as all eyes were fixed on the judge, waiting for his decision.

Cameras clicked, capturing the moment, while a crowd of people held their breaths in anticipation. The judge, with a stern expression, knew what his decision would be even before this court case began. He had weighed the evidence meticulously, analysed every detail, but Elisa's testimony had stirred something within him.

"You may be seated," said the judge, his voice steady and commanding.

As everyone took their seats, the judge's gaze shifted to the defendant, Donald Prince, who sat confident in his finest suit. With a smile on his face, he met the judge's eyes, undeterred by the gravity of the situation.

"Can the defendant please rise?" said the judge, his voice echoing through the courtroom.

Donald Prince obeyed, his demeanour unwavering, as if he already knew what the judge was about to say. The judge took a moment, his eyes scanning the room, observing the anxious faces and the expectant silence. His decision was clear, his conviction unshakable. But as he prepared to deliver his verdict, a flicker of doubt flashed through his mind. Elisa's testimony had touched his heart, revealing a side of the defendant that was unforeseen, but there was nothing he could do about the situation, it was never his decision to begin with. The judge cleared his throat, the room becoming still as he began to speak. He recounted the evidence, dissecting each argument with precision. The tension in the courtroom only intensified as the judge's words hung in the air, waiting to be absorbed by both the defendant and the spectators.

"I understand that this must be a very difficult time for everyone involved," the judge began, his voice firm but empathetic. The room leaned in, captivated by his commanding presence. "And I appreciate your hard work and dedication with this case," he continued, acknowledging the prosecution team.

The tension in the courtroom skyrocketed as the judge's words hinted at the severity of the crime. The collective imagination of the jury started painting vivid pictures of the harrowing events of that fateful night. Whispers filled the room, amplifying the sense of dread that pervaded the atmosphere.

"I can't fathom to think what the victim in this case must have gone through that horrible night," the judge's voice resonated with a mix of sympathy and disbelief. The gravity of the situation became visible, weighing heavily on the hearts of those present. The room fell silent, as if trying to shield itself from the horrors that had unfolded.

"But the fact of the matter is," the judge paused, his gaze sweeping across the room, "there was not enough evidence to convict Mr. Donald Prince today."

A hushed murmur rippled through the crowd. Confusion etched on the face of the prosecution team, disbelief etched on everyone's face. The defense team exchanged glances, unable to hide their relief. How could it be? How could justice slip through their fingers? The accused, Mr. Donald Prince, stood motionless, his eyes filled with a mix of gratitude and perplexity. The weight of uncertainty lifted off his shoulders, yet questions lingered in his mind. Did the world truly believe in his innocence, or was this merely a stroke of luck? What secrets remained buried in the shadows of the courtroom?

The judge's final words echoed through the chamber, sending shock waves through the hearts and minds of those present.

"I hereby find you not guilty."

An abrupt chaos descended upon the courtroom. Conflicting emotions swirled in the room – relief mingled with doubt, celebration juxtaposed with sorrow. The air was thick with unanswered questions, leaving everyone wondering, searching for the elusive truth. As the courtroom erupted in a frenzy of disbelief and confusion, Sergeant Soliman and Detective Moony stood rooted to the spot, their faces a mask of astonishment. The words that had just escaped the judge's lips echoed in their ears, defying every ounce of logic they possessed.

"How could the judge find Donald not guilty?" Sergeant Soliman muttered under his breath, his eyes narrowing with a mixture of frustration and anger.

Detective Moony simply shook his head, unable to comprehend the turn of events. They had been so sure, so convinced of Donald's guilt. The evidence had seemed insurmountable, painting a vivid picture of his involvement in the heinous crime that had rocked the town. But now, as Donald and his lawyer, Boxall, embraced each other in celebration, the Sergeant and Detective couldn't help but feel a sense of defeat and injustice wash over them. The courtroom seemed to spin around them as the reality sank in—Donald was walking away a free man. Melissa, watched in disbelief as Donald cast an evil smile in her direction, his eyes filled with a sinister triumph. Her heart sank, her faith in justice shattered, and a chilling fear gripped her soul. How could this be happening? Could Donald truly have gotten away with it?

Leaving the courtroom, Sergeant Soliman and Detective Moony stormed out, their fury barely contained. They had invested countless hours, sleepless nights, and relentless determination into building the case against Donald. It felt like the very fabric of justice had been ripped apart before their eyes. Silently, they made their way to Elisa's house, their hearts heavy with the burden of delivering the devastating news.

Forty-Three

Timing is Everything

E lisa lay in her bed, her eyes fixated on the television screen. The news of Donald Prince's acquittal echoed through her ears, shattering her hopes for justice. Confined within the walls of witness protection, she felt an overwhelming sense of helplessness. How could he have gotten away with assaulting her? As she looked around her room, everything seemed distorted. The once cozy space now felt cramped and suffocating. The small coffee table appeared immense, as if ready to crash down on her at any moment. The furniture, once familiar and comforting, now seemed to cave in, mirroring the weight of her despair. Elisa buried her head under the covers, seeking solace from the world that had failed her. Tears streamed down her face, mingling with the pain that consumed her. It was an agonizing reminder of the injustice she had endured. How could a human being be subjected to such brutality, only to witness their assailant walk free?

In this twisted tale of betrayal, Elisa had lost more than just her faith in the system. Her friend, her confidante, had been brutally murdered, leaving her with a void that could never be filled. The void of having no one to talk to, no one to share her fears and frustrations. Life, it seemed, had dealt her an unfathomably unfair hand. In the darkest corner of her soul, a seed of despair had taken root. The weight of her anguish was unbearable, threatening to crumble her fragile spirit. Tears flowed freely down her face, a testament to the pain that devoured her. In that moment, it felt as though the world had lost all colour, all hope. With an anguished cry, she stumbled towards the balcony, seeking solace in the chilling night air. The door creaked open, releasing a rush of cool breeze that danced upon her tear-stained cheeks. She stood on the ledge, a figure cloaked in vulnerability and despair, her white night-gown clinging to her pregnant belly. Thoughts swirled in her mind, a tempest of doubt and fear. How could she possibly carry on, burdened by the weight of a traumatic experience? How could she bring a child into a world so filled with cruelty and suffering? Doubts gnawed at her heart, threatening to take away the last vestiges of her strength.

As the wind tousled her hair, her hands fell gently to her side. The cool breeze whispered tales of distant lands and whispered secrets, momentarily offering respite from her pain. She closed her weary eyes, allowing her mind to escape to a place where happiness once resided. In her imagination, she roamed through sunlit meadows, her laughter echoing through the air. She saw herself surrounded by loved ones, their warm embraces filling her heart with joy. There, in that moment of serenity, she glimpsed a flicker of hope. But reality soon tugged at her, reminding her of the challenges that awaited her return. The pain of her past haunted her, refusing to let go. Her unborn child, innocent and yet burdened by her scars, stirred within her womb, as if sensing her turmoil. Elisa stood on the ledge of the tall building, her heart pounding in her chest. Tears streamed down her face as she contemplated the unthinkable. Her life had become a never-ending nightmare, filled with heartbreak and despair. She had reached her breaking point, and the darkness seemed to demolish her.

As she looked down at the bustling city below, memories flooded her mind. She remembered her best friend Charlene, the laughter they shared and the adventures they embarked on together. She thought about her parents, who had always been there for her, until they tragically lost their lives in a car accident. And then there was her first boyfriend, the one who broke her heart and made her question her worth. Elisa yearned for peace, not only for herself but for her unborn baby. She couldn't bear the thought of bringing a child into a world filled with pain and suffering. The weight of her burdens threatened to suffocate her and jumping seemed like the only way to find solace. But just as she was about to take that fatal leap, a familiar voice echoed in her head. It was her mother's voice, gentle and loving, as if she was right there beside her.

"Elisa," her mother pleaded. "You are stronger than you think."

Those words halted Elisa in her tracks. The voice of her mother had always been a source of comfort, even in her darkest moments. It was a reminder that she was not alone, and there were people who cared about her, even if they weren't there physically. Sergeant Soliman found himself standing outside a familiar door. With a police officer by his side, he knew he had a difficult task ahead. The air was heavy as he raised his hand and knocked. To his surprise, there was no response. Soliman's heart skipped a beat as he slowly turned the knob, allowing the door to creak open.

"Elisa, where are you?" he called out in a soft, concerned tone.

Thoughts raced through his mind as he pondered how he would break the devastating news of Donald's verdict to her. As he cautiously made his way further into the apartment, his eyes caught sight of an open balcony door. Panic gripped his soul as he prayed to God that no harm had befallen her. With trembling steps, he approached the balcony, fearing what he might find. And there she was, Elisa, standing on the edge, her arms outstretched, ready to leap into the abyss. Soliman's heart pounded in his chest as he fought against the fear coursing through his veins. Without a moment's hesitation, he lunged forward, and with strength he didn't know he possessed, managed to grab hold of her just in the nick of time. Elisa collapsed into his arms, tears streaming down her face, her sobs echoing through the empty apartment. Soliman held her tightly, providing shelter from the storm that raged within her tormented soul. In that moment, he knew he had saved her from the brink of self-destruction.

As the tears subsided, Elisa looked up at Soliman with eyes filled with a mix of gratitude and confusion.

"Why did you save me?" she whispered, her voice tinged with both despair and curiosity.

Soliman's gaze softened as he met her searching eyes.

"Because life is full of second chances," he replied, his voice filled with sincerity. "You may not see it now, but there is hope. There is a future for you beyond this darkness. You are not alone."

As a seasoned sergeant, Soliman had been witness to the harsh realities of life, the unfairness that often plagued the innocent. But Elisa was different. She was just a woman, who still haven't experienced life yet. In that moment, he didn't know what the future held for Elisa, but he made a silent promise to himself that he would try his best to help her every step of the way. He knew that within this broken system, the odds were stacked against her, but he refused to let that extinguish his determination.

Forty-Four

Yours Mine & the Truth

It was a dreary morning, and Sergeant Soliman found himself slouched on the sofa, his eyelids heavy with fatigue. The events of the previous night had left him emotionally drained, as he had been faced with the horrifying sight of Elisa attempting to take her own life. Determined to ensure her safety, Soliman had decided to keep a watchful eye on her. As he drifted off into a restless sleep, his mind burdened with thoughts of Elisa's fragile state, a sudden loud bang on the door jolted him awake.

His heart raced, and his instincts kicked in as he leaped off the sofa, instantly fearing the worst. In his half-asleep state, he imagined an intruder, a sinister figure lurking outside, ready to pounce and harm Elisa. With adrenaline coursing through his veins, Soliman dashed towards the door, reaching for the gun he kept close by. His mind clouded by fear and urgency, he cautiously peered through the peephole to identify the source of the disturbance. With guns drawn, he prepared for the worst, bracing himself for the imminent confrontation.

To his surprise, it was Detective Moony relentlessly pounding on the door. Confusion mingled with relief as Soliman unlocked and opened the door, slightly lowering his weapon. Moony's face wore an expression of urgency and concern. Something was amiss, and Soliman's curiosity piqued.

"What's going on, Moony?" Soliman inquired, his voice still tinged with sleep.

Moony's gaze darted nervously as he quickly composed himself.

"Sarge, we've discovered something.... something that could change everything."

Soliman's brow furrowed as he absorbed Moony's cryptic statement. His mind raced, desperately trying to connect the dots between Elisa's suicide attempt and Moony's mysterious revelation. There was an undeniable sense of intrigue, as though a puzzle was slowly unravelling before his eyes.

"Did you see the video?" said Detective Moony, his face etched with panic.

"What video, and why are you banging like that? Is everything okay?" Detective Soliman questioned, his eyes narrowing in concern.

"It was true, it was true! Every fucking word she said was true," Moony gasped, his voice trembling with a mix of fear and bewilderment. He paced around the room, his gaze darting from one corner to another, searching for any sign of confirmation.

Unsure of what was happening, Soliman watched as Moony retrieved an iPad from his bag. With haste, he pulled up a video and handed it to Soliman.

"Look," he whispered, his finger pointing emphatically at the screen.

Curiosity now at an all-time limit, Soliman pressed play. In a daze after just being woken up, Sergeant Soliman rubbed his eyes, struggling to shake off the remnants of sleep. His mind was clouded, and confusion washed over him as he tried to make sense of the commotion around him. Detective Mooney's urgent voice echoed in his ears, but the words slipped through the fog in his mind. What was Moony on about, and what the hell was going on? As Soliman stumbled towards the source of the commotion, it was almost like watching a movie. The footage started off by showing Elisa, giving a testimony, just like she did in court. As the video played on, Soliman's disbelief turned into astonishment. The scenes depicted were unimaginable yet undeniably real. It could be seen all over the world, parents, teenagers, news reports – everyone was captivated by the video. It was broadcast all over the internet and news stations, spreading like wildfire.

Sergeant Soliman watched intently as the video played before him. As the footage continued, a sense of curiosity instantly gripped him. In the video, Elisa, with a radiant smile, entered Donald's lavish apartment. She seemed genuinely happy, her eyes filled with excitement, as she explored the beautifully decorated space. Removing her jacket, she strolled around the room, admiring the intricate details. The camera angle switched, revealing Elisa engaging in conversation with Donald. His charming manner seemed to captivate her, his words weaving a spell around her unsuspecting heart. Their laughter filled the air, creating an illusion of a perfect moment frozen in time.

But as the video played on, Sergeant Soliman's unease grew. Donald excused himself, disappearing into the bathroom. Just as the camera angle shifted, a chill ran down the Sergeant's spine. There, sitting on the bathroom counter, was another man who bore an uncanny resemblance to Donald. This mystery man exuded an air of confidence and authority, his eyes shrouded in mystery. He leisurely puffed on a cigar, sending swirls of smoke dancing through the air. His presence raised a multitude of questions in Sergeant Soliman's mind. Who was this doppelgänger? What was his connection to Donald? Minutes later, the door creaked open, and the man stepped out of the bathroom. His eyes met Elisa's, and there was an air of mystery around him, and she couldn't help but be captivated by his presence. They began a conversation that would consume hours of the night. As the evening progressed, the audience watched intently, curious about the nature of their interaction. Little did they know, a sinister plot was unfolding before their eyes. Unbeknownst to Elisa, the mystery man discreetly slipped a white powder into her drink. The audience gasped, their curiosity now tinged with concern.

Hours passed, and what had started as an evening of intrigue turned into a nightmare of pain and anguish for Elisa. She was subjected to unspeakable acts of violence, beaten and whipped mercilessly. The mystery man took advantage of her vulnerability, leaving her broken and devastated. But the horror did not end there. Elisa was led to a secret room, a black room she had testified about, a place of unspeakable darkness. Bound and drugged, she became a pawn in a sadistic game. The audience, their eyes glued to the screen, watched in horrified silence as she screamed in pain, her torment lasting for agonizing hours. The video played on mute, but the visuals spoke a thousand words. The audience, unable to tear their eyes away, were left to imagine the sounds accompanying the horrifying scenes before them. Elisa's suffering seemed endless, her spirit crushed under the weight of unimaginable torture and assault. Sergeant Soliman held his breath as he slowly sat down on the couch, his eyes fixated on the screen. The video played before him, revealing a horrifying scene that made his blood run cold. A drugged-out mystery man was taking advantage of Elisa, over and over again. The brutality of it all left Soliman speechless.

"Where did you get this video from?" he finally managed to ask, his voice trembling with a mix of anger and concern.

"It was leaked, Sarge," Detective Moony replied, his voice filled with distress. "It's all over the internet."

Soliman's heart sank as he realized the implications of what he had just witnessed. He reached for the remote, his hands shaking, and turned on the television. He waited anxiously for the news to unfold, hoping against hope that it was all just a horrible hoax. But as he switched to the news channel, his worst fears were confirmed. There, on the screen, were Donald's and Elisa's faces plastered all over. The news anchor's voice carried a sense of urgency as they reported the shocking revelation.

"Who could have leaked this?" he muttered to himself, frustration etched across his face. Detective Soliman leaned against the doorframe, his eyes filled with determination.

"I don't know, but we have to get that motherfucker man," Detective Moony exclaimed. "And who is this mystery guy anyway?"

Sergeant Soliman paused for a moment, deep in thought. Suddenly, it hit him like a bolt of lightning. There was something both Elisa and Jack had mentioned – the mystery man looked different.

"He looked different," Sergeant Soliman repeated aloud.

"What? Who looked different?" Detective Moony asked, confusion evident in his voice.

"That's what they kept saying," Sergeant Soliman replied, his mind racing. "One day his hair was a bit longer, and the next it wasn't. This mystery man, it has to be his twin brother or something."

Detective Moony eyes widened in realization.

"How the fuck did we not see this sooner?" he exclaimed.

Detective Moony stood in the dimly lit room, his eyes wide with astonishment. He couldn't believe what he was hearing. The pieces of the puzzle were finally coming together, but they formed a picture that was too twisted to be real.

"And that's not all Sarge," Detective Moony continued, his voice filled with a mix of excitement and disbelief. "The fire squad came back with a DNA match on my patrol car when Smith died. The same person that killed Charlene, also killed Smith, my guess is, it's this mystery man right here." He pointed at the television screen. "They wouldn't pay anyone to kill a cop, no...that was too risky, they knew that someone would snitch sooner or later. And the way that Charlene's neck was cut, it had to be a professional."

The room was thick with tension as Sergeant Soliman flung the iPad across the room, his anger reverberating off the walls.

"Motherfucker!" he bellowed, his frustration clear as day.

Detective Moony watched, wide-eyed, as Soliman paced back and forth, his mind racing with a newfound realization. Soliman turned to his partner, Moony, a look of determination in his eyes.

"Didn't Mrs. Prince say that she had two boys? One was Donald, and the other one was disabled, in a nursing home, right?" he asked.

Moony nodded cautiously.

"Yes, that's right, a very expensive one too, she said, that bitch. But what does that have to do with anything?" he responded curiously.

Soliman took a deep breath and looked at his partner, the weight of his theory becoming clear.

"Well, what if that arsehole isn't as disabled as we think he is? What if he's just mentally sick? What if Donald lures these women in with his charm and looks, only for his brother to live out all of his sick fantasies?"

Detective Moony looked on in astonishment, his mind swirling with the possibilities. The pieces of the puzzle were starting to come together, forming a disturbing image that left them both reeling. Detective Moony stared at the television in front of him, his mind racing with the implications.

"So, the baby could potentially be his brother's?" Moony's voice trembled with an unsettling mix of shock and curiosity. "That's why the DNA test came back inconclusive, the test couldn't determine which fucking brother it was. Then we had Boxall, who said that the DNA proved that the baby was not Donald's, but he didn't say that it was inconclusive." He paused. "But what about the person who collected her at the door in the video? We need to find them too." Continued Moony.

Sergeant Soliman's face mirrored Moony's astonishment.

"I don't know who collected her, but I'm guessing it's one of his little goons. I doubt we will be able to find them now. What I want to know is, how could Ronald, the brother, sneak out of the nursing home to take part in these crimes?" Soliman asked.

Moony's eyes narrowed as he connected the dots.

"I think this whole damn family is involved. I think they knew Ronald was a sick fuck, and they paid millions to help his dysfunctional brain. You can try and help the mentally ill, but you can't cure a sexual predator. They will always be sick fucks until they go to hell."

As Moony and Soliman continued to investigate the twisted family, details emerged that sent shivers down their spines. Ronald, the seemingly innocent brother, had been the mastermind behind a series of heinous crimes. His family, aware of his deranged nature, had orchestrated elaborate plans to protect him and enable his sadistic desires. As they discussed the case unfolding before them, Elisa, sensing the commotion, cautiously entered the room, her concern etched on her face.

"What's going on?" she asked, her voice trembling slightly. Sergeant Soliman quickly scrambled to turn off the television, desperate to shield Elisa from the turmoil that had unfolded. He couldn't bear to see her face plastered all over the news and internet, not after everything she had been through.

"Erm, nothing," the two men stammered, their attempts to remain composed falling short.

Elisa, undeterred, grew more suspicious as she walked towards Sergeant Soliman and gently took the remote from his grasp. Her intuition told her that something was amiss, and she was determined to uncover the truth. With a resolute click, she switched on the television, bated breath filling the room. As the screen flickered to life, Elisa's eyes widened in disbelief. The news anchor's voice boomed from the speakers, reporting a shocking revelation that made her world come crashing down. Images of her assault, once buried deep within the depths of secrecy, now danced across the television screen, exposing her darkest secrets for all to see. Elisa stood frozen, her eyes fixed on the screen before her. Her heart pounded in her chest, threatening to burst through the ribs that caged it. The video played on, each second a relentless reminder of the night that had haunted her every waking moment. But this time, it was not a figment of her imagination. It was not a flashback. It was real. As the grainy footage unfolded, Elisa could hardly believe her eyes. She watched in terror as her own body, dressed in the same clothes she had worn that fateful night, was subjected to unimaginable violence. Her mind recoiled, but her eyes remained transfixed. The man on the screen, showed no mercy as he brutally assaulted her. Time ceased to exist as Elisa's world crumbled before her.

Every bone in her body screamed for her to look away, to shield herself from the horror playing out on the television. But something compelled her to keep watching, to bear witness to the embodiment of her worst nightmares. The man's fists pummelled her lifeless body, leaving no doubt about the extent of the pain she had endured. And then, the scene took an even darker turn. A bottle, once harmless and innocuous, became a weapon of unspeakable violation. Elisa's gasp was stifled by her trembling hand as she watched the bottle penetrate her, defiling her very essence. The shock of it was suffocating, threatening to swallow her whole. She desperately wished to look away, to escape the torment, but a gripping curiosity held her in its clutches. Tied up, helpless, and teetering on the edge of death, Elisa watched the video through her tear-filled eyes. The relentless assault played out with a cruel precision, each blow chipping away at her already shattered spirit. And as the seconds stretched into eternity, Elisa's soul cried out for justice.

The room around her was filled with the anguished silence of the police officers, their eyes locked on the same horror that Elisa watched unfold. They were witnesses, too, to the raw vulnerability of a soul that had been stripped away, piece by piece. The weight of their empathy was palpable, a shared pain that transcended words. Elisa's hand slowly moved from her mouth to cover her heart, as if seeking solace in its rhythmic beat. Her mind wrestled with a whirlwind of emotions, a maelstrom of anger, fear, and disbelief. But amidst the chaos, one question lingered, etching itself into her very being—how had this private hell become public? As she watched on with tears in her eyes, the world around Elisa felt as though it had come to a standstill. The room seemed to fade away, leaving only the piercing reality before her. She felt a sharp pain in her stomach, a sensation that cut through her like a knife. The baby, there was something wrong. Water leaked out of her as she stood and looked at the officers in front of her.

As panic began to rise within her, Elisa's trembling hands clutched her abdomen, her heart pounding with fear. The room suddenly filled with the urgent voices of the officers standing in front of her.

"Elisa, are you okay?" Detective Moony's concerned voice broke through the chaos, filled with a mix of worry and confusion.

"No, she's not," Sergeant Soliman responded urgently, his tone filled with urgency and determination. "Her water just broke. We need to get her to a hospital."

As the officers rushed Elisa to the hospital, their sirens blaring through the night, the news continued its announcement of the breakthrough in the case. The city was captivated by the unfolding events, and everyone was on the edge of their seats, desperate for some closure.

....

Meanwhile, in a quiet neighbourhood, Donald's door was kicked down by a ring of officers. They stormed into his house, their determination evident in their eyes. Every nook and cranny was thoroughly searched, as they meticulously tore apart his hidden apartments. The search seemed never-ending, with each room revealing secrets and surprises. But it was in one particular apartment that the officers came across something that shook them to their core. Hiding in the shadows was Donald's twin brother, Ronald. He had been living a secret life, detached from the world and invisible to everyone. No one, not even those closest to Donald, had any knowledge of Ronald's existence. The news of Ronald's arrest spread like wildfire, causing an uproar among the townsfolk. How could such a sinister secret remain hidden for so long? The once peaceful neighbourhood was now filled with whispers and speculations, as people grappled with the revelation.

As the investigation into Ronald's life began, the similarities and differences between the twins unravelled, painting a perplexing picture. Ronald, the elusive counterpart, carried a mysterious aura that intrigued everyone involved. Journalists, psychologists, and curious onlookers delved into the lives of the twins, trying to uncover the truth behind this baffling discovery. Questions flooded the minds of the people. How could Donald and Ronald lead such different lives without anyone noticing? Did they share the same dark secrets, or was Ronald the puppet master behind it all? The news outlets feasted on this newfound tale of intrigue, presenting it to the public like a tantalizing puzzle. Conversations buzzed with theories and assumptions, as the city became obsessed with the enigmatic twins. In the small city of Cleveland, days turned into weeks, and with every passing moment, the truth began to unravel.

Corruption had infested the very foundations of justice, and the people could no longer turn a blind eye. As the news spread like wildfire, exposing the intricate network of corruption, the wheels of justice began to turn. Arrests were made, and the guilty were brought to light. It was a moment of reckoning, a time for the corrupt to face the consequences of their actions. One by one, the pillars of corruption crumbled. The judge, who had once held immense power, now found himself at the mercy of justice. Sergeant Soliman, a relentless enforcer of the law, marched into his home in front of his children, handcuffs clicking ominously. The fraudulent judge's face was plastered all over the news, a symbol of the fall from grace.

As the men were thrown into prison and convicted, Sergeant Soliman stood by, a mix of satisfaction and sadness in his eyes. He was finally witnessing the right people being held accountable, but it came at a heavy cost. Too many lives had been taken unnecessarily, their voices silenced by the corrupted system. But justice, like a double-edged sword, had its limitations. It could not bring back the lives lost or undo the pain endured. The town, once filled with hope for a fair society, now felt the weight of the scars left behind.

Forty-Five

The Beauty of Nostalgia

Sergeant Soliman stood in the graveyard, rain softly falling on his clothing. He knelt down and placed a bouquet of flowers on Detective Smith's grave, a small tribute to the memories they shared. His heart heavy with sorrow, yet a flicker of satisfaction warming his soul.

The two had been inseparable partners, solving countless crimes together and forging an unbreakable bond. But their partnership was cruelly cut short when Detective Smith was brutally murdered in cold blood, a crime that had haunted Soliman for far too long. For months, Soliman had tirelessly pursued the truth, leaving no stone unturned and no lead unexplored. He faced countless obstacles, fighting against a system that seemed determined to let the case fade away into obscurity. But his determination was unwavering, fuelled by the memory of his fallen partner. Finally, he had managed to bring the perpetrators to justice. Each one of them was now behind bars, their crimes laid bare for the world to see. The satisfaction of knowing justice had been served was bittersweet, for it could never bring Detective Smith back. Standing there, shrouded in the misty rain, Soliman couldn't help but feel a mix of emotions. A sense of closure washed over him, yet the ache of loss remained. He whispered to the grave, the words barely audible among the falling raindrops.

"We did it Smith," he murmured, his voice filled with both sadness and triumph. "We finally brought them to justice." He paused, his mind feeling at peace. "And Elisa, yeah, she sued the fuck out of the city, she's due to get millions. I hope they all rot in hell for what they have done to you all. I've missed you my old friend."

As he stared at the gravestone, memories of their time together flooded his mind. The late nights poring over evidence, the adrenaline-fueled chases through city streets, and the camaraderie that only partners in crime-solving could understand. It was a chapter of his life that had ended, but its impact would forever be etched in his soul. Soliman looked around the desolate graveyard, the solemn silence mingling with the sound of raindrops. His heart ached for the conversations they would never have, the cases they would never solve together. But amidst the sorrow, a question lingered in his mind. What now?

He had fought so hard for justice, dedicating years of his life to unmasking the truth. But with that battle won, a void loomed ahead. The thrill of the chase, the adrenaline rush of piecing together clues, it seemed to dissipate with the rain. Putting on his hat, Sergeant Soliman felt a wave of relief wash over him. The rain had finally subsided, leaving behind a drizzly mist that hung in the air. As he looked out at the cityscape, a thought crossed his mind - it was almost as if the rain itself was trying to communicate with him. With a sense of accomplishment, Sergeant Soliman made his way to his favourite bar, the O'Brien's. It was a place where he could escape the pressures of his job and unwind with a drink. Today, however, was different. Today, he would raise his glass not only to celebrate the closing of the case but also to bid farewell to his life as a Sergeant. As he sat at the bar, the patrons around him were oblivious to the weight of his final triumph. To them, he was just another person seeking solace at the bottom of a glass. But Sergeant

Soliman knew that underneath his calm demeanour, an extraordinary story was coming to an end. He looked back on his twenty years of service, remembering the lives he had touched and the lives he had saved. Every day had been a battle, but today, he felt a sense of peace he had never experienced before. The weight of the world had been lifted off his shoulders, replaced by a deep gratitude for having made a difference.

Chatter and celebration filled the air as Sergeant Soliman's retirement party roared to life. Colleagues and friends clinked glasses, sharing stories and laughter, reminiscing about the good old days. It was the end of an era, and everyone wanted to make the most of it. Amidst the festivity, Detective Soliman found himself seated at the bar, a glass of whisky in hand. He looked over at the empty seat beside him, where Smith, Moony, and himself used to gather almost every day, solving cases and sharing camaraderie. Smith, who had tragically passed away, seemed to materialize before Soliman's eyes. His face was radiant, a smile of gratitude etched upon it. Was Soliman imagining things, or was this a miracle? His heart swelled with joy as he gazed at his friend, who appeared to be alive. Detective Smith raised his glass, a gesture of cheers to their years of friendship and shared experiences. A smile escaped Soliman's lips, a genuine reflection of the happiness he felt in that moment.

But just as suddenly as Smith had appeared, his figure dispersed into thin air. The illusion shattered, leaving Soliman in a state of bewildered wonder. What had just happened? Was it a figment of his imagination, a trick of the light, or something beyond his comprehension? Detective Moony, noticing Soliman's dazed expression, walked over and gently patted him on the back.

"Lost in your thoughts my old friend?"

His gaze shifted to his friend and partner, Detective Moony, who stood beside him. They had been through it all together, chasing down leads, cracking tough cases, and supporting each other through the darkest hours. Soliman turned to Moony, a mixture of nostalgia and reflection in his eyes.

"Lost, nah, not anymore," Soliman said softly, almost to himself.

Moony, understanding the weight of those words, smiled back at him. They both knew that this retirement party marked the end of an era. It was the last time they would stand side by side as colleagues, as warriors fighting for the greater good. But in their hearts, they were grateful for the journey they had shared and the impact they had made. As the night wore on and the festivities continued, Soliman's mind once again drifted back to the countless lives he had touched, the stories left untold. He couldn't shake the feeling that there were still mysteries left unsolved, secrets yet to be uncovered. The world was vast and filled with infinite possibilities, and he couldn't help but wonder what lay beyond the confines of his retirement party.

Sergeant Soliman stood at the threshold of the bar door, his hand pressed against the wooden frame for support. The sound of laughter and clinking glasses filled the air as his colleagues celebrated his retirement party. He hated goodbyes, but deep down, he hoped that everyone knew how appreciative he was to them all. Taking one last glance over his shoulder, he could see the familiar faces of those he had worked with for years. The brotherhood the shared experiences, all encapsulated in that single room. It was bittersweet to leave it all behind. Stepping out into the cool night, Sergeant Soliman's eyes were drawn to the vast expanse of the sky above. Stars twinkled and danced, as if aware of the significant moment in his life. His eyes widened with a mixture of curiosity and hope. With every step away from the bar, he felt a weight lifted off his shoulders, and a sense of freedom washed over him.

As he placed his hat on his head, the wind embraced his long coat, billowing it behind him like a cape. This was a new chapter in his life, one he hoped would be more relaxing and fulfilling. Away from the chaos and demands of his career, he yearned for the peace that had eluded him for so long.

Stories Yet To Be Told

In a mystical land far beyond our reach,
Lived a maiden with eyes as brown as sand on the beach.
Her heart was filled with love and delight,
Always seeking a love that felt just right.

~

Her name shined bright, a maiden so fair,
With brown locks cascading like a sunlit flare.
Every day, she wandered through the enchanted wood,
Hoping to find love, something that felt so good.

~

One summer's eve, as the moon shone bright,
She stumbled upon a beautiful sight.
A man with eyes as deep as the sea,
Stood there, his gaze fixed upon a tree.

~

Intrigued by his presence, she drew near,
Her curiosity ignited, filled with both excitement and fear.
"Good sir," she said, her voice soft and low,
"What is it that captivates you so?"

~

His eyes met hers, filled with an ancient sorrow,
He spoke of a love that was lost, gone by tomorrow.
"I loved once," he said, his voice filled with pain,
"But my past mistakes caused my love's disdain."

~

She listened intently, her heart fluttered fast,
Could this be the love that was meant to last?

She vowed not to let his past taint her view,
For she believed that their love could be true.

~

Days turned into weeks, and weeks into months,
Their love blossomed like enchanted flower bunch.
Hand in hand, they strolled through the meadow,
Their dreams intertwined, like an eternal shadow.

~

But one fateful day, as the sun began to set,
The man vanished, leaving behind only regret.
She called out his name, but no answer she found,
Her heart shattered, crashing without a sound.

~

Years passed, and memories began to fade,
She continued her journey, her spirit still unswayed.
But deep down, a question always remained,
What happened to her love, where had he been detained?

~

With tears in her eyes, she bid him farewell,
Knowing their love story would never run its final spell.
She walked away, heartbroken yet still strong,
For the future held secrets, still untold, where she belonged.

~

We never know what the future may bring,
But in their hearts, a love forever would sing.
For it's in the unknown that life's mysteries unfold,
Leaving us wondering, stories yet to be told.

Forty-Six

Uncharted Territory

I t was a warm summer's evening, the gentle breeze caressing the neighbourhood. The houses stood proudly, their grandeur shining under the golden rays of the setting sun. Each residence in this beautiful neighbourhood was a testament to wealth and success, standing alone in its splendour. The manicured lawns were a vibrant shade of green, glistening as the sprinklers rotated gracefully, adding a touch of magic to the scenery. As the sun dipped lower on the horizon, the neighbours prepared for another day of hard work, rising early and dressing in their finest suits. It was a neighbourhood where success was cherished, and ambitions ran high. The morning hustle and bustle filled the air as cars hummed to life and people rushed to their offices, the sound of their footsteps echoing with determination.

Curiosity fuelled the imagination of the neighbourhood's residents. Who were the fortunate individuals who called this mansion their home? Whispers and tales swirled through the community, adding to the air of mystery that surrounded the magnificent estate. Some claimed it belonged to a renowned celebrity seeking refuge from the prying eyes of the media. Others believed it to be the residence of a successful entrepreneur, their wealth amassed through innovative ventures and shrewd investments. Despite the rumours and speculations, the mansion's inhabitants remained an enigma. The windows were always adorned with lavish curtains, concealing any glimpse into the lives within. The grand double doors, crafted from the finest mahogany, seldom opened, keeping the secrets of the mansion tightly locked away. The residents of the neighbourhood grew even more intrigued as time passed. Parties were held within the mansion's sprawling halls, the sound of laughter and clinking glasses seeping through the cracks in the silence. Elegant soirées and gatherings took place beneath the glow of chandeliers, leaving the observers outside yearning to be a part of the exclusive world behind those closed doors.

Elisa, opened her front door and ventured outside, immediately inhaling the refreshing air. She descended the steps gracefully, her yellow polka-dot dress swaying with each step, her hair elegantly styled in a bun. A smile played upon her lips as she strolled towards the mailbox, anticipation filling her heart. Every week, like clockwork, Elisa received the same white envelope in her mailbox. It had become a routine for her - the anticipation, the curiosity, and the slight apprehension that accompanied each delivery. She knew what was inside. Every time she opened it, her heart would race with a mix of excitement and uncertainty. Today was no different. Elisa took a deep breath and tore open the envelope, her eyes fixed on the contents. As she unfolded the letter, she saw it again - a stack of money neatly placed inside. This was not the first time she had found this unexpected windfall, nor was it the second. For several years now, the mysterious benefactor had been sending her money, without a word or explanation. Elisa's mind raced with questions. Who was behind these generous gestures? And why her? She had never encountered such a situation before. The money was a blessing, undoubtedly, but it also raised a sense of unease within her. She couldn't simply accept it without knowing the motive behind it, especially knowing that she didn't need it.

Lost in her contemplation, Elisa looked up from the letter to absorb her beautiful surroundings. She was standing her picturesque home, surrounded by lush green trees and vibrant flowers. The tranquillity of the place offered a temporary respite from the chaos in her mind. Just as she allowed herself a moment of peace, a sudden commotion caught her attention. A little girl, around eight years old, came rushing towards her. Without any hesitation, she threw herself into Elisa's arms, wrapping her tiny arms tightly around Elisa's neck. Elisa couldn't help but look at her beautiful blue eyes each day. They sparkled like sapphires, reflecting the innocence and joy that only a child possesses. They were a constant reminder of the pure love that existed in her life. As Elisa held her daughter close, a rush of warmth flooded her heart. She couldn't help but marvel at the magic of motherhood. It was as if her entire being had been transformed the moment her daughter came into this world. Her love knew no bounds, and she cherished every moment she spent with her little one.

"Look at you, baby," Elisa spoke softly, her voice filled with tenderness. "You are so beautiful. Let's get you ready for school."

Her daughter nestled in her arms, snuggling closer, cherishing the warmth of their embrace. The scent of fresh flowers wafted through the wind, adding a touch of serenity to their morning routine.

"Okay mummy," her daughter said, her voice filled with excitement as if she too sensed the hidden wonders awaiting them.

Finally, dressed in her school uniform, her daughter stood before Elisa, radiating an innocent joy that melted her heart. Elisa brushed a stray strand of hair away from her daughter's face, her touch gentle and loving. With a sigh, Elisa realized that time was slipping away, and they needed to embark on their daily routine. But something in the air made her pause, a flutter of anticipation that whispered of extraordinary possibilities. Hand in hand, they walked through the front door, their footsteps blending with the melody of nature. The morning sun, still low in the sky, painted the world in shades of gold, casting a magical glow upon everything it touched. Elisa was a woman of routine. Every morning, she would wake up early, make her daughter's lunch, and walk her to school. As they strolled down the street together, Elisa couldn't help but soak in the beauty of the world around her. The way the sunlight filtered through the trees, casting a warm glow on the sidewalk, filled her with a sense of peace and contentment. After bidding her daughter goodbye, Elisa continued her daily ritual with a leisurely walk through the nearby park. The sound of children's laughter filled the air as they ran and played, bringing back memories of her own carefree days as a child. She smiled nostalgically, cherishing the innocence and joy that radiated from the youngsters.

As she wandered further into the park, Elisa's eyes caught sight of a vibrant flower bed. The colours were so captivating that she couldn't resist venturing closer. Inhaling deeply, she allowed the sweet scent of the roses to fill her senses, transporting her back to her grandmother's garden, where she would spend hours surrounded by blooming flowers. Feeling rejuvenated, Elisa decided to take a break at the nearby coffee shop. She found her favourite spot, a cozy nook by the window, and settled down with her book. The bustling atmosphere of the café provided a backdrop of constant motion as people came and went, engrossed in their own lives. Elisa relished the solitude, feeling like an inconspicuous observer in the grand theatre of human existence. Time passed unnoticed as Elisa lost herself in the pages of her book. The waiter approached her table, breaking her reverie. She ordered her usual coffee, grateful for the interruption that brought her back to reality. As the aroma of freshly brewed coffee wafted through the air, Elisa took a sip and felt a surge of warmth spreading through her body.

With her coffee finished and her book read, Elisa gathered her belongings and bid farewell to the coffee shop. The rest of her day unfolded in a series of familiar tasks and chores. Cleaning her home was a cathartic experience for her, a way to find peace and order in her surroundings. Yet, there was one room that Elisa always lingered in a little longer — her daughter's room. It was a sanctuary of dreams and imagination, filled with toys, books, and drawings that showcased her daughter's vibrant personality. Elisa found herself lost in the memories of her daughter's laughter, the sound of her footsteps running down the hallway, and the feeling of her tiny hand intertwined with hers. As Elisa meticulously arranged the toys and tidied up the room, a sense of longing washed over her. She wondered how her daughter was doing at school, what adventures she was embarking on, and what dreams were filling her mind. It was in this moment, surrounded by her daughter's cherished possessions, that Elisa's heart filled with a bitter-sweet mixture of love, pride, and a tinge of melancholy. With a sigh, Elisa completed her task and left the room, closing the door gently behind her. The house seemed strangely quiet, as if it too sensed the absence of her daughter's presence. There was a yearning in the air, an unspoken desire for her return.

As the day drew to a close, Elisa couldn't help but reflect on the passage of time and how quickly her daughter was growing up. She pondered the inevitable journey of life, the moments cherished and lost, and the beauty that lies in every fleeting experience. And so, as Elisa settled into her bed that night, her mind brimming with questions, she found solace in the mysteries of the future. Who would her daughter become? What adventures awaited them both? Only time would reveal the answers, leaving Elisa with a sense of anticipation, wonder, and an unwavering love for the journey that lay ahead.

Forty-Seven

The Future of the Unknown

It was a day like any other for Elisa. After bidding her daughter good-bye at the school gates, she walked back home, her mind focused on the mundane tasks that awaited her. There was never a moment of respite in her busy life, and today was no exception. As she reached her doorstep, she noticed the mailman had left a stack of letters in her mailbox. Elisa absentmindedly collected them, flipping through the envelopes without much interest. Bills, the same envelope with money inside, advertisements, and the occasional invitation to a neighbour-hood event. Nothing out of the ordinary. With a sigh, she decided to take a break from her chores and headed towards the nearby park.

The sun was shining, casting a gentle warmth upon the green grass and blooming flowers. Elisa strolled through the park, taking in the sights and sounds, finding solace in the serenity that surrounded her. After a leisurely walk, she made her way to the local coffee shop. To her surprise, the place was buzzing with activity today. The usual tranquil atmosphere had been replaced by a lively chatter and the clinking of coffee cups. Elisa's curiosity piqued, but she managed to find her favourite seat, a cozy corner where she could observe the bustling crowd. As she sipped her coffee and settled into her seat, she started reading the much-lauded book she had recently purchased. The words on the pages transported her to a different world, captivating her with their beauty and depth. Hours slipped by unnoticed as Elisa became engrossed in the story, losing herself in its enchanting narrative. Time stood still for Elisa until she glanced at her watch in a moment of realization. She had completely lost track of time and now had to rush to pick up her daughter from school. Hastily closing the book, she gathered her belongings. As she rushed to gather her things, the urgency within her grew. She needed to get to the bathroom to clean herself up before leaving. The stain on her blouse was a glaring reminder of the chaos that had ensued just moments before.

In her haste, she darted through the crowded cafe, weaving in and out of people. And then it happened. A jolt, a collision, a disastrous spill. Elisa had bumped into a man, causing her coffee to cascade over his perfectly tailored suit. Barely registering the commotion around her, Elisa looked up, her breath caught in her throat. There, standing before her, was a man she had not noticed until that very moment. He towered over her, his presence commanding attention. Dressed impeccably in a dark navy-blue suit, his shiny shoes gleamed as if they were polished to perfection. His hair was slicked back, highlighting his chiselled features and adding an air of sophistication to his already elegant appearance. But it was his eyes that truly captivated Elisa. Those mesmerizing eyes held a depth and intensity that she couldn't tear her gaze away from. They seemed to carry stories and secrets, as if they had witnessed the wonders and tragedies of the world. Elisa felt an unexpected connection in that moment, a soft spot growing in her heart for this stranger.

Regaining her composure, Elisa stammered out an apology, feeling a rush of embarrassment for her clumsiness.

"I'm so sorry, I didn't see you, oh my goodness, I'm so very sorry," she said, her voice filled with genuine remorse.

In that moment, time seemed to stand still. He was captivated by Elisa's beauty, her delicate features and warm smile making his heart skip a beat. A strange but undeniable connection formed between the two.

With a charming smile, the stranger reassured her.

"It's okay."

Not wanting to leave him in a sticky mess, Elisa insisted.

"Please, let me help." She quickly grabbed some napkins and began to gently clean the coffee off his clothes.

"It's okay, please. Accidents happen," he responded, his gaze focused solely on her.

Though flustered, Elisa couldn't help but notice the tender way he looked at her. It was as if he saw beyond her physicality, finding something deeper that resonated within their souls. A spark ignited between them, and their interaction became more than just a coffee mishap.

Feeling a sense of gratitude, the stranger took the napkins from Elisa's hand, insisting, "I got it, I got it. Thank you."

"I'm so sorry," Elisa apologized once again. "I'm running really late, but if I see you again, I promise to buy you another coffee."

With those words, Elisa hastily gathered her belongings and made her way towards the exit. The gentleman, still captivated by Elisa's charm and grace, watched her disappear into the busy street. He couldn't help but feel a sense of curiosity and an inexplicable connection to this woman. Her beauty, her politeness, and the gentleness that radiated from her intrigued him. But it was something else that resonated within him - a feeling that there was more to Elisa than what met the eye, that she carried a story of strength and resilience. He had to see her again. As he stood in the dimly lit coffee shop, the aroma of freshly brewed coffee wafting through the air, his eyes were fixed on her as she walked away. Her beauty was unmatched, her smile like no other he had ever encountered. It captivated him, pulling him in like a moth to a flame.

Her presence added a touch of enchantment to the room, making it impossible for him to look away. Every movement she made was graceful, her laughter echoing like music in his ears. He couldn't help but wonder who she was and what stories lay behind those mesmerizing eyes. Lost in his thoughts, he promised himself that he would come back to this very coffee shop. With only God on his side, he would meet this beautiful stranger again. It became an undeniable obsession, a burning desire that he couldn't ignore.

Forty-Eight

A Serendipitous Encounter

As the morning sun cast its warm glow on the bustling streets, Liam found himself in the familiar embrace of the cozy café. The aroma of freshly brewed coffee filled the air, intertwining with his anticipation. With a steaming mocha cradled in his hands, he settled into a worn-out armchair, his gaze fixed on the world outside. For three consecutive days, Liam had embarked on a pilgrimage to this very spot, hoping for a serendipitous encounter. Fate had brought him here time and time again, a silent whisper urging him to wait patiently. Today, however, his hope hung on the slimmest of threads. Dressed impeccably in his tailored suit, Liam's appearance juxtaposed the casual ambiance of the café. He glanced at his watch, his mind racing with each passing second. The hands seemed to mock him, slowly ticking away the precious moments he couldn't afford to waste.

The café buzzed with life, a symphony of laughter and animated conversation filling the air. Patrons formed an ebb and flow, their voices rising and falling like the tides of a distant sea. Yet, amidst this delightful chaos, one person remained conspicuously absent. Through the windowpane, Liam's gaze wandered into the bustling city. Each fleeting figure seemed to hold the possibility of her presence. He yearned to see her smile and fall once more into the enchantment of her emerald eyes. Minutes turned into hours, yet the dance of fate evaded Liam's outstretched hand. With each sip of his cooling mocha, his hope waned like a flickering candle in the early morning breeze. The weight of reality settled upon his shoulders, suffocating the last vestiges of optimism. Reluctantly, Liam rose from his seat, a spectre of defeat etched across his face. He adjusted his tie and prepared to face the consequences of his tardiness. But just as he turned to leave, a hush fell upon the bustling café, as if time itself held its breath.

And there she was, Liam couldn't believe his luck. For days, he had been eagerly awaiting the moment he would catch a glimpse of her. And now, in this moment, there she was. A few hours later, dressed in her summer dress, her hair tied up neatly, her lipstick bright red, and her perfectly manicured nails. She was the epitome of beauty. Her presence was like a breath of fresh air, captivating everyone who laid eyes on her. Liam couldn't help but be drawn to her, mesmerized by her elegance and grace. Elisa settled into her seat and retrieved a worn-out book from her bag. It was as if the book held the keys to a secret world, a world she eagerly delved into every day. As she immersed herself in the pages, Liam observed her with fascination. He couldn't help but wonder what story lay within the pages of the book she held so dear. Was it a tale of romance, adventure, or mystery? He yearned to know the secrets hidden between those pages that had the power to transport her to another world. Lost in his own thoughts, Liam studied her every move.

He watched as a friendly waiter approached Elisa, his eyes conveying admiration and respect. Liam admired her politeness and the way she reciprocated the waiter's kindness. With every interaction, Liam felt his heart flutter, as if Cupid had struck him with a love arrow all over again. As time passed, Liam's enchantment grew stronger. He longed to know Elisa's story, to unravel the mystery that surrounded her. What was it about her that made her stand out from the rest? What secrets did she hold behind that captivating smile? He finally mustered up the courage to approach her, his heart pounding loudly in his chest. The cafe was buzzing with the sound of chatter and clinking cups, but his focus was solely on her. Elisa, with her captivating presence and mesmerizing eyes, was completely absorbed in the pages of her book.

With a hopeful smile on his face, he moved closer and took a seat beside her. As he gently placed his hand on her shoulder, hoping to catch her attention, he couldn't help but feel a rush of excitement mixed with nervous anticipation. Her deep concentration broke for a split second, and she turned her head towards him, her eyes filled with curiosity. He took that as an encouraging sign and mustered up the courage to speak.

"Pardon me, but are you the special lady who accidentally spilled coffee all over me a few days ago?" he asked, unable to contain his smile.

Elisa's eyes widened, as if a secret had been revealed. A blush slowly crept up her cheeks, and she closed her book, seemingly captivated by the unexpected encounter. With a smile that mirrored his own, she nodded.

"Yes, it was me, how are you?" Her voice carried a mixture of embarrassment and intrigue, as if she couldn't quite believe they had crossed paths again.

His heart skipped a beat, both relieved and excited that she remembered the incident. As he mustered up the courage to speak, he managed to utter,.

"I'm very well, thanks. Mind if I sit?"

She smiled warmly, her eyes twinkling with familiarity.

"Yes, please. I do owe you a coffee, don't I?" Her gaze lingered on his big blue eyes, filled with a sense of connection.

"That's correct," he replied, a hint of playfulness in his voice. "And a suit too, please. That would be great." They both laughed, the tension dissipating into the air. Elisa joined in with a childlike giggle, suddenly feeling at ease in his presence.

"I'm Liam," he said, extending his hands towards Elisa.

His gesture was a mixture of formality and an invitation for a fresh start. She hesitated for a moment, as if contemplating whether to take his hand or not. Without breaking eye contact, she finally reached out and clasped his hand, creating a spark of electricity that neither of them could deny.

"Nice to meet you Liam, I'm Elisa," she said, her voice filled with warmth and genuine interest.

Liam was immediately captivated by her presence once again. Her soft demeanour and friendly nature made him feel instantly at ease. As he shook her hand, he couldn't help but notice the way her eyes seemed to light up when she smiled.

"Elisa, that's a wonderful name," he replied, a genuine smile now gracing his lips as inquisitiveness started to get the better of him.

Elisa couldn't help but ask, "I've never seen you around here before."

Liam chuckled lightly as he replied.

"Well, I've just moved here actually, wanted a better view," his eyes meeting hers, a subtle hint of mischief dancing within them.

Elisa felt a warmth in her heart that she hadn't felt in a long time. The troubled past she had endured seemed to fade away with every word spoken. She couldn't help but be drawn to this man, who had become a beacon of hope in her otherwise weary existence. Liam too, was enchanted by Elisa. He had never met someone who understood him so effortlessly. The connection they shared was undeniable, and he couldn't bear the thought of parting ways with her. As he glanced at his watch, he realized he wouldn't make it to work on time. But in that moment, it didn't matter. Without hesitation, Liam made the bold decision to cancel his plans for the day. The message to his boss was quickly typed and sent as he continued listening to Elisa's every word. He didn't want to let this opportunity slip away. For the first time in a long time, he felt alive.

Elisa noticed Liam was engrossed in his phone. Intrigued by his apparent distraction, she couldn't help but be curious about what was capturing his attention. A smile danced across her lips.

"Have to run off to work?" she asked, her tone laced with playfulness.

Liam looked up, his bright eyes meeting hers. A smile tugged at the corners of his lips as he replied.

"Erm, no, not today."

Elisa continued the conversation.

"What do you do for work, if you don't mind me asking?"

Liam chuckled, his smile growing wider.

"You can ask me anything you want. I work in the trade service. I used to work in transport before I moved here, but I like the quiet life.

It's peaceful. Plus, I get to see the most beautiful woman I've ever set my eyes upon. So I guess it's a win for me."

Elisa's cheeks flushed with a mix of surprise and contentment. Her heart fluttered as she absorbed his words. In that moment, the world seemed to fade away, leaving only the two of them in a bubble of lust. As the hours blended into one another, the café buzzed with life around them. Their conversation continued to thrive, filled with laughter, shared dreams, and unexpected confessions. The world seemed to fade away, leaving only the two of them in their own little bubble of happiness.

Lost in the moment, Elisa and Liam barely noticed the waiter approaching their table. Startled, they looked up, caught off guard by his presence.

"Can I get you anything else?" the waiter asked, his voice gentle. It took a moment for the words to register with Elisa and Liam, their minds still swimming in their conversation.

Elisa's eyes widened.

"Erm, yes please, one..." she pointed at Liam, her eyes meeting his momentarily before returning to the waiter.

Liam smiled at Elisa as he knew she wanted to still buy him that coffee. He looks at the waiter and responded.

"Yes, one hot chocolate for me please, thank you."

The waiter nodded, a small smirk playing at the corner of his lips as he wrote down the order.

"Ahh, hot chocolate, my absolute favourite," Elisa remarked, her eyes sparkling with anticipation.

With their orders taken, the waiter gracefully retreated, blending into the background of the bustling café. Elisa and Liam exchanged giggles, their conversation picking up where it had left off. Hours melted away as they delved deeper into their thoughts and stories, their voices intertwined with laughter and shared experiences.

Forty-Nine

The Deepest Connection of All

Elisa's life had taken another incredible turn. After meeting Liam, everything seemed to fall into place. They went on countless dates, each one more magical than the last. From dinners at fancy restaurants to bowling nights and romantic walks in the park, their bond grew stronger with every shared experience. Liam had a way of making Elisa feel like the most important person in the world. He would playfully lift her petite frame and twirl her around as they laughed under the golden sun. No one had ever understood her the way Liam did.

He seemed to know some of her deepest desires and darkest secrets, even the ones she had left behind in her past. But there was one thing Elisa hadn't yet revealed to Liam. It was a part of her life that she had tried to bury, to forget. She was afraid of what he might think, afraid of losing this perfect love she had found. Yet, as their connection deepened, Elisa couldn't deny the growing certainty in her heart. She wanted to spend the rest of her life with Liam. The thought of a future without him seemed unimaginable. But she couldn't shake the nagging feeling that her secret might shatter the idyllic world they had created together.

Days turned into weeks, and weeks turned into months. Elisa and Liam's love only blossomed further, becoming a beacon of hope in their lives. It was a love that felt timeless, unbreakable. They were inseparable, their souls intertwined. But as Elisa delved deeper into her feelings for Liam, her secret began to haunt her every waking moment. She knew she had to tell him, to let him see the shadows of her past. The weight of it all consumed her, threatening to tear apart the delicate fabric of their relationship. As she carefully dressed up, her mind raced with thoughts of how he would react. Would he be surprised? Overwhelmed? Would he still love her after knowing the truth? She couldn't bear the thought of keeping anything from him any longer. Before leaving, she quietly tiptoed into her daughter's room, planting a gentle kiss on her forehead and whispering a soft goodnight. With a reassuring nod from the babysitter, she stepped into the waiting taxi, the engine humming with a sense of urgency that mirrored her own.

The journey to Liam's house felt like an eternity. Every minute seemed to stretch on forever, her thoughts intertwining with the passing streetlights. What if he didn't feel the same way? What if her confession changed everything between them? But she couldn't ignore her heart's relentless desire to be honest and vulnerable. As the taxi pulled up outside Liam's elegant home, her hands trembled with a mixture of nerves and anticipation. Stepping out, she took a deep breath and gathered her courage. And there he was, standing at the door, dressed in his impeccably tailored suit. Liam's eyes sparkled with genuine delight as he saw her. Without a moment's hesitation, he pulled her into a warm embrace, his arms enveloping her like a shield against her fears. Their lips met in a tender kiss, a silent reassurance of the connection they shared. They exchanged smiles, the unspoken love between them shimmering in the air. Liam gallantly paid the taxi fare, an act of chivalry that made her heart flutter even more. Hand in hand, they entered his luxurious home, the door closing behind them with a quiet click. Walking into Liam's home, Elisa couldn't help but be overwhelmed by the sight that greeted her. Liam had planned a romantic dinner, but this was beyond anything she could have imagined. His beautiful house, lavishly decorated in red, felt like stepping into a fairy-tale. Red petals rolled through the house, leading her into the kitchen, where a well-dressed cook waited for her.

As Liam guided her through the doorway, Elisa's eyes widened in awe.

"Wow, this is incredible," she breathed, unable to contain her astonishment.

Liam smiled, his eyes sparkling with affection.

"It's all for you, my love. I wanted to make tonight special."

Elisa couldn't help but blush at his words. Liam had always been thoughtful and attentive, but this was on another level. She moved further into the kitchen, mesmerized by the exotic scents that filled the air. Shocked, she covered her mouth as she took in the sight before her. There, standing at a spotless marble counter, was a Chinese chef, ready to create the most extravagant meal she had ever had. The chef, dressed in traditional attire, looked up and greeted Elisa with a warm smile. Elisa was at a loss for words, her mind racing to comprehend the effort Liam had put into this surprise. As the chef began to cook, Elisa could only marvel at the precision and skill with which he moved. Each chop of his knife was executed with grace, each ingredient added with a precise measure. The kitchen was a symphony of Flavors and aromas, and Elisa felt like she had been transported to a different world.

As the evening progressed, Liam and Elisa enjoyed a delicious meal, their laughter filling the air. They shared stories, dreams, and the love they had for each other. The atmosphere was alive with warmth and happiness. Elisa had never felt more loved and cherished than in that very moment. The night was fading into the shadows, but Elisa could feel the weight of unspoken words hanging in the air. She found herself sinking into the plush sofa, her legs draped over Liam's lap, as they savoured the remaining moments of the evening. The taste of wine lingered on her lips, a bittersweet reminder of the confession she longed to make. With a nervous laugh, Elisa took a deep breath and looked into Liam's eyes. They sparkled with interest and affection, giving her the courage to speak her truth. She knew that now, in this intimate moment, she needed to bare her soul and reveal the depths of her love.

"Liam," she began, her voice hushed yet determined, "there's something I need to tell you. Something that I've been holding onto, afraid to share, but tonight, I realize that it's time."

Liam's brows furrowed slightly, his attention fully captivated by Elisa's words. He set his glass of wine aside, giving her his undivided attention as she continued. Unable to resist any longer, Liam leaned in and pressed his lips against hers. The world around them faded away as they surrendered to the intoxicating passion that enveloped them. Elisa's heart fluttered as she allowed herself to fully embrace the kiss, feeling a surge of emotions that she had long forgotten. With each touch, each caress, a dormant desire awakened within Elisa. For years, she had closed herself off, guarding her heart and body from the pain and disappointment that love often brought. But Liam had managed to break through those walls, making her feel alive again. It was a vulnerability she had never experienced before, but one that she welcomed wholeheartedly.

In that moment, as their lips parted, Elisa looked deep into Liam's eyes. There was an unspoken understanding between them, a silent promise of trust and acceptance. Without hesitation, she took his hand and led him towards the sanctuary of the master bedroom. The room was dimly lit, casting soft shadows on the walls. Elisa slowly removed her dress, revealing the scars that adorned her body. Each mark told a story, a painful reminder of battles fought and wounds healed. Liam's eyes traced the lines, but instead of judgment or pity, they held a genuine admiration and tenderness. No words were exchanged as they stood before one another, baring not just their physical selves, but their deepest vulnerabilities. It was a moment of raw truth, where their pasts collided with their present, intertwining their souls in an irrevocable bond. Liam cautiously approached Elisa.

The air was heavy with an unspoken sorrow, and as he drew nearer, he observed a solitary teardrop slowly making its way down her delicate cheek. Liam's mind raced, he silently wondered what had brought her to this moment of vulnerability. His eyes fixated on her weary form, he then gracefully sank to his knees. With gentle hands, he delicately removed her high heels, one by one. Elisa, a picture of strength, gracefully stepped out of each shoe, her height diminishing with every passing moment. One could almost feel the weight of the world being shed with each step she took.

Liam, now mesmerized by the woman before him, decided to offer a form of solace that transcended the physical realm. He tenderly pressed his lips against her toes, one by one, carefully moving upwards towards her thighs. Every scar that adorned her body received a kiss, as if he was attempting to erase the pain etched into her very being. As Liam continued his intimate gesture, he couldn't help but notice a transformation. Elisa's head fell back, her eyes closed as if in a moment of bliss. It was as if his kisses held a power beyond comprehension, a power capable of healing not just her physical wounds, but the scars that ran deep within her soul. The room seemed to hold its collective breath as Liam's lips caressed each mark, marking a journey towards redemption. Time stood still as the ethereal connection between them grew stronger, the weight of their shared pain slowly dissipating.

And then, Liam stopped. Still on his knees, he looked between Elisa's thighs, a mixture of excitement and nervousness filling his veins. This was the moment he had been waiting for, dreaming about, for what seemed like an eternity. He had forgotten the anticipation, the longing that consumed him each day until now. As he stares at Elisa's pussy lips, time seemed to stand still. The world around them blurred, and Liam focused solely on her vagina. He could see the universe reflected in her irises, a vast expanse of unknown possibilities. The weight of their history and unspoken desires hung in the air, creating a charged atmosphere that crackled with electricity. His intense gaze pierced through her, as if he knew every secret she held within her soul. He spoke not a word, yet his eyes conveyed a story that intrigued her beyond measure. It was an unspoken invitation to a world she had never known, and her heart couldn't resist its allure.

He pressed his lips against her pussy, gently parting them with a light thrust of his tongue. His beard brushed against the delicate skin of her outer labia, tasting like the sweet nectar of her arousal. Elisa moaned in pleasure as he kissed her intimately, his hot breath tickling her clit and sending shivers through her body. He moved slowly and deliberately, like a conductor leading an orchestra from the podium. He feasted on her like a hungry animal, plunging deep into her folds while his lips tugged at her clit. His stubbled beard scratched her delicate skin, driving her wild with pleasure as his hot breath sent sparks racing through her body. He changed pace abruptly, taking control as if conducting an intense symphony of pleasure for Elisa to enjoy while the crescendo built up and peaked until she was overwhelmed with joy.

Elisa's breathing quickened as he slowly knelt and tasted her abdomen, tracing his tongue along the ridges of healed scars. He then made his way up her torso, planting small tingling kisses on each of her breasts. Her moans grew louder and she dug her nails into his back, trying to control the pleasure that was coursing through her body. His lips moved up to her neck, creating a trail of sweet love marks as he went. Finally, their lips met and Elisa felt every sensation, from his velvet tongue inside her mouth to the warmth of his embrace enveloping her completely. Elisa couldn't help but be mesmerized by the allure of Liam's face. It was a face that portrayed not only physical attractiveness but also a kindness that resonated deep within. His eyes, like pools of reassurance, held a mysterious shade of red that sparked curiosity in Elisa's heart.

Liam carefully picked Elisa up and placed her on the bed. He gazed at her as if she was everything he had ever dreamed of in a woman. Her perfect ten face was framed by long brown hair that cascaded down to her shoulders, and her hourglass curves were enough to turn any head. She had an amazing body--her thirty-six double-D breasts were the most beautiful thing he'd ever seen, and something about her brown eyes and cheery smile made him feel alive. He then began removing his garments, standing right above her. Elisa watched breathlessly as Liam dropped his pants and revealed his six-foot four-inch frame. His impressive manhood rose at attention for her. She marvelled at it--it was just like she imagined it would be: eight inch hard with throbbing veins and a flushed pink head that glistened with pre-cum. In that moment, he knew it was not about him tonight; this was all for Elisa.

Liam gripped Elisa tightly, his hands stroking her skin as if it was delicate silk. He smothered her body with kisses before spreading open her thighs and feasting on her anus, eliciting low moans of pleasure from deep within her. His masterful technique sent waves of ecstasy through her body, forcing her to surrender to the sensations he evoked. She was temporarily blinded by a dazzling blue light that appeared in her mind's eye until Liam abruptly pulled her up into an embrace and headed towards the hot tub. Without hesitation he submerged himself beneath the steaming water, and began hungrily devouring her vagina. The intensity of Elisa's cries echoed off the summer night like thunder. Time drifted by as if suspended in a dream, until Liam's lips suddenly crashed into Elisa's with a rough intensity. His hands found their way to her throat, creating an unexpected moment of vulnerability. Elisa's face showed a mix of surprise and concern, unsure of the sudden change in the dynamics, her past quickly bringing back memories of that fateful night.

Sensing her unease, Liam immediately stopped, his eyes searching hers for understanding. As he released his grip, his touch transformed from rough to gentle, like a wave turning from a tempest to a caress. He then slowly slipped his fingers inside of her, allowing the water to flow in with them. Elisa could tell that she wanted him now. Moments later, Elisa and Liam were locked in a passionate embrace in the shower. She felt him push her around and bend her over slowly, before inserting himself inside of her. Elisa's eyes widened in amazement at the size of him. Her legs quivered from the sensation—it had been many years since she wanted someone this badly. She felt as if she were in some other realm, a heavenly place, as he moved deeper into her and she welcomed it. Taking deep breaths, she embraced his size. For hours they engaged each other passionately and Elisa was amazed by the healing power of their connection. Eventually, as she lay on his chest, watching him drift off to sleep, Elisa's entire being filled with love for him; a feeling so deep that it seemed like he already knew her deepest secrets without her having to tell them. And in that moment, she knew with every fibre in her being, that she wanted to spend the rest of her life with this man.

Fifty

The Aroma of Cinnamon

As the sun streamed through the kitchen window, casting a warm glow on the countertops, Elisa hummed a tune while she prepped the ingredients for dinner. It was a Sunday, her favourite day of the week, and she felt a sense of peace and contentment as she moved about the kitchen. After marinating the chicken with her secret blend of spices, she carefully placed it in the oven, making sure to set the timer just right. As the savoury aroma of roasting chicken began to fill the kitchen, Elisa turned her attention to the dessert. She mixed the batter for a decadent cinnamon cake and slid it into the oven, the scent of cinnamon and sugar mingling with the appetizing notes of the chicken. As she tidied up, wiping down the countertops and loading the dishes into the dishwasher, a feeling of satisfaction washed over her. Everything was falling into place, and she couldn't wait for everyone to gather around the table and enjoy the feast she had prepared.

With time ticking away, Elisa eagerly awaited the moment when the meal would be ready. She checked the oven again, ensuring that the chicken was cooking to perfection and the cake was rising beautifully. Just as she was about to take a well-deserved break, the timer beeped, signalling that the chicken was done. She opened the oven door and a smile spread across her face as she marvelled at the golden-brown chicken and the perfectly puffed cinnamon cake. As the delicious scents filled the air, Elisa's mind wandered, contemplating the joys that the day would bring. She imagined the smiles and laughter of the people she loved the most, as they gathered around the dinner table, enjoying the fruits of her labour. As the warm aroma of freshly baked cookies filled the kitchen, Elisa's daughter came running through the door, her eyes sparkling with excitement.

"Mummy, mummy!" she exclaimed, wrapping her tiny arms around Elisa.

"Hey there, my little nugget," Elisa replied, lifting her daughter into her arms.

"Something smells wonderful," her daughter remarked, her nose twitching with anticipation.

"Well, that must be the cookies, or is it the cinnamon cake? Either way, I promise that when they're all finished, you can have the first special cookie, okay?" Elisa said, playfully pointing at her daughter's nose. "Now, go and get ready. You're meeting someone very special today."

"Is it Santa?" her daughter asked, eyes wide with wonder.

"No, silly, it's not even Christmas yet," Elisa chuckled.

"Is it the tooth fairy?" her daughter inquired, eyes wide with wonder as she clutched her tiny tooth in one hand.

"Noooo, I don't think you'll ever meet the tooth fairy, baby. Now remember I said it was a surprise, so let's get you cleaned up and ready," Elisa replied playfully, a mischievous glint in her eyes. She scooped up her daughter, who erupted into giggles as they made their way to the bathroom, the sound of music trailing behind them.

As Elisa bathed her daughter, the air filled with laughter and the scent of soap, creating an atmosphere of warmth and joy. With her little one fresh and sweet-smelling, Elisa wrapped her in a fluffy towel and carried her to the bedroom. As she began to dress her daughter, the anticipation in the room was clear. After the final buttons were fastened and the last strands of hair were lovingly combed, Elisa scooped her daughter into her arms and twirled merrily, both of them caught in a moment of pure happiness. The evening stretched ahead of them, full of promise and mystery.

Fifty-One

The Power of Blue

As Elisa placed the final earring into her ear, she couldn't help but marvel at the reflection staring back at her in the mirror. Dressed in a long, elegant black dress accentuating every curve, with a vibrant red cardigan adding a pop of colour, she looked nothing short of spectacular. A delicate bow nestled in her hair completed her enchanting ensemble. As she sprayed a hint of perfume, a soft smile graced her lips. For a moment, she pondered how she had arrived at this contented place in her life. Elisa had made a conscious effort to leave the past behind, embracing each day with renewed optimism.

However, there were moments when memories of bygone days lingered, haunting her like a persistent shadow. She stood in front of the mirror, her hand gently caressing her face. Her eyes searched for answers, delving into the depths of her soul. With a deep breath, Elisa closed her eyes, relishing in the tranquillity that surrounded her. As she opened them, a radiant smile illuminated her face. She knew that despite the trials and tribulations, she had found solace within herself. The journey hadn't been easy, but it had led her to this beautiful, serene moment.

As she stood in the dimly lit hallway, she felt a peculiar sense of fulfillment creeping over her. She was about to speak the words aloud, to make sense of the swirling emotions when the doorbell rang, breaking her reverie. Hurrying down the staircase, she flung the door open to reveal Liam, standing there with an air of quiet confidence. His presence was a balm to her disquieted mind, and she found herself instantly drawn to him. Two separate bunches of roses, one pink and the other red, were cradled in his arms, adding a pop of colour to the otherwise dull setting.

Liam, usually impeccably dressed in a sharp suit, was now clad in casual attire. His blond locks, slightly longer than usual, framed his chiselled features, and she couldn't help but admire his rugged yet refined appearance. As their eyes locked, a familiar warmth settled in her chest, and she was reminded of the depth of her affection for him. Without a word, Liam leaned in and planted a gentle kiss on her lips, enveloping her in a tender embrace. In that moment, the world around them seemed to fade away, leaving only the undeniable connection they shared. As she melted into his arms, she realized that she truly loved the man standing before her.

"You look beautiful, baby," Liam said, his voice filled with genuine admiration.

Elisa laughed softly, the sound like music in the air.

"You too. I love the casual wear today," she said, her eyes lingering on him.

"Well, I thought about it, and I didn't want to look too businessy. Maybe that would scare her," Liam joked.

As Liam stepped through the doorway of Elisa's home, a rush of conflicting emotions swirled within him. Excitement and apprehension tangled together, creating a bittersweet sensation that seemed to echo through the walls. His heart raced with nervous anticipation, as if he were about to encounter something of immense significance. Yet, in reality, he was simply about to meet a six-year-old girl. As he took in the surroundings, the warmth and coziness of Elisa's home welcomed him, offering a sense of comfort amidst his uncertainty. But before he could gather his thoughts, a sudden movement caught his eye. A small figure darted into the room, heading straight for Elisa.

"Mummy!" the little girl exclaimed, throwing her arms around Elisa in an exuberant hug.

"Hey, baby," Elisa greeted her daughter with a smile. "There's someone I want you to meet." Cradling her daughter in her arms, she turned to Liam. "Charlene, this is Liam. Liam, this is Charlene—my very precious cheeky little nugget."

The rest of Elisa's words faded into a hushed murmur as a wave of realization washed over Liam. The pieces fell into place, and a profound sense of awe and disbelief settled upon him. He gazed at the little girl with wide eyes, trying to comprehend the inexplicable truth that was unravelling before him. There, in the innocence and purity of Charlene's gaze, he saw something extraordinary. It was as if time itself had looped back upon itself, weaving an enigmatic web that connected the past, present, and future in a way that defied all logic and reason. Liam gazed at Charlene, nestled in Elisa's arms, and felt a surge of emotions welling up inside him. Her red and black Mickey Mouse dress was an adorable contrast to her tiny frame, with her hair neatly tied up in a bun and a red bow perched atop her head. Every detail about her seemed perfect, but it was her eyes that captivated him the most. They were the deepest shade of blue, reminiscent of the vast expanse of the ocean. It was as if he could lose himself in those mesmerizing eyes forever. In that fleeting moment, something profound stirred inside Liam. He felt an overwhelming desire to protect and cherish Charlene for the rest of his days, and beyond. He made a silent promise to himself, vowing to be her guardian and confidant, to support her through every joy and sorrow.

As Liam extended his hands to greet Charlene, a spark of curiosity flashed in her eyes.

"Well, hello Charlene, it's very lovely to meet you," he said with a warm smile.

Charlene, still in her mother's arms, eyeing him intently.

"Well, you're not Santa," she responded wittily, causing laughter to fill the room.

The dinner proceeded, filled with shared jokes and heartfelt conversations. Elisa skillfully passed around the delicious dishes as everyone enjoyed the flavours of the meal. Liam felt a sense of contentment wash over him as he looked at the joyful faces around the table. This was exactly what he had longed for—a sense of belonging, a family of his own. Despite his past mistakes, he found solace in this moment, realizing that this is what he wanted for the rest of his life. As the evening drew to a close, Liam couldn't help but reflect on the events that led him to this point. His journey had been a tumultuous one, marked by trials and tribulations. Yet, as he looked at the loving faces of his newfound family, he knew that every struggle had led him to this exact moment. In the quiet of the night, the soft glow of the TV illuminated the room as Liam watched over young Charlene, her gentle breaths lulling him into a sense of peace. He could feel her tiny frame nestled against him, her innocence radiating in the stillness of the room. The movie had come to an end, but the magic of the moment lingered, casting a spell of warmth and tenderness over them all. As Elisa joined them, Liam couldn't help but steal a glance at her, a silent exchange passing between them. He gently gestured for her to carry Charlene to bed, but to his surprise, Elisa insisted that they do it together.

"She's fast asleep," Liam whispered, not wanting to disturb the tranquillity that had settled around them.

"It's alright," Elisa replied, her voice filled with a quiet understanding. "Let's take her up together."

With careful movements, Liam lifted Charlene, her peaceful slumber a testament to the joy and wonder she had experienced that day. Liam felt a surge of tenderness as they carried her to bed, the weight of her trust and innocence resting gently in their arms. As the moonlight seeped through the curtains, Elisa crept along the hallway, her feet barely making a sound on the plush carpet. Liam followed close behind, his heart heavy with the weight of the tiny, slumbering girl in his arms. Charlene had been through so much, and now it was up to them to give her the love and care she deserved. As they reached Charlene's room, Elisa paused, allowing Liam to enter first, as she switched on the lights. The room was a kaleidoscope of colours and dreams, with its walls adorned with pink paintings of ponies and butterflies. It was a sight to behold, a sanctuary for a little girl's imagination. Charlene's large princess bed beckoned, adorned with flowing drapes that danced in the gentle night breeze.

Liam carefully laid Charlene down, tucking her in with the soft, warm covers. As he bent to kiss her goodnight, Charlene stirred, her eyes fluttering open for a brief moment. In that fleeting instant, she saw the love and tenderness in Liam's eyes, and felt the warmth of a newfound family surrounding her. As Elisa stepped out of Charlene's room, a warmth enveloped her heart. Her daughter lay there, peaceful and serene, her sleeping form bathed in the soft glow of the nightlight. With a gentle smile, Elisa switched off the lights, casting the room into a gentle darkness. She paused for a moment, looking at the little universe her daughter had created within those four walls – the posters of her favourite colour ponies, the stack of books on her bedside table, and the cherished drawings on the walls. Her heart swelled with a deep sense of love and gratitude. As they made their way down the hall, Elisa left the door slightly ajar, allowing a sliver of light to spill into the hall-way. It was a small gesture, a silent promise of protection and love.

As Liam stepped into Elisa's bedroom, he was immediately struck by the elegance and opulence of the room. The large, beautiful bed was the centerpiece, exuding an air of luxury and comfort. The soft glow of the bright white lights from the chandelier added a dreamlike quality to the atmosphere. His gaze settled on Elisa, who stood before him with a mysterious smile. Their eyes met, and without a word, she approached him, her movements graceful and hypnotic. As she leaned in, her lips met his in a tender yet passionate kiss. He was taken aback by her boldness, but he couldn't deny the magnetic pull between them. He responded to her embrace, feeling a rush of emotions and desires that left him breathless. In that fleeting moment, time seemed to stand still as they were lost in each other's embrace. The intensity of their connection was undeniable, transcending any logical explanation. But as quickly as it had begun, the kiss ended, leaving him longing for more. Without a word, Elisa unbuttoned her dress and slipped it off of her shoulders. He looked down at her breasts and softly kissed their pink roundness. Lifting his arms, he pulled his shirt over his head and stripped out of his pants and underwear before spreading his legs slightly and opening himself to her.

She teased him with gentle strokes that slowed every now and then, enough to stoke the fires but not quite cause an eruption. When she was sure he was moist from the attention she had been giving him, she took him in both hands and started to slide them up and down his shaft while licking its underside. Liam tried desperately to stifle his moans knowing that Charlene was in the other room. Just before he could ejaculate, he took it out of her mouth, standing her up and bending her over the bed. Kneeling down on the floor, he licked her clitoris tenderly until she softly moaned in pleasure. Stimulating her clit for what felt like hours but was really only minutes, he stood back up slowly. Reaching one hand around to feel where they were joined, he gently pushed forward entering her warm wet valley slick with passion juices. Minutes later they were lying on the bed curled into each other's arms watching the sun rise on a new day holding onto each other as if neither of them would survive if something should happen to the other.

Fifty-Two

Eternity's Promise

As the moon cast its gentle glow over the park, Elisa and Liam strolled hand in hand, their laughter mingling with the soft rustle of leaves. The evening had been a tapestry of joy, filled with shared secrets, stolen glances, and the warmth of kindred spirits. This night held a magic that seemed to whisper promises of forever in their ears. As they found themselves at their favourite spot in the park, the world seemed to stand still. Elisa could feel Liam's nervous energy, and she couldn't help but wonder what he might be thinking. As they sat down on the familiar bench, the air crackled with prediction. Suddenly, Liam rose to his feet, a playful glint in his eyes. Elisa's heart skipped a beat as he knelt before her, the moonlight bathing them in its ethereal embrace. With trembling hands, he produced a glistening ring, and his eyes shone with a love that transcended words.

Amidst the calm, Liam suddenly stopped, his eyes shining with a mix of nervousness and overwhelming love. His voice shook as he uttered the words that had been weighing on his heart for so long.

"Elisa, I love you more than anything in this world," Liam's voice trembled with emotion, "I want to spend the rest of my days making you happy. From the moment that I met you, I knew that I wanted to spend the rest of my life with you. I know that I'm not perfect, but who is? You are the love of my life, and I promise to make you the happiest woman each and every day. I promise to communicate with you, to feed you seafood and cherish you." They both smiled in that moment, knowing how much Elisa loved seafood. "I want to continue to kiss your pain away, I want to make love to you for the rest of my life. I love you, and only you. Will you marry me?"

Elisa stood speechless, her heart pounding with a mixture of joy and disbelief. Tears glistened in her eyes as she nodded, unable to find the words to express the overwhelming rush of emotions coursing through her. As Liam slipped the ring onto her finger, the park echoed with the birds' chorus, as if nature itself was celebrating the union of two souls bound by love. Elisa' breath caught in her throat as tears welled up in her eyes. Her lips curved into a radiant smile, and she nodded, unable to find her voice amidst the overwhelming rush of joy and love. As Liam slipped the ring onto her finger, they embraced, the world around them disappearing into a symphony of love and hope.

In the weeks that followed, Elisa and Liam busied themselves with planning their upcoming wedding, each moment filled with excitement and love. The air was filled with happiness, and every detail seemed to fall perfectly into place as they prepared to embark on the next chapter of their lives together. As the big day approached, their hearts beat in unison, echoing the rhythm of their deep love for each other. Finally, the moment arrived when they stood before their friends and family, ready to exchange vows and declare their everlasting love. The sun-bathed the outdoor ceremony in a warm, golden glow, casting a magical aura over the couple as they spoke the words that bound their souls together. In the midst of the celebration, Charlene, Elisa's delightful daughter, danced and twirled with unbridled joy to the music that filled the air. With her laughter mingling with the harmonious melody, the scene radiated pure happiness.

Elisa's heart swelled with love and gratitude as she kissed her daughter's forehead. Surrounding her, the room was filled with joyful faces of their loved ones. This moment of bliss was everything she had ever dreamed of. Her heart overflowed with contentment, and yet, there was a lingering ache within her. On this, one of the happiest days of her life, Elisa wished her parents could be here to witness it. Their absence weighed on her heart, a void that could never be filled. She longed for their warm smiles and comforting presence. She missed their wise counsel and unwavering support. Her best friend, Charlene, was another person Elisa yearned for at this precious moment. They had been inseparable since childhood, sharing laughter, tears, and dreams. However, fate had snatched Charlene away far too soon, leaving Elisa with only memories of their adventures and secrets.

As Elisa scanned the room, her eyes caught a glimpse of the night sky outside the window. The stars twinkled like diamonds against the velvety darkness.

'Maybe, just maybe, her loved ones were watching over her from above.' She thought to herself.

With a renewed sense of hope, Elisa whispered to the sky, "I hope you're proud of me, Mom and Dad. I wish you were here to witness this beautiful day. And Charlene, my dear friend, I miss you more than words can express."

She closed her eyes, feeling a gentle breeze caress her face, as if carrying her words to her loved ones in the heavens. A sense of peace washed over her, reminding her that the bonds of love never truly vanish.

Fifty-Three

Timeless Footprints

Years passed, and Charlene blossomed into a remarkable young woman, embodying the grace and kindness that her mother had always admired. She had grown from a curious and adventurous child to a compassionate and strong-willed individual, ready to make her mark on the world. Meanwhile, Elisa and Liam's love only deepened with time. Their bond had weathered storms and celebrated countless joys, and they couldn't imagine life without each other. They supported each other's dreams and aspirations, nurturing their relationship with love and understanding. Then, just when life seemed to settle into its comforting rhythm, a new revelation dawned upon them – Elisa was pregnant once again.

The news sent ripples of astonishment and delight through their family, and as they embraced this unexpected twist of fate, they found themselves filled with a renewed sense of wonder and love. As the months passed, Elisa's belly grew round with life, and the house was filled with a buzzing energy. They prepared the nursery, choosing colours and furniture that would welcome their new bundle of joy into the world. Charlene, brimming with excitement, began reading books on siblings and helping her parents prepare for the arrival of her baby brother or sister.

The day finally arrived, and Elisa's labour was intense but filled with excitement. Liam stood by her side, holding her hand and whispering words of encouragement. Charlene paced outside the delivery room, anxiously awaiting news of her new sibling. And then, a cry pierced the air, announcing the arrival of their baby. Elisa's eyes filled with tears of joy as the newborn was placed in her arms. Liam couldn't contain his emotions, his heart swelling with love for the tiny being they had brought into the world. As the family celebrated the new addition, they marvelled at the miracle of life. They watched as Charlene held her baby sibling, a mix of awe and protectiveness in her eyes. The circle of love expanded, intertwining their lives in a tapestry of joy, challenges, and endless possibilities.

Years passed once again, and the family thrived. Charlene and her sibling shared adventures and secrets, forming a bond that would withstand the test of time. They laughed, they cried, and they grew together, each day filled with love, support, and cherished memories. But amidst the laughter and innocent chaos, a question lingered in Charlene's mind. She couldn't shake off the feeling that there was something more, something hidden beneath the surface. It was as if the universe held a secret for her, whispering its mysteries into her ear. The sisters grew older. Charlene embarked on her own journey, her dreams taking her to far-off places, and yet, the question remained. It followed her like a loyal companion, tugging at her heart-strings, urging her to seek the truth. But for now, she was happy with life, until God was truly ready to answer her questions, she was content with life and its never-ending mysteries.

Fifty-Four

A Love That Endures

Charlene's heart raced as she sped towards the hospital where her elderly mother was staying. Tears streamed down her face, the radio playing 'Florence And The Machine, Never Let Me Go', blurring as she weaved through traffic. Gripping the piece of paper in her hand, she knew time was of the essence. As Charlene's car screeched to a halt in front of the hospital, She parked the car haphazardly and ran towards the entrance, her mind consumed by a single thought. Her chest heaved with anxiety, her mind raced with a multitude of fears, but one thought dominated all others – she had to find her mother, and she had to find her fast. Tears blurred her vision as she clutched the crumpled piece of paper, her fingers trembling with urgency. She navigated the unfamiliar corridors with determination, her heart pounding in her ears. The weight of the unknown pressed heavily upon her, driving her forward with unrelenting fervour. She sprinted through the hospital, her heart raced with a mix of panic and disbelief.

'How could this be? there could be no way.' She thought to herself. She finally reached her mother's room and pushed the door open with trembling hands.

Her mother was sitting by the window, bathed in the golden light of the setting sun, her eyes fixated on something outside. The sight took her aback. Her mother looked happy, with a gentle smile gracing her lips. Her confusion escalated, knowing her mother suffered from dementia. But in that moment, she didn't have time to dwell on the sorrow of her mother's condition. This was her chance to share the astounding revelation that had shaken her to the core, and to express the emotions that were consuming her.

"Mom," she began cautiously, her voice wavering with a blend of urgency and trepidation. Her mother turned to her, her eyes holding a glimmer of recognition amidst the fog of her illness.

"Mother, how could you? How could you do this to me?" she exclaimed, her voice trembling with emotion. "I can't believe you've kept this from me for so long," Charlene continued, her voice quivering with hurt and betrayal.

The weight of the revelation hung heavily in the air, casting a shadow over the once peaceful hospital room. The seconds ticked by, each one filled with an unspoken tension that threatened to engulf them both. As the sun began to set, casting a warm orange glow through the window, Elisa sat in the armchair, lost in thought. Her wrinkled hands clasped a cup of tea, but her mind was far away, wandering through the corridors of her memories. She gazed at the photographs adorning the walls of her room, each snapshot a testament to a life well-lived. In one corner, a picture of her husband, Liam, stood proudly, his vibrant smile capturing a moment of pure joy. How she missed his laughter, the way his eyes crinkled at the corners when he smiled. The image of him brought a bittersweet ache to her heart, a longing for the days when they were young and in love. Beside it, a photo of her best friend Charlene beamed back at her, their arms linked in a timeless bond of friendship. Oh, the adventures they had shared, the secrets they had whispered under the stars. Charlene had been her rock, her confidante, and the laughter in her life. As the scent of cinnamon wafted through the air, Elisa's thoughts turned to her parents. Their comforting presence seemed to linger in the fragrance, a reminder of the love and guidance they had bestowed upon her. How she wished she could hear their voices once more, to feel the warmth of their embrace.

But it was Liam who occupied the forefront of her mind, his absence a palpable presence in the room. She knew that soon, she would join him in the vast beyond, where their love would be reunited in eternity.

"Mother, I'm talking to you. You knew about this, didn't you? Didn't you?" Her accusatory tone reverberated off the walls, causing Elisa to look up in surprise.

Elisa regarded Charlene, her heart aching at the pain etched on her face. Who was this fiery young woman with piercing blue eyes, and why was she so incensed? Elisa's mind raced as she struggled to comprehend the source of Charlene's anguish.

"Mum, I know you can hear me. Tell me what the heck is going on. All this time, you had me believing that Liam was my stepfather, only to find out that he was my real father all along. Why, mother? Why?" Charlene's voice quivered with raw emotion, her hands trembling as she confronted her mother.

As Elisa gazed into her daughter's tumultuous eyes, memories flooded her mind like a torrential downpour. What was she talking about? Slowly, memories began to resurface - the night she was assaulted, the tall figure that brought her home, the piercing blue eyes that haunted her dreams, that day in the coffee shop when Liam told her that he worked in transport a few years back, was he transporting for the rich? And then there were the years of anonymous money that arrived in the mail, only to stop abruptly after Liam had entered their lives. Elisa took a deep breath, her heart racing with the weight of her secret. She had vowed to protect her daughter, but now it seemed that the truth was finally catching up to them. The truth that Liam, the man who had been a pillar of their family, was indeed Charlene's biological father.

Elisa struggled to find the right words, to untangle the web of half-truths and omissions that had threatened to engulf them. In a daze, Elisa found herself staring out the window, seeking solace in the familiar sights of the world outside. The gentle sway of the trees and the soft glow of the sun offered no comfort, and she felt a pang of despair deep within her chest. Suddenly, a sharp pain gripped her, sending her crashing to the floor. From across the room, Charlene watched in horror as her mother crumpled to the ground. Panic surged through her as she rushed to Elisa's side, her mind reeling with fear and confusion. As she knelt beside her mother, Charlene's thoughts were consumed by a flood of questions. What had prompted Elisa's sudden collapse? And what could possibly explain the bewildering revelation that had shaken their lives to the core?

As Elisa lay on the floor, the world around her seemed to blur and fade. The truth she had uncovered had ignited a storm of emotions within her, but now, as darkness tugged at the edges of her consciousness, she was left with more questions than answers. Her mind whirled with the weight of the revelation, and the final, enigmatic smile on her lips left Charlene wondering about the untold secrets that had shaped her mother's life. The air was electric with tension, unsaid words hanging heavy like the prelude to a thunderstorm. One thing was certain, life was not going to be the same again.

The corridors of the old hospital were echoing with the urgent, resounding footsteps of a desperate daughter. Charlene, with her heart pounding in her chest, was racing against time to fetch the doctors. Her mother, Elisa, an aged epitome of grace, lay in her room, her feeble body tethering on the brink of the life and the great beyond.

The gravity of the situation amplified as Charlene burst into the room, doctors in tow. The medical professionals darted toward the fading soul, immediately immersed in a battle against the impending silence of mortality. Charlene stood at a distance, her gaze locked on her mother. Elisa, on the other hand, was lost in the torrent of thoughts traversing her deteriorating mind. The room filled with the bustling noise of medical directives, yet Elisa focused on the woman before her – her beautiful Charlene.

But in this moment of crisis, Elisa found herself tangled in a web of confusion.

"Why was she so angry?" Elisa wondered. A flicker of fear ignited in her heart. The memories, like sand, were slipping through her fingers, blurring the recognition of her own flesh and blood.

Despite her internal turbulence, Elisa shared a faint smile with the worried woman. Somehow, on an innate level, she recognized the love and concern mirrored in Charlene's eyes. With that sense of comfort, Elisa gently closed her eyes, a serene acceptance of her fate washing over her.

As Elisa's eyes fell shut, her lips moved in a whisper.

"Liam."

She was ready to reunite with her beloved husband in the world that lay beyond. The room, once bustling with frantic efforts, fell into an eerie silence as Elisa succumbed to the inevitable.

They placed her on the hospital gurney, her frail body barely making a sound as it glided down the sterile corridors. Charlene, her daughter, looked on with a mixture of hope and fear etched upon her face. It had been a long and difficult battle for Elisa, and now she was being whisked away into the unknown. Elisa found herself in a state of wonderland, surrounded by an ethereal glow. She scanned her surroundings, her eyes widening in disbelief as she saw Liam standing in front of her. His smile, so familiar and comforting, washed away all her pain and worries.

"Liam," she whispered once more, her voice filled with love and longing. He held out his arms, beckoning her closer. With a mixture of excitement and trepidation, Elisa stepped into his embrace. As their bodies intertwined, she felt a surge of warmth and familiarity, as though they had never been apart.

But there was something even more special about this reunion. As Elisa held onto Liam, she could feel a weight being lifted off her heart. In that moment, she knew that she had forgiven him for what he had done so many years ago, she had no choice. The pain and resentment that had once consumed her melted away, replaced by a deep sense of understanding and acceptance. She understood why he did what he did, why he came back to her, and most importantly, she understood the love they had for each other. They stood there, locked in an embrace that transcended time and space. The world around them seemed to fade into the background as they basked in the purity of their love. Elisa couldn't help but wonder how she had been granted this extraordinary opportunity to be with Liam once again.

With a deep breath, Liam knelt down on his knees, a gesture of infinite devotion. His lips tenderly kissed her from her toes, moving upwards, leaving no part of her untouched, almost as if he was healing her scars all over again. Elisa surrendered to his touch, overwhelmed by the intensity of their love. It was a kiss imbued with a thousand stories and lifetime of shared memories. The weight of their separation and the sorrow it had brought melted away, leaving only the purest joy. Elisa had longed for this moment, to be reunited with her love. Finally, she felt happy again, a warmth filling her soul, but most importantly, she felt free.

Together, they looked at each other, their souls entwined, ready to embark on a new adventure. Hand in hand, they walked towards the horizon, disappearing into the ethereal glow. The garden, once alive with vibrant colours, shrank into the distance as they faded away, leaving no trace behind.

Forever Love

In a land where love reigned supreme,
There lived a couple, their souls agleam.
Hearts entwined, their love knew no bounds,
A love so pure, a love to astound.

~

But alas, darkness lurked in the shade,
A secret, a lie, that couldn't be swayed.
For in this tale of love and despair,
Betrayal's venom tainted the air.

~

She discovered the truth, hidden away,
The lies that he told, day after day.
Her heart shattered, her trust broken,
Yet forgiveness in her soul was awoken.

~

And so they stood, face to face,
Torn by pain, seeking solace, seeking grace.
She looked into his eyes, filled with remorse,
Unsure if love could ever run its course.

~

But love, it has a mind of its own,
Forgiveness prevailing, seeds were sown.
For in her heart, the love remained,
Their souls intertwined, never to be tamed.

~

They embraced the pain, hand in hand,
Facing the storm, together they would stand.

Their love grew stronger, with each passing day,
Defying the odds, come what may.

~

In the afterlife, their love did reside,
Unbreakable, eternal, forever side by side.
They danced among the stars, never growing old,
A love story that would forever be told.

~

And so it goes, the tale of their love,
A story of forgiveness, rising above.
In the realm of love, miracles do occur,
Leaving you to ponder and infer.

~

For love, it's a force that never dies,
A mystery that ignites hearts and skies.
In the end, it's love that defines our age,
Leaving us wondering, turning that last page.

Until it's my turn, I will write.

With Love
Chavanese Wint

Milton Keynes UK
Ingram Content Group UK Ltd.
UKHW020609170124
436176UK00002B/15